"With *The Void*, Ms. Jacobs has written a remarkable first novel. The savory prose overwhelms your senses, the story itself darkly beautiful and wholly decadent. It is a story that you won't soon forget."
—Monica O'Rourke, *Black October*

"Nightmarish, surreal and wonderfully poetic, *The Void* will surely propel Jacobs into the horror limelight. Make way for the new Mistress of Terror!"
—Tim Lebbon, author of *The Nature of Balance*

"With her debut, *The Void*, Teri A. Jacobs unleashes fully the furious promise of her excellent short fiction. *The Void* is an adrenaline rush of re-imagined myth and all-too-real terror. Read it and be awed."
—Gary A. Braunbeck,
author of *The Indifference of Heaven*

"Teri A. Jacobs understands that mythology lies at the core of who we are and how we interact and—most importantly for the fan of horror literature—what truly frightens us. Teri knows these demons by name, and she's not afraid to use them."
—Brian A. Hopkins, author of *Cold at Heart*

"A stunning debut from a new voice, *The Void* not only earns Teri A. Jacobs a place at the table, it solidifies her position there as one of the hottest up-and-coming talents in the genre. And deservedly so."
—Greg F. Gifune, author of *Down to Sleep*

"There is nothing slow or ordinary about Teri A. Jacobs's *The Void*. This is otherworldly madness at its most disturbing. I had to keep stopping to get my bearings—making sure the world was still as I remembered."
—Charlee Jacob, author of *This Symbiotic Fascination*

The Dark Gods' Demand

He recognized their disguises and knew how they dealt out their wrath. He would not anger them and be wiped out.

"Tell me what they want from me," he said.

Solid ground evaporated into air, and he fell into a vacuum. He was sucked out of the threshold and thrown back into his body with such force that he slammed against the wall and his nose bled.

Drop after drop of his blood landed on the open pages of the yearbook, a sanguine rainfall drowning out the human faces. His testicles tightened up and his skin quivered in anticipation of wearing the skin of his victim.

"Command me, my Masters," he said as he licked the blood from the glossy paper. Leslie's picture appeared from the ruby puddles.

"Take her to Xibalba and hand her over to the Bat-God," they answered from the shadows.

TERI A. JACOBS

THE VOID

LEISURE BOOKS NEW YORK CITY

A LEISURE BOOK®

June 2002

Published by

Dorchester Publishing Co., Inc.
276 Fifth Avenue
New York, NY 10001

ISBN 0-8439-5024-2

Visit us on the web at www.dorchesterpub.com.

*Every child dreams of that grown-up day
when he/she walks beyond the childhood world
of fantasy into reality. But I chose to remain
behind—in a world of the dark fantastic,
where anything imagined is possible.*

*I'd like to thank my parents for giving
me that belief that anything was possible for me;
my family—Mike, Arden and Emory—
for giving me the time to devote to my dreams;
Monica O'Rourke for her writerly support,
because dreams don't come easily;
and Don D'Auria, my editor,
for making my dream a reality.*

THE VOID

Chapter One

He crept into her mind. In her blue-water dream, his dark ether seeped like spilt oil, blackening her sea of mermen with their emerald flesh and crystal grins, poisoning her vision with his inhuman, skull-like face, which floated before her own. A scream of bubbles erupted from her gaping mouth as he gripped her dreaming self, her soul, and dragged her through a chasmal cave, through the darkest channel into another world. A place of phantoms, the underworld called Xibalba.

Beyond the passage, a desiccated stretch of land lay before them. Towers of barren rock walled against the ghostly silver horizon, and twin peaks, in the form of monstrous talons, rose on each side of the pass. Dry winds rushed and snaked through the pass, whispering his secret name.

"Coatl, Coatl," came the airy slitherings, and the ground rumbled beneath their feet as one of the clawed hands of rock reacted to his presence and curled into a fist. The Lord of Mictlan, the God of the Dead, wanted to take his offering in his hand.

His offering cowered with her ivory arms draped over her head of golden hair, and her cherub mouth opened wide with silent screams as rocks fell upon her. With edges like glass shards, the rocks cut into her shoulders and arms. Black gashes appeared, and Coatl's own black-death wounds along his astral body spread wider, as if they were hollow mouths grinning.

The tzitzimime demons of this dead abode slunk from behind boulders, shadows casting shadows, murmuring foul hunger. Capacious mouths snapped open and shut, their razor rows clicking sharply, and Coatl clamped his jaws in greeting, for they were his chosen brethren.

"Give her to us," they spat.

Hands tight upon her bony shoulders, he pushed her toward the tzitzimime, and she fell on her knees before them, supplicating with tears and screams as they grappled her with razor claws and stripped off ribbons of her flesh. Inch by agonizing inch of creamy skin came off wet and pink. The demons wrapped the fleshy bows around their tongues, and her blood dripped from their cavernous mouths like spit. Slathering tongues slurped in the stringy noodles of her flesh until her body lay on the sands, fleshless and gleaming bright red, the pulp of her still screaming.

Coatl gripped her beneath her arms of warm, sticky muscles and grisly tendons, and dragged her down the pass. Her raw heels left sanguine trails.

"Oh God, oh God, oh God . . ." she muttered in shock and pain, her eyes rolling in their bony sockets, looking almost as if they'd roll out without their lids to hold them in.

With his ebon-boned fingers, he held her chin and whispered in her ear, "Meet my goddess."

Her eyes focused before her, on the terrible sight of a leviathan serpent. It rose upon cobalt coils, reaching ten feet into the bright, dead-gray sky, and exposed its massive hood, its sapphire scales gored with carmine mouths, infantile snakes hissing out like vomited curses. In minutes, hundreds of blue cobras surrounded them.

Seductive songs seethed into his soul.

The air was alive with hisses, as if the very wind could strike with invisible fangs, and Coatl swayed to the snake-cadence. He learned long ago, during his first visit to Xibalba, the sinuous dance of the serpent. Appeasing the snake-goddess this way was better than the other . . .

. . . wound tight within the springs of her oily scales, ribs spearing crisscross through flesh and bulbous organs, sternums cracking into the pulpy hearts, bodies pressed and squeezed like olives, red plasmic oils and ruddy pits of innards extracted through both opened ends.

3

Arched downward, the serpent pressed a cold nose against him, tongue flicking out of a lipless mouth, tasting him. Obsidian-mirrored pupils reflected his face—a cobra himself. His cowl hid most of his skull-face, and he grinned striking fangs. Breathing his name, Coatl, the Aztec word for serpent, he prayed for her gifts. The leviathan stretched open its mouth, fangs of curved swords pierced from the pink gums, its throat quivering like a cock in the throes of orgasm, spraying ocher venom. The venom splashed onto his face, burning into the marrow of his bones, and Coatl licked the acid-bitter reptilian juice off his lips. His tongue bubbled and exploded inside his mouth. *Exaltation*.

His victim whimpered in his arms as serpents wriggled up her legs and dangled from her waist, fangs in her guts, tails whipping like silky strands of a blue skirt upon her. Only one thing was missing from her new image. Coatl unsheathed a stone knife and cut off her hands. Her severed hands dropped to her feet, and blood splayed out from her wrists in long red fingers.

There she stood, like Coatlicue, mother of the War-God, Devourer of Filth, with her skirt of serpents and disembodied hands.

The snake-goddess approved and settled upon coils again, and Coatl ushered his sacrifice toward the shore of the blood river. Clumps of rotting flesh floated by, and Xochitonal lifted her snout from beneath the current and snatched bits of carrion, sharp jaws crushing the waste as easily as squeezing mud through a fist. Even the bones crumbled into dust in her steel maw.

Xochitonal was a fast and fierce alligator, but she paid no attention to them as she crawled to the shore, her belly bloated with yowling souls. Coatl shuddered to think of the infinite agony of those souls, churning in sulfurous acids, eternally digested in the pit of her stomach.

Waiting by the shore, he watched the suns drip onto the horizon and sink into the infertile womb of Hell, and the night sky birthed itself in howling darkness. He hoisted her skinless bones over his shoulders and walked onward, skulking in the dark.

He was the roadrunner in the eight deserts. He was the panther in the eight mountains. Invisible, he walked through the whirlwind sharp as swords toward the gates of the Lord of Hell, gates fashioned from the ribs of a monolithic beast, with chains formed from the petrified links of its intestines.

The Lord of Mictlan dwelled within, as well as all the other dreaded lords. Inside the gates, a myriad of structures patterned the ground, fallen ruins, even the palatial temple of Mictlan. Ivy and moss clung to the sandstone blocks and marble columns, but, as Coatl drew closer, he noticed it wasn't plant but another organic material winding up the columns and stretching across the stone. Decay spread across the outside of the temple: sacrificial skins, yellow and thinned into the finest parchments by the arid winds, had been glued to the walls with gangrenous pus; entrails roped around the columns, and moldy growths sprouted along the pink-rot slickness, releasing foul spores into the air; and thousands upon thousands of putrid tongues were nailed into the stone, slurring hideous mysteries in the wind.

His own tongue curled in his mouth, as though to swallow those mysteries, mysteries he yearned for, mysteries he would kill for. His sacrifice to the gods weighted his shoulders.

"The God of the Dead awaits you in his dead temple," he told the girl. The Lord of Mictlan waited for the dawn of the eternal night—the god's wishes revealed in Coatl's dreams, of darkness devouring the light, of chaos in their reigns, a certain salvation from evolution toward extinction. Because didn't everything die out eventually, even gods? Worse to be forgotten than destroyed. But Coatl wouldn't forget the dark deities, nor their commands. "Or would you rather meet doom in the Houses of Ordeals?"

The House of Bats loomed in the courtyard, windowless, foreboding with its leathery walls and gothic spires raised like the Bat-God's hooks. Camazotz, the ruler of the bats, would swoop down upon any visitor, his leathern wings whirring, his claws hooking under chins and taking off heads. He syphoned the blood from the stumps of the necks. Coatl remembered the sounds within that house, the horrible sucking and gurgling sounds.

"Nightmare," she croaked.

Indeed, the nightmare of a god strolled through the temple's doors, surrounded by the tzitzimimes. Snails, slugs, and leeches covered his monstrous skull like skin, and worms of every kind squirmed upon his limbs. Little gods, little devourers of death and filth.

"Lord of Mictlan," Coatl said in a hushed tone.

"I know you," she said, struggling in his arms. He dropped her to the ground, offering her to the Lord of Mictlan and the sands crusted upon her seeping body like new gritty skin. She grimaced as she tried to find his human face within the rough contours of malformed bone. "Your voice, your eyes . . ."

"Yes, you do, Charlotte. You always complained that I never took you to any nice places. Didn't I prove you wrong?" He smirked and put his hand over her mouth and nose, silencing her for eternity. "Time to prove to the rest how wrong they've been about me."

Once more, he used his knife on her as he sliced her tongue from her slack mouth and added it to the temple's walls. Her shrieks were carried away by the awful winds. Kowtowing before the God of the Dead, Coatl allowed the god to brush his hand upon him and barely trembled when the godly leaches wiggled into every orifice.

The demons regurgitated the pieces of Charlotte's flayed skin onto the ground, and the sodden ribbons of flesh swirled in the muck with disgusting vigor. Heads of hookworms had grown on the ends, their hooks and suckers opening and clenching the air, searching for a soft hold.

"Feast with the god," they snarled at him.

Instead, Coatl vomited the worms that had burrowed inside him, adding more to the half-digested larval brew, and stole away through the darkest tunnels with a stolen prize from the wall tucked in his palm.

He was angry with himself. *Rejecting the food of the gods.* Before he opened his eyes, he inhaled deeply, trying to cleanse the negativity from him. Sweet sage burned into his nostrils, sooting his membranes with its blackish smoke. He always lit a bowl of sage leaves for his trances. The scent invigorated and calmed him.

In a haze, the bare room came into view. Plaster dusted the pine floor, and mildew stains speckled the yellowing walls. Timber and leaves cluttered before the stairwell, which had collapsed long before he came, and he was surprised the second floor hadn't come crashing down yet. The hundred-year-old home had weathered at least one fire, its burnt roof opened up to the night sky and like a mouth caught the rain and snow and swallowed them into the rotting beams. He'd broken into the abandoned farmhouse years ago to practice his trances and his faith without fear of prying eyes; although, if the eyes could see as his could, then he wouldn't be safe anywhere.

He lifted the loose floorboard and retrieved a hardbound Owen County High School yearbook. A red ribbon saved the place he visited most often, page thirteen, Leslie Starr's senior picture. Tracing the curve of her face, he marveled at how simple her beauty was. Soft brown curls framed her delicate oval face, and he could still remember how it felt like stroking velvet when he touched her hair, how it smelled like apple blossoms when the wind blew through it. Though her face was plain by most men's standards, he adored her big bright hazel eyes, sparks of spirit fire glinting around her dark pupils, and longed to kiss her cherry-pop–colored mouth. His lips tingled whenever he was around her.

His anger returned.

"What do the gods want with you? What makes you special in their eyes?" he asked the smiling portrait.

She was once inseparable from Charlotte Schneider, the vain creature beaming next to her in the book. From his pocket, he withdrew a knife, flipped its blade up, and carved out her eyes with its tip.

Staring at Charlotte's picture, he projected his sight to where she lay dead.

Darkness shrouded her body. Her sprawled outline on the bed reminded him of a doll tossed carelessly, limbs askew. A Barbie he'd grown tired of playing with.

An approaching car filled the room with shifting caramel light, illuminating Charlotte's prone body.

Teri A. Jacobs

Necrosis in her tissue, she resembled an unwrapped mummy, still fresh from the embalming and not quite dry. Unnatural decay peppered her skin, and, by psychic-mutilation, her eye sockets were empty, little voids staring at the ceiling. It was strange how the body changed when the soul never returned, the rapid chemical degradation that made him suspect the soul contained chemical or physical elements that scientists had yet to discover, almost as if the soul was the acid for the battery. Corrosion happened when the acid went bad or was completely used. In Charlotte's case, he emptied her soul. *Sip-sip*, gone.

Good-bye, he whispered in his mind, knowing it was the first of many good-byes. He'd broken the eternal circle around Leslie and planned to strip away her old support one by one until no one was left. *Trisha Watkins, Robin Merle, Bonnie Johnson.* Flipping through the pages, he watched their pictures disappear as quickly as their ghosts would exit their bodies.

Words and images blurred on the pages, bringing to mind other books with words and images of death, the Mayan *Popul Voh* and the Mexican *Book of the Dead*. Ancient tomes filled with sweet poetry, sweet like the scent of rot. Once they were in his possession, he ravaged the pages with great interest, learning more than he had ever hoped about the gods of his dreams and the worlds he visited in spirit, if not in some other body. Learned things like the ritual of Xipe-Toltec, Tezcatlipoca to the

10

Yopi, the red god, the god of human sacrifice who wore the skins of the flayed man.

Thinking of the ritual, he went in search of Leslie, his eyes closed, his vision turned inward, and tumbled through astral space, allowing the beacon of her soul's chrome-black pulsing light to guide him. He stepped into her reality, unseen and unformed, a smudge upon the wall. A smudge as small as a fly.

Her eyelids fluttered in dreaming sleep, and he remembered the first shock of his mind melding with hers, into her dreams. It was strange because she dreamed in black and white.

Dreams as monochromatic as her soul.

Her cat arched its back, raising hackles and hisses with his presence, but she didn't stir from her dream, and he slipped into her mind as if he were her very breath inhaled.

She dreamed about climbing a mountain, snow-capped peaks brilliant white against the dark slate of the stone beneath it. Jagged holds cut through her gloves, and her fingers bled raw. Still, her face beamed with the blush of sunshine joy.

An eagle screeched in the distance, silhouetted against the clouds, almost menacing, like a demon trying to sneak into the heavens. His shadow passed over Leslie. She lost her footing as if the shadow had pushed her.

Beware the shadows, her mind-voice said, as she struggled to steady herself. Her foot only kicked loose pebbles free.

Coatl appeared to her then, dressed in a black cloak, his white face hidden beneath the dark flowing folds. He reached for her hand.

Leslie shook her head, resisting him, fear-etched frown furrowed on her brow.

Beware the shadows, she mouthed again. She released her hold and fell from the face of the mountain, and her dream shifted into a nightmarish gape as her mind stretched and yawned black.

Its darkened edges flowed upon him. Celestial blackness, empty spaces, yet he was suffocated by its unfathomable density, and soon its cold, vapid stench of eternal death broke upon him, waves of horror within him. Gripped by primal fear of the ultimate unknown, Coatl fled from her mind. Fled from what was inside her.

Chapter Two

Into a darkness unlike the night, more of a deep cavern-pitch, but without the wind hushing through its vast spaces, without the echoic drip of water or settling sigh of rock, into a black, absolute stillness, Leslie went terrified.

This place muffled her heart. Slowed to a dreaded stop, her life was stifled and suspended into nothing in this place of nothing. No sight, no sound, no thought, no breath. Empty as death.

The Dark Man had vanished from her mind, but then she did as well, and everything was void.

No, not quite so, spoke the subtle thought that formed somewhere else than here.

In the darkness beyond dark, things stirred, and the ancient enemies of all worlds seeped alongside her, touching her obscenely with unseen hands, whispering to her with unheard voices. Rot tainted their seething laughter as they dragged her deeper within the Void.

Leslie woke, gasping for breath because her thumping heart seemed lodged in her throat. Sweat and chills drenched her dream-fevered body, and the way the room shifted in surreal angles made her believe she still dreamed. She knew though she had escaped the dream, the *vision* of that cosmic crypt, and had ventured back into real time with real space and matter. Away from the domain that left physics behind.

Sucking on her lower lip, listening to her breath hitch and quiver through her slitted mouth, she understood the Frankenstein monster's disorientation when he came alive—of being brought back from the nothing he'd become. Every cell in her body shook. Live-wire flesh strapped down and electrified, she felt trapped in a limbo between living and dead, and, as shadows converged in the corners, she wasn't sure which side was worse.

The shadows formed faces against the stark wall, of deformed and inhuman features, of death masks and carnival-leers, of hideous, loathing eyes. Parading, circling the room, they taunted her.

She clasped her hands over her eyes, pretending it was her own mind projecting these lurid images, but the viscid hissing surrounding her denied her that comfort.

Even behind closed lids, she saw them dancing with the flitting light as they crawled the walls, slipped into the air, and stole through her skull. Dancing, dancing, singing abrasive, "Ring around the rosies, pocket full of posies, ashes, ashes, you'll fall down!"

Down she felt their hands pull her.

Mouth opened to scream, Leslie tasted the grave-dust on her tongue and choked on the dry ashes.

"Ring around the corpses, pocket full of kisses, ashes, ashes, dead on your lips."

Wind generated within the room. A maelstrom of droning voices and swirling ice hailed upon her, tiny nips into her skin, icy shivers in her hot blood, and she jerked her hands away from her eyes when she recognized her father's voice within the torment.

"Beware the shadows," he said in a tone pierced with sadness and pain. "Beware the shadows." Then the winds died, and her father disappeared within a mass of hungry darkness once again.

In an unsettled quietude, Leslie sat upon her bed and allowed the tears to flow down her face. Strange how her suffering felt warm on her cheek when it was so damn cold in her heart. She trembled as she wept, feeling those raw wounds of her father's death ooze and sting as if it had happened a moment before. Scabs of old terrors broke off, and she pulled the blankets to her mouth, muffling her wails with them. It was happening again, and she knew it wouldn't stop until her ghost joined her father's.

The glittery dawn did little to dispel the darkening fear within her. Rather, its golden touch upon the floor and walls disturbed her because she knew where there was light, there were shadows.

Wandering into the gallery with vapid stare and dragging steps, Leslie ignored the greetings and headed for Bruce's office. She entered without knocking and unceremoniously dropped the package on his desk.

"Leslie, you make a wretched prima donna. So, I gather the photos didn't turn out?" he asked as he tore into the envelope. Proof sheets slid out onto his desk, and he scanned the pictures with sincere enthusiasm. "God, they're incredible. Why the glum face then?"

"Bad night," she said. Words flat, quick, devoid of the sick quivering memory of the night's events.

"No sex, huh? Understandable, sounds like my life." He sighed comically, glancing up from the pictures, catching her eyes, telling her without words that he understood more than she wanted.

Leslie stared at the twenty-by-twenty photograph above his desk in order to ignore his imploring eyes. Eyes the color of a stormy sea, with the intensity of one as well. Eyes that could peer behind her tough exterior, beyond the steel wall around her soul, and into the secret, soft, vulnerable parts of herself. His gaze unnerved her as much as her photograph disturbed viewers.

"Cross Dresser in Rapture" had hung behind his desk for over a year, after he purchased it at her first art show and signed her onto his gallery. The photo depicted a man being crucified on a wooden cross. It was Easter, and Leslie had traveled to Central America to witness the religious fanatics' reenactment of Christ's crucifixion. Just as Mary Magdalene washed and kissed the feet of Jesus, a young boy of about seventeen, a beautiful specimen to Leslie, with his brown curls dipping over his long-lashed eyes, sucked on the toes of the condemned. The man's body responded. If not for the nails being positioned above his wrists, Leslie would've joked it was the erection and not the resurrection.

She'd felt the pull of the scene and started snapping the pictures. The one that struck her the most when she developed them was the first one she took—as the hammers drove in the long iron nails, the man arched his back, shut his eyes, and opened his mouth to scream. The image, however, portrayed him in near ecstasy. Whether the boy or the hammer caused the erection, it was unclear.

The crown of thorns added vivid contrast, spikes blooming in his temples, red rosebuds of blood opening on his face. She remembered his scarlet perfume on that humid day. It overpowered the stench of unwashed bodies and open sewers, even though it was the most delicate of scents upon the sweating breeze. Golgotha visions swooned within her, and she had gotten swept into the act before her, almost believing as that young boy did that nameless saviors truly died over and over in this remote town for their sins. Such an aching, desperate need for salvation.

When she looked at the picture for an extended period of time, it seemed the head of the penis glistened and glowed with the setting sun in the background. Glorious blasphemy as a song played in her mind, its phantom singing, "I am the God of Fuck."

"You'll shock Cincinnati more at your second show, judging by these proofs. That trip to the London fetish club paid off in terms of creativity." Bruce tapped the center image. "She/he has won my heart. Love the serpent tattoos twining around the breasts, and the bulge beneath the vinyl Speedo . . . well, I'm jealous. But I have to ask, are the metal spikes real?"

Leslie cringed as she nodded, and Bruce shuddered with a mixture of disgust and joyful greed in his expression.

"To even portray this stuff as beauty makes you a freak, you know that, don't you?" he asked, continuing his oohing and aahing down through the frames.

Her lips twitched into a little grin, knowing his way of complimenting her was hidden within the chiding. *Beauty* was not how many would define her work, but if she stepped back and took an objective look at her prints, she would agree she found an unexplainable allure in the grotesque. Masochistic torture, self-mutilation, haunting agony, repetitive themes developed throughout the copies for sale. Denial subdued, she saw bits of herself in every photo, scars no longer veiled but made plain to the world in rich images.

She was the girl with midnight-blue hair, black tear drawn beneath her eye. Of black sorrow, Leslie held inside and refused to shed, for fear it would drown her and the world.

She was the cross dresser in rapture, with burdens upon her.

She was all her images, freakish by nature, pained, caught in a still frame of disturbing details.

Upon the glass that covered the Rapture print she saw her face reflected in distortion, and she smiled at herself, finding it a better likeness than the mirror, until she noticed another image beside her own.

Waxen-faced and hooded, the Dark Man stared at her.

Leslie gasped and shrank back from the desk, pinning her back against the wall. His image disappeared, but she sensed his presence in the room, his ox-blood eyes watching invisible from the recesses.

"Roach?" Bruce asked as he leaned forward against the desk, scanning the ground for the nasty bug. "Damn things actually like the insecticide, I think. Might as well call the stuff steroids for city roaches."

Teri A. Jacobs

"Roaches. Right."

"Saw one the other night scramble out from beneath a box—thought it was a mouse at first. Did you know the things chirp when they run toward you? Must be the meal bell."

"Scary." *Pound, pound*, her heart agreed as a faint chattering erupted within the wall.

"Yeah, well, until they get bigger than my shoe, I'm okay."

Sounds like water and air flushing through a tank, a gurgling, a grumbling, hushed conversations of demons seemed to come from behind the wall. Then the sounds vibrated through the plaster into her skin. As if music thrummed and throbbed from loud speakers, palpable sound waves upon the air, the rhythmic muttering pushed against her, crossing the barrier of flesh into her veins, pulsing. Blood fluttered instead of flowed, and her heart beat arrhythmic discord of her terror.

In her ears, her pulse turned hellishly symphonic. Pipe-organ veins filled with long-drawn sanguine notes, and the phantasm opera played, chorus of demon song in her mind, blaring curses and warnings. Her body resonated with it all.

Leslie slapped her hands over her ears and screamed.

Bruce was shaking her, his mouth moving without sound, his fearful eyes blinking away from her sight as darkness bordered her mind. She fled into the fade, to the place of no sounds.

*　　*　　*

20

With delirium-tinged awareness, Leslie found herself in a hospital bed. A blood pressure cuff was being pumped by a serious-looking nurse, her severe cropped hair tinted with gray, heavy glasses perched on a sharp nose, thin lips pinched hard enough to drain away their color. In the corner of the egg-white room, Bruce had tucked himself into a chair, accounting ledger open on his lap, pen stuck between his lips.

She searched for the fan, for the comforting hum that had awakened her. Nowhere to be seen but still heard, its plastic blades rotated in a quiet whir, and she longed to feel its artificial wind upon her.

The hum reminded her of her father. Every night, he would turn on his fan, positioned beside the bed, because he said it would help blow the nightmares into the dream catcher hung above the headboard. Sometimes, after her own bad dreams, she would slink out of her bed, sneak into her parent's room, and stand in front of the fan, listening to it shush her scares, feeling the air hit her, pretending it was her father blowing kisses to make the hurt go away.

Where was the fan? She needed the bad things to go away.

"Welcome back," the nurse said in the softest of tones.

"Where was I? What happened?" *Where's the fan?* She heard the noise of a high-speed motor running, faster, faster until it began to echo like wails.

"Fainting spell, as far as we can figure, but we'd like to keep you overnight for observation."

With a *shred-rip* of the Velcro strap, Leslie jerked as the cuff came off her arm. For a split second, she thought it was the seams of reality tearing apart.

"Your blood pressure is very low, and you've had a series of heart palpitations that concern us," the nurse continued. "I'll bring the doctor in—"

"No, no need. I won't be staying." Leslie turned down the stiff white sheets and wobbled to a standing position.

"I wouldn't advise—"

The screams cut her off.

Down the hall, a woman shattered the hospital-tomb quiet, and her siren charged the nurse into calm efficiency. She rushed out of the room, her rubber soles padding away as silent as shadows. Leslie feared for the woman down the hall.

"Will you take me home?" she asked Bruce, who only nodded in confusion. She found her stashed clothes and dressed in haste, not caring if Bruce saw her pale nakedness.

Hanging on to his arm, Leslie left the room and headed down the death-stalked corridors to the exit, where she finally breathed in relief. She hated hospitals, with their antiseptic care and sterile cold. Only once had her parents brought her in for tests—needles, tubes, radioactive serum injected in what blood they'd left inside of her, a trip into the CT-scan machine and the breathless panic it set upon her. But once was all it took to poison her against hospitals. She hadn't felt safe as the tray, *its tongue*, slid back, *swallowed her*, and held her motionless inside its churning hollow *belly*. Like the Void, the machine was a vacuum of nothing, sucking away her very breath and everything else but her fear.

Winter night air filled her lungs.

She stopped in mid-stride, checked her watch, and shuddered at the lapse of time—the longest black spell yet. Five hours out of her mind.

"You really should've stayed," Bruce said.

"No, no, I can't . . . no, no," she stammered, staggering under a dizzy whirl. Fast revolving world of moonlight streaks and wintry trees reached around and around and around for her. The parking lot was on turbo-spin. Her mind flashed round to the memory of CT scans, her body stationary, everything else moving, making her sick.

Light-headed, she allowed Bruce to lead her to his Mazda Miata. He drove her home without speaking, but every once in a while she caught him glancing her way, assessing her.

Would he believe her if she told him it was the brewing storm that wrecked her equilibrium? Far away, a storm gathered, atmospheric pressure intensifying, its long reach winding within her. Her childhood doctor had refused to accept her ability to sense the storms, even though one clear day she had announced it would snow any moment, and the doctor had shaken her head, lecturing her on how stress was to blame for her headaches and spells. *Children of alcoholics* went the sober talk. But the snow had begun to fall as soon they had stepped out of the door. Leslie had worn the doctor's haughty grin the rest of the afternoon, knowing she, a hick-town child, was right, and the doctor with all her advanced degrees was wrong.

Another reason for her to quit the doctors and the tests and the science of something they probably could never explain.

Seemed she'd run away from everything.

"Here you go, ma'am. Twenty-dollar fare, please," Bruce announced.

Leslie couldn't help chuckling. Bruce was a wise-ass, but the dearest friend who honored her reclusive life, never probing too deep, always keeping an open mind.

"Up for another favor?" she asked. Her Mount Adam's apartment loomed on the slope, a stone facade for the stony heart that beat within. She couldn't face the apartment yet, not with the shaded windows leering down on her and waiting for her to come inside.

"Name it, it's your dollar." Bruce grinned wide and drummed his fingers on the steering wheel to the radio's tune—Bruce's favorite, Celtic folk music. In his car, it was always a May Fair festival.

"I've changed my mind about the party. Want to escort me and Moon?"

"Do you have to bring the cat?" Bruce groaned, eyes glassing over even before the cat had a chance to spread its allergenic dandruff.

"Oh, he'll make a great accessory in the photos. What graveyard is complete without a black cat?"

"You're taking pictures? Oh, hell, bring the cat, bring his fur balls, bring his fleas!"

Giggling, she held her finger up for him to wait while she went into her place and gathered her things.

"Don't forget," he called from the car as she inserted her key, "it's a celebration of the night. Put on a Gothic costume. Time to learn to fit into a crowd, sweetheart." And he laughed, because he had no intention of dressing for the party. Bruce wouldn't be caught dead in anything but his jeans and white oxford.

"Right," she said as the door swung open, and the sallow-lit stairwell greeted her.

Heels clicking on the wooden steps, she made her way to her fourth-floor apartment. The aroma of her neighbor's dinner wafted into the hall, ginger and onion spice making Leslie's stomach grumble with hunger. As she slipped into her apartment, the walls groaned with their own hunger.

Leslie flipped on the lights, quelling the dark but not her unease, and she jumped when Moon rubbed his welcome against her legs. Bending, she scooped him into her arms and nuzzled the silver-white crescent of fur between his eyes, the moon upon his midnight face for which he was named.

"We're going to a party, Moon," she said, carrying him into her bedroom, judging him for the slightest reaction to something amiss. Ears perked, golden eyes alert, drool-drop on his lips, Moon showed little sign of danger.

She trusted Moon to perceive the watcher in the empty spaces, as he had proved over and over that he could, the flattened ears, the hissing, the corner attacks with his paws thwacking fast and furious every time she felt spooked by invisible prying eyes. Did pets share their owners' madness? she wondered.

Dressed in black leather pants, red bustier, and her snazzy leather jacket, she was ready to go. Off she went with camera and Moon in hand, leaving the lights on behind her in the hope that dark things wouldn't encroach upon her when she returned.

Bruce whistled his approval as she slid into the car and handed her a mask, its feathers fanned like scarlet flames.

"It's a masque ball, Leslie. The game is to decide which ·is the true face." Bruce slipped a baboon mask over his face. His eyes were bestial behind the mask, and Leslie's heart gave a start because she never would've expected so perfect a transformation.

The tiny hairs on her arms stood at attention, little soldiers waiting for the battle. His breath snorted from the air holes, and she couldn't help but think of the jungle—twilight hunters swinging down from the trees, screeching; gray blurs roaming in the darkness with eyes aglow; crimson and corpse-blue faces snarling, long teeth exposed. The true face behind the wild mask.

She brushed the chills from her arm and turned her mask in her hand, finding it bland in comparison to his extraordinarily real image.

"And you give me a simple feather mask?"

He answered with a deep growling voice, "You need no elaborate display. You hide your face in the shadows well enough."

Something other than his own voice resonated in his tone. Something more ancient and mysterious than the seas. Something she'd wished she'd never hear again.

Camera-flash quick and blinding, he grinned at her, mask beneath the mask, of long white teeth and evil.

Moon yowled in her lap, and his sleek body trembled in fear.

"What's wrong with your cat?" Bruce asked, all signs of the other intruding face gone, leaving only a fake, vinyl beast.

Warped reality, a phenomenon she dreaded. A slip through the cracks, and she feared she might never come back.

"Spooked by your mask, I think," Leslie said, settling Moon with gentle strokes. Moon's starry eyes blinked at her, pupils shrinking as he relaxed, but she noted his eyes' wariness and the way they accused her of lying.

"Ha! Serves him right. Payback for the time he freaked the shit out of me by clawing my arm just because it dangled over the side of the couch." Bruce pulled the mask off and snarled at Moon.

Moon yawned.

"Coward," Bruce said as he shifted the car into gear and sped off toward the Cemetery Masque.

Leslie watched the houses blur by, windows dotted with lights. She thought about how life went on inside the houses, of families gathering for dinner, of mothers reading bedtime stories to children, of friends laughing and playing cards, of lonely hearts dating their televisions, and how she was always on the outside, looking in. She was a ghost even before her body rotted in a grave, flitting through life without any ties to the lives around her.

Life was passing her by, and the tires whooshed on the black road like the revolving doors of birth and death. Someone enters the world; someone leaves the world; someone enters the world; someone leaves the world. Endless comings and goings. Turning away from the window, she bit her lips as fears repeated, as she felt trapped between the living and the dead.

A string of cars lined up outside Spring Grove's Cemetery and Arboretum. The perfect haunt for one of Trixie's parties. Writer, painter, Goth-grrl, Trixie held a party for each season, celebrating some aspect of the dark side. Last autumn, on All Hallow's Eve, she rented a river boat, an old-fashioned steam queen, and had the invitees wear period clothes. It was a strange night of gambling, drinking, and seances to call the Delta Queen's ghost aboard.

It wasn't until after Leslie developed her film that she realized the Delta Queen's ghost had appeared, a shimmery form with silver flowing clothes and hair, anguish on her pallid face as wispy hands failed to steer the paddle ship. "Wraith at the Wheel" sold for fifteen hundred dollars, bought by Trixie herself.

At the gate, a security guard asked for their invitation, took their embossed flyer, and directed them toward the century-old chapel.

Impressive, yet simple and medieval in design, the chapel sat gloomily on the snowy ground. Did grief mortar the stones of the walls? Narrow arched windows and doorways cut dark slits into the coarse walls, and the triple-arched main entrance opened into a large vaulted area. Candlelight flickered within the chapel, though still dim from the mass of mingling bodies blocking the glow. Along the red velvet aisle, masked celebrants danced together, Goth-rhythm grinding to a Covenant song.

Upon the granite altar, a woman wearing an antique-white, tattered lace gown and pale feline mask swayed between two vampire-clad men. Black capes opened and embraced the woman, and the men ravished her with their raven faces. A ghastly smile spread across her face, with ebon lips of the long dead, with fangs of the panther.

Trixie. Her skin-art showing on her exposed back—the cat-headed goddess Bast, the lover of pleasure and dance.

Teri A. Jacobs

Leslie snapped several shots of the grim scene, catching each twisted expression, each seductive coil of arms and tongues as they groped one another like adders mating. The title of the series formed in her mind as she clicked the shutter: "Night Shall Overtake."

Phantoms and every form of the risen dead surrounded Leslie—one man in black tuxedo, formal top hat, and alabaster mask, sulking in the corner; a group of women with their colorful taffeta and peacock faces putting razor-kisses on their pallid skins; "Blue Boy" reclining on a wooden pew, blue suede shoes propped up, dull eyes staring from behind his drowned-flesh vizard.

The Cemetery Masque offered her Mardi Gras decadence without a trip to New Orleans. There was its voodoo zombie princess in the arms of a Victorian Count, gold-dusted breasts exposed and bitten, bloody milk at her nipple, her hand upon his leprous cock.

The camera chattered on and on until the end of the roll.

As Leslie changed the film, the sounds of laughter altered, replaced by hacking and chortled songs, and she glanced up from the camera. Cigarette smoke swirled in the chapel like graveyard mist. Affected by whippet fumes and cloves, her vision swooned. False faces leered, and beasts within beasts strolled toward her, malignancy in their pithy eyes, silent secrets on their grinning lips.

30

Dragging Moon on his leash, she bolted from the chapel and raced across the slippery ground, across the bridge, and into the maze of gravestones. The brisk air stung her tight throat. Moon panted as she slowed her pace, and she released him from his leash, feeling guilty.

He bounded up the hill, stopping before a crypt, meowing loudly. A figure rested against the door of the mausoleum. On either side of the door stood a marble angel, lengthy sword in arms, guarding the entrance. They frowned upon the man on the steps. He wore a dusty Union uniform, its gold piping dull with age against the navy, and his cap had slipped over his eyes. If he wore a mask, it was the second skin of misery.

"Everything okay?" Leslie asked, figuring him for drunk.

With a slow movement, he tipped his cap back, eyeing her briefly before casting his gray steel gaze downward. "Aye, everything's as it should be."

"Mind if I take your picture?" The image had hit her when he looked at her—broken soldier placed between two armed angels like some kind of prisoner of God. Heaven was a concentration camp.

"I'd rather you take my tale." Lifting up from the steps, he walked toward her and extended his hand, as if he meant to introduce himself.

His fingers, palm, wrist slid through her hand.

And his tale was told with every breath she took. . . .

. . . *Red brick buildings lined the shore of the green Chaplin River, and the prosperous merchants greeted him as he walked by, waving him inside to sell their wares. Perryville was a quiet, pretty town before their enemy fought at its doors.*

Canon blasts echoed through the cobblestone streets. Merchants closed their shops. His troop readied for war and headed toward the smoky clouds that rose from beyond the hill.

By the time they reached the valley, the battlefield was strewn with fallen soldiers. Their feet sloshed through the blood-sodden ground, and they recognized their comrades in the charred faces. Unblinking eyes saw no Heaven in the haze.

Winds brutalized them with the stenches of acrid gunpowder and slaughtered flesh, and, before they recovered from their shock, gunfire sounded.

Bullets zinged into their bodies. Blood spurted from fresh wounds, and his troop dropped dead within a few hours.

As he lay dying, a little girl, an eerie glowing spectre in the bright sunlight, whispered in his ear.

"*James Harberson failed to return to the caves one night.*

"*Like you, he had disappeared over the hills after hearing the whoops of the raiding Indians. He never returned. Mrs. Harberson found his severed head a mile from the fort, beside a tree carved with their initials. She kept his head in a complete state of preservation for many years.*

"On certain nights, the people swore they saw him dancing with Mrs. Harberson beneath that tree."

The little girl with freckles splattered across her cheeks took a knife to his hand and cut off his pinky.

"For your wife," she said.

With the same knife, she cut off his thumb.

"For our guardian of spirits," she said, *and skipped away with her fleshly trinkets.*

The man stepped away from Leslie, and she shuddered as though long needles had been withdrawn from her fingers.

"Avoid shadows, my dear. By the time you hear the battle, you're already walking among the dead," he said, vanishing into the stone structure.

Avoid shadows echoed in her head, and she was afraid, afraid of standing alone in the cemetery.

A bronze plaque adorned the door of the family sepulchre, reading:

Charles Beaumont Somner, born 18 July 1830, died 10 October 1862 during the battle of Perryville. "From the valley of death comes the shadows of life."

Winding back along the paths, she carried Moon, who had his claws dug into her leather jacket, but she didn't care about the tiny holes, only about her wretched past puncturing in the shell of her new life.

The snow crumpled under her steps. Her breath steamed into the frigid air. Within a few numbing minutes, she made her way back to the party and borrowed Bruce's cell phone to call a taxi service.

Exhausted. An easy enough excuse to give and 100 percent the truth. She was tired of the nightmarish chaos and of trying to escape it. As the cab pulled out of Spring Grove, as headstones dwindled from her sight, she doubted that she would find peace in the grave.

Lights extinguished in the homes, it was a dark way home.

Whiskers twitching, ears flicking, Moon slept in her lap during the ride and chased his dream-mice. There was no stalker in his mind, and she envied him. Envied even the warmth of his body as she shivered with a cold deeper than the winter.

Her apartment looked no different than when she left, but still she stood outside, holding cat and camera, unable to move inside.

Her head throbbed with images not her own.

She has no eyes, only shadowy pits, but she is not blind to Hell.

Pulled by macabre strings, she entered her apartment building. Moon's tail bushed in fear-electrified response.

The Dark Man has his hands upon her.

The key unlocked the door with a hollow click as empty as her apartment. Or maybe not. She stepped through the open door and found words written on her wall in wet burgundy.

Gasping for breath, she clutched her chest and pushed on the knife pressure within.

Words screamed in blood, *Come back to me or die.*

Her mouth filled with the copper taste of those words. Growling, Moon leapt from her arms and scurried away with clicking nails under the bed.

Blood on his hands.

The phone rang, jarring her.

For whom the bell tolls, something whispered.

"Hello?" Inaudible word on the crackling line.

"Leslie? It's Mom." Echoes of nightmares in the familiar voice, of pain, of betrayal.

He holds the blade.

"How did you get my number?" Leslie blinked as the words dried and crumbled to the floor like brick dust.

"I saw an article about your upcoming photography exhibit in the *Cincinnati Enquirer.* I called your agent's office, told them it was an emergency, and got your number."

Silence, save her ragged breath. One second, two, breathless waiting now for the news . . .

He cut her eyes for him to see.

"Charlotte's dead," her mother said. "Funeral in two days. You need to come home."

Grief wrenched her heart. Terrible wails formed in the pit of her stomach, and her whole body tightened, depressing, squeezing out the immense feeling, and a strangled cry was released. Her best friend dead. It was like losing a sister.

"Sam needs your help."

"Why?" Leslie sobbed.

"Because they suspect him of Charlotte's murder."

The line went dead and in the static his laughter cackled. Slamming the receiver into the cradle, she dropped to the floor and hugged her knees. She had to return to Elk Lake. To reconnect with the horrors of her past and face the new ones of the future, but she wouldn't let Sam fall prey to the legions of Shadows.

Madness drove her away, and madness would bring her home.

When the bough breaks, the cradle will fall.

Exactly where *he* wanted her.

Down will fall baby, cradle and all.

Chapter Three

Coatl withdrew from her, lingering at the gray threshold before he plunged back into the world. Lightning sparked like silver webs through the ashy ether, and the viscera-pink matter, which swirled suspended in air, flashed into view. The myriad of eyes within the embryonic tissues caught the light, all winking bright and storm-violent.

Beyond this threshold, all things unformed dwelled. Indescribable and alien, slick horrors bubbled up from the murk below, and he realized every living creature had a touch of monster within it, being fashioned from this unnatural material, the stuff of slaughterhouse wastes. He dubbed the gray abyss the Reincarnation Factory.

The loathsome assembly line flowed by him, and their seeping vapors stuck to him, coating him with albumin as though this place meant to remold him in its womb.

Coatl hummed a lullaby, inspired by Leslie's mind and the fetuses-in-wait, and the lurker in the deep, the mother of all abominations, sighed. With *her* breath, the uterine waters swelled. Ripples churned on the gray-blackish surface, and waves of malformed demons spewed forth.

"Ring around the rosies, pocket full of toesies, ashes, ashes, we all fall down."

The demons circled him, throwing the abattoir bits at him.

Faster and faster, they rounded him until flames, orange like old gold, rolled along the circle and formed a wheel of fire. They showed him the fires of creation, magma belching from the bowels of the earth, red, hot liquid flowing, steaming, cooling from the rains into blackened lands. They showed him the fires that consumed his home, fiery tongues licking away the timbers like blood off a wound, smoldering cries from his family within the smoky embers, choking pain within him. They showed him the fires waiting to consume him. Charred figures were hidden within the smoke, eager for his crispy flesh.

With shrills and snarls, the shadow creatures said, "Our dreaded lords command your obedience. Else we devour you entirely."

"I will obey," he said as the pitch-dark fiends stepped closer to him, slavering loudly. His jaw locked in fear.

"No, give up your ghost for us. We promise you won't suffer . . . much," they bargained.

Shuddering, he remembered how they came upon him on the day he sealed the pact with them.

He stood in centerfield, overheated in the glare of the afternoon sun, breathless from the dry air. Flies buzzed about, and he continually brushed them away from his ball cap. The cheers, the drone of insects and distant mowers, seemed to stuff his ears, deafening him with their monotony. His sight fogged as he faded in a whiteout. In his peripheral vision, grim specters flew toward him, darkening his view until he was cast in a gloomy shroud of their embraces.

They violated him, penetrating his ears, mouth, nose, and anus. He had bitten his lower lip as the malignancies rankled through his body.

Even now, Coatl chewed his tongue as the pain's eight-year-old memory festered in his mind.

He had collapsed in a broken reap of sweat, insanity mumbling from his lips. Their whispers echoed in his mind.

"Give us a part of you, and we'll give you a part of us. Else we devour you entirely."

"Yes," he had muttered, not truly aware of what his promise entailed, only wanting their fangs removed from his innards.

Gases twisted in his intestines, painful bubbling within, and he lost control of his bowels. Doubled over, he clutched his cramping gut as erupting gases and burning shit spurted out of his ass. His friends gathered around, first jeering, then silent when the gases became words. His teammates heard the flatulating voices, "devour you," and ran shrieking from the field. In the bleachers, the pretty girls hid their pretty faces in their pretty hands, screeching ugly with disgust.

Coatl was sprawled in the grass, rocking, shaking with pain, gagging on his septic odors, reeling from the bloated thing inside him. He heard a confusion of tongues—the static of the people in the background speaking, not with their mouths but their minds, their thoughts within his head; the cacophony of demons, their hissing laughter, their slithery murmurs; and his own mind in noisy bedlam. Coiled in his gut, a demon tugged on his viscera and wrapped himself in it.

The demon pressed its cold lips against his inner ear.

"Listen to the lonely heart. Its ragged rhythm."

And, in the haze, he caught the flub-dub of a heart. The beat grew louder and louder, and he noticed a female figure approaching through his half-closed eyes.

"Feel the heat between her legs."

And her warmth poured from her body and touched him as she knelt beside him.

"Touch her empty spaces. Fill her."

And with a strength not wholly his, he pulled her to the ground, ripped her yellow shorts off her bone-knobbed hips, her screams barely heard over the din of the demon's glee, and weighed her down with his shit-smeared body.

"Taste her fear."

And he bit into her lips, crushing her screams into pulp and blood.

Hands grappled him, dragging him off her, and he saw her face, that narrow face with its pallor in her hollow cheeks, the nurse's homely face, a perfect mirror of the sickness she administered to. Tears wet those hollows, and her blood finally gave her the color she so long missed.

Heat stroke, they explained. He giggled a bit, and the doctor had frowned, as if reconsidering his diagnosis, but released him to the world again with the something inside him begging for more *heat stroke*.

The flames died around the demons.

"Light has been subordinated to the gloomy beings," they snickered.

Light, the warmth and joy of life, had given over to the dark, the night, the gloom, the fear of the darksome death.

As an agent of darkness, Coatl acquired the power to steal into bodies, like these black-smoke demons, through the breath, and to shroud their souls from the light and take them into the dark. *Xibalba*. The phantom place begged his return, and the demons reminded him of the task ahead. Reminded him how important it was for him not to fail as they brought darkened skies upon him.

The threshold became a black space of obsidian rock and cavernous pits.

Giant bats with carmine-glowing eyes swooped down from the rafters, and the blades of their wings razed his astral flesh, splitting new death wounds upon him.

"The Bat-God has a command," the demons said.

Coatl bowed upon the ground, waiting.

"Do you remember the rites?"

"Yes," Coatl answered, remembering the day he stumbled into an irreal world and was handed the book of rites.

Some days he would forget himself as he wandered up and down Main Street, flitting into one small shop after another, picking up residual energies of patrons and even the artifacts sold. He particularly enjoyed the library. Not that many of the town's folk visited, but the books seemed to call from the shelves, not the stories within but the hands that had held them.

While a severe thunderstorm raged outside, amid the rattling windows and hail-pelted roof, he had run his fingers over the volumes' spines, drifting into hallucinations. The books' leather or cardboard bindings changed beneath his fingertips. He was fingering backbones.

Nancy McMullen glanced up from the desk and smiled in her efficient and unfriendly manner. She had one of those smiles that was more like a reaction to painful abdominal gas. As if nothing unusual was happening to the books, she returned to her paperwork, scribbling out notes of late dues. The chocolate truffles she nibbled on looked like eyeballs to him. One by one, they went into her wrinkled lips, and she sucked the white pulp out. He broke out in a cold sweat.

A frail set of bones, bent and brittle with disease, almost splintered from his touch. These were the bones of decay. Worm pockets pitted the browning surface, and a voice seeped from them as if they were mouths.

"I am trapped in my death of this dream, dreaming of Sartre's Argos. I had wept one time reading his works, so dark and utterly damnable. Sin. My sin was living in the books. Now I am dead in the books," the voice said, continuing in her dead voice like the buzzing of flies. "This eternal passage, '. . . Then those blood-smeared walls, these swarms of flies, this reek of shambles and the stifling heat, these empty streets and younger god with his gashed face, and all those creeping, half-human creatures beating their breasts in darkened rooms, and those shrieks, those hideous bloodcurdling shrieks—can it be that Zeus and his Olympians delight in these?' And I say yes, they do. As does every soul, its very nature clotted with darkness. We all know the greatest works and lives are tragedies."

He remained silent, a little scared of the talking bones. Around him, the partial skeletons shifted on the shelves, clacking like seashells snapping apart. The room stank of mildew and sulfur.

"You delight in those, don't you? Yes, I can tell. I can see the blight in your soul, the sliver of black pus putrefying in your heart." She cackled like a rank old witch. "Those half-formed creatures found a darkened abode in you! I like my Hell much better than yours."

The storm punctuated her sentence with a thunderclap, heaven smacking the bare ass of earth. The lights blinked out, and he was surrounded by darkness and cornered by things darker.

"Free us. Else we devour you entirely."

And he bolted from the library, frightened of the things he couldn't see.

Running in the cold, stinging rain, he had headed for the lake. Elk Lake was a private resort, for people who liked seclusion and nature but not the inconveniences of camping. He'd found a rend in the fence at its back perimeter. Since then, he'd come to the lake whenever things got rough. He couldn't think of a better time to collect his wits before madness settled in his mind.

He entered the first empty summer home in sight. Stripping off his drenched shirt and jeans, he threw them in the dryer next to the bathroom. He turned on the hot water and hopped into the scalding shower, shrieking as the water scorched his flesh. It was no different than the demon's infestation within him.

When he stepped from the stall, he cringed as he toweled off. His back was bright pink, and he popped the few blisters that had begun to form. At least the pus wasn't black.

A figure sat on the bed. He cried out in surprise, thinking the homeowners had returned.

The figure growled, "Read and learn. Knowledge is power." He set a book on the bed, rose, and sauntered out of the cabin, easy and carefree, like it was the most natural thing to be a dead man walking. He watched the man's long black hair whip in the wind, his red scalp dangling against the back of his neck. Millipedes and beetles burrowed in the furrows of his green-graying brain.

He almost wanted to follow the man and throttle him, but he didn't know how to kill a man already dead. Heading back to the bed, he wondered if the book held some of those answers.

It was the *Popul Voh*. He opened the book and understood the Mayan words as he read about the ritual of Tezcatlipoca, the equivalent of the Aztec Xipe-Totec. He had his first clue as to what the shadow creatures expected of him.

It was the uprising of two ancient civilizations, united and not as long dead as scholars believed, and he was their key to unlock the dark future.

Overwhelmed by the unreal, he had blacked out.

Coatl had long since given up his childish dread of the unknown and the dark. His second sight also allowed him to spot the dying. Their death masks grinned at him, and he took it as a challenge. He came to them on their final nights, taking their souls from their still-breathing bodies and setting them on the course to Xibalba. It was like ball practice to him. Until the real games began.

The Mexican *Book of the Dead* was also rich in poetry and heroism like the *Popul Voh*, and it detailed Xibalba enough for him to navigate its tests. Now it was like coming home.

"We look forward to the torture," the demon brood cut in, erasing his memories.

Wisps of black smoke curled out of their mouths and stretched toward Coatl, forming a lattice around him, like threads of a web. They held him immobile. One raked its talons against his back, gouging his astral flesh. The demon tied the ribbons of his skin around its neck like a bow tie.

"Wear the skins, and the scars will heal." Its foul breath exhaled into his open, screaming mouth, choking him. "You have picked your victim for sacrifice, yes?"

"Yes," he grunted.

"Blood Gatherer will come as soon as the arrows pierce the body. The body should rain blood, remember. Else Blood Gatherer will rip your heart out instead and devour it entirely."

"I remember." He also remembered the story of creation, how Tezcatlipoca and the dreaded gods destroyed the first man. The mannikins, carved from wood, angered the gods with their irreverence. Then Hurakan caused the waters to swell and flood upon the mannikins. The bird Xecotcovach tore out their eyes, the bird Camulatz cut off their heads, the bird Cotzbalam devoured their flesh, the bird Tecumbalam broke their bones and sinews and ground them into powder. The only remnants of the first man are their progeny, the little monkeys, dwelling in the woods.

He recognized their disguises and knew how they dealt out their wrath. He would not anger them and be wiped out.

"Tell me what they want from me," he said.

Solid ground evaporated into air, and he fell into a vacuum. He was sucked out of the threshold and his astral self was thrown back into his body with such force that he slammed against the wall and his nose bled.

Drop after drop of his blood landed on the open pages of the yearbook, a sanguine rainfall drowning out the human faces. He was the symbolic god, Tezcatlipoca. His testicles tightened up in little excited balls, and his skin quivered in anticipation of wearing the skin of his victim.

"Command me, my Masters," he said as he licked the blood from the glossy paper. Leslie's picture appeared from the ruby puddles.

"Take her to Xibalba and hand her over to the Bat-God," they answered from the shadows.

Chapter Four

With a cup of hot tea warming her hands, Leslie curled into the bay window's seat and counted the dim stars in the night sky. Something to keep her mind focused before it unraveled. Every time she had tried to close her eyes, images of blood-washed hands throttled her sleep, and she decided not to fight with them and gave up the idea of sleeping this night.

This night; she sighed. Across the room, a small lamp lit an Ansel Adams frame—round moon lonely in the black sky, streaks of white clouds on the horizon above the snow-tipped Rocky Mountains, gray sagebrush bristling along the desert, a adobe-mecca chapel and its burial ground's white-gleaming gravestones. Ethereal, ghostly. The dead highlighted with the rising sun—the dead seeming the only life in a deserted land. It was a conflicting image, but she loved it. Maybe Ansel Adams saw more than the empty graveyard, maybe he saw what she had seen, the dead rise instead of the sun and walk with the night.

A shriek came from beyond the window and a shadow flew by.

Leslie jerked, spilling her tea on her wrist, its steaming water dripping into her lap, but she didn't feel it as she watched bats soar around the courtyard. A flock? A fleet? A swarm? Was there any word to describe the sheer number of bats flying? But swarm they did, in black droves in the sky, circling with eerie song.

With his hackles raised, Moon growled and slashed at the window, and the night-flyers picked up on his nails tapping ferocious against the glass and, in mass synchronicity, headed for them. Leslie screamed at their approaching faces.

Their *lack* of faces. Hundreds of bats without features, only black hollows between their leathery wings. Though mouthless, the bats emitted terrible shrills, splintering the glass with their pitch, and delicate lace patterns spread outward like beautiful ice crystals on a dangerous pond.

She jumped off the seat and backed farther into the room. Black bodies smacked into the window, with scores of thuds and tinkling chimes of shards hitting the floor.

Wind rushed into the room, carrying the odors of the black plague, of sulfurous rot and sickly burnt death. As she covered her head with her arms, the bats vanished into the wind. Only her clutter of papers flew about the room, pages flapping like wings.

A rock lay on the floor, beneath the window, upon a shattered mess. Someone had painted a face upon the rock—onyx eyes and ruby-moist mouth.

And shrill screams came from the unmoving mouth.

Seconds passed before Leslie realized it was the phone ringing, and she gave a whimpering laugh.

She picked up the receiver, her hand shaking and nerves wrought.

"Come home, or we will devour you entirely," the phone hissed, and then there were only legions of crackles and white noises and slavering sighs.

Tearing the phone from the wall, she threw it to the floor, and it scattered in plastic clangs toward the rock.

This night would never end.

Leslie grabbed her travel bag and stuffed her clothes, still on their hangers, into it, making sure she packed her black suit for the funeral. Trodding behind her, Moon carried his toy mouse in his mouth and looked quite happy to be leaving the apartment.

But where they were headed would prove to be worse than a hundred nights like this. She was certain of that, more certain than of anything in her life, but until she found a way to escape her own shadow, she had to stop running. She had to return to the beginning, the only place for it to end. *Full circle*, her father's favorite theory.

She threw her bags into the Jetta, glanced at her apartment, and wondered if she would ever set foot in it again. The rising sun set its gilded light upon the building, but her windows remained dark, reflecting her foreboding future. She was scared.

She called Rod from her cell phone to let him know she'd left.

"Left where?" he grumbled, his tongue thick with sleep.

"I'm going home, to Owenton. A friend has died." The phone cut out as she headed through downtown, skyline interference.

". . . the shadows have come . . ."

"What?" Leslie yelled into the tiny receiver.

"I asked, do you want me to come?"

The tires whined over the steel deck of the suspension bridge, dreadful noise coming from below. *From the deep, dark waters of the river*, she thought.

"No, I prefer to go alone. Too many issues to deal with, and I don't want to burden you with them," she said as she crossed the state line, feeling as if Ohio crumpled behind her, never to exist again. "You have your audition anyway."

"I'd skip it for you. You know that." She heard the hurt in his voice.

"Yes," but she couldn't muster any more; her guilty heart twisted her tongue. Rod tried every measure to break through her walls, even a fraction would do for him, and she never let him in. Maybe it was his kindness and caring that kept her pushing him away when he got close because she couldn't bear losing him, and she couldn't be sure, if he knew the truth about her, that he would be so kind.

"Why do I feel like you're running away from me?" he asked.

Because I am.

"I'll be back after the funeral in a couple days, at the most a week. Don't worry, and good luck on your audition. I'll be thinking about you. 'Bye."

"I love you, Leslie."

But she'd already hit the end call button before she could respond. *If she could've responded.* Her shy heart pounded nails through her lips at the slightest impulse of expressing words of love.

I-75 stretched gray and empty at this early hour, dawn at the edge of the world still, and her mouth became drier the farther south she drove. The deer warning sign with its red-nose sticker didn't elicit a smile from her as it usually did. Rudolph lay bloated and stiff in the grass median.

"Daddy, what makes the dead raccoon's belly swell? Does it still eat?"

"No, it's the gases trapped inside."

"Did it eat something that made it gassy, like with you and red peppers?"

Her father had laughed. "No. The dead don't eat."

"Oh. I thought I had seen it suck dark things into its mouth yesterday."

Her father hadn't laughed the rest of the day.

By the time she made it to the Dry Ridge exit,

the sun had risen a pale orange, muted by the rain or snow clouds, depending on the wind and the mood of the lands, she supposed. It wasn't unusual for the temperature to soar into the seventies during February. The weather might be unpredictable, but they could always predict a warm spell during this winter month.

She went through McDonald's drive-thru and ordered a cinnamon roll and an orange juice. She contemplated Shoney's breakfast buffet to stall her inevitable arrival, but she wasn't that hungry. With her stomach in knots, she forced down what little food she bought. The sticky icing reminded her of Jake, her stepfather. Pulling her Jetta over, she opened the door and vomited.

This is a huge mistake, she thought. *I'm as foolhardy as Dad walking back into the monster's lair, and probably just as dead.*

When she was a little girl, with her brown hair tightly wound in braids and sunflower patches on her jeans, her dad had called her "his little weed flower" as they hiked through the woods, searching for tender saplings of dogwoods, or clumps of yarrow, to sell to local vendors. He didn't have a regular job. He fixed roofs, raised barns, did some caretaking here and there on the summer homes, and worked on the tobacco farms with the immigrant Mexicans.

Leslie liked to tag along behind her dad, imitating his bowlegged walk, marveling at how adventurous his life seemed to an eight-year-old. He was a scraggly man with an unkempt beard peppered with gray, and he wore loose-fitting denim overalls to hide his severely thin frame, but she didn't mind his scarecrow appearance. He always had a twinkle in his deep-set blue eyes and a smile to brighten her day. To keep her entertained, he told her stories. His favorites centered on campfire tales of ghosts and demons, but he swore some of them were true. He couldn't stress enough how evil influences had taken root in Owenton. And he wasn't referring to the illegal aliens.

As she sped down Route 22, taking the *S* curves like a stock car racer, she lost her focus on the road; instead of seeing trees reaching high branches over pavement, she saw her dad gripped by unseen hands and tossed into a brambling honeysuckle bush. He had spewed blood from his mouth as his chest caved inward. The doctors called it heart failure. Before he died in her arms, he called it the shadows.

Only one person could give her enough of an answer to satisfy her child's curiosity. Everyone called him L.W., which stood for Lone Wolf. He had the look of a wolf—long nose, sharp slate eyes almost like silver cataracts, and a wide grin. He was a Mexican Indian who had worked with her dad, and she had witnessed him "dance the fire tongue," as he liked to call storytelling.

She remembered her dad was particularly interested in the one about the challenge from the Kiche Hades, how the rulers of the dread abode tricked the sons of their enemies into coming down to the Underworld for a game of ball.

The hero brothers, Hunhun-Apu and Vukub-Hunapu, discovered quickly that the Lords of Hades had fooled them and had meant to ridicule them further. After they crossed the river of blood, they came upon two figures sitting within the palace courtyard. They thought the figures were Hun-Came and Vubuk-Came, the sovereigns of Hell, and saluted them, but they were merely wood carvings. The inhabitants jeered at the brothers, offending them further.

They invited the brothers to sit in the seats of honor. To their dismay, Hunhun-Apu and Vubuk-Hunapu sat on red-hot stones. Next they were imprisoned in the House of Gloom, waiting for their sacrifice. Vubuk-Hunapu was finally buried in the House of Gloom, but Hunhun-Apu's head was hung from a tree branch that grew crops of gourds like the dreadful trophy head. The Lords forbade any one in Xibalba to eat of the fruit.

L.W. had winked at her when he finished, saying, "But what is a good story without a woman to disobey and go after what is forbidden? Some other day I will tell you of the princess and the divine children who eventually tricked the tricksters and avenged Hunhun-Apu and Vubuk-Hunapu."

After her father died, that day never came. She didn't visit the fields much, except with Charlotte to scope out Buddy and his friends, and then she didn't have the heart to speak to L.W. The stories were so much a part of her dad, and it pained her to be reminded of what was once a joy shared between them.

Leslie wondered how Buddy was handling Charlotte's death, considering the news in Sam's last letter that they had eloped.

What else did I miss in my absence? she thought as she hit the brakes to avoid a baby raccoon. In her rearview, she saw the car behind her smash its little round body, rolling it in separate pieces to the other side of the road.

Leslie cried out, in surprise and also pain. It was as if its disembodied spirit flew into her and hit her heart. According to her dad, her great-great-aunt was what he called a sensate, something of a clairvoyant, with the ability to sense things, like energy, omens, spirits, feelings, something more than an empath. *Something of a freak, just like me.*

Though, at times, sensing had its rewards. She slowed around the bend, anticipating the canopy ahead. The tree limbs had grown over the road, like bark-skinned arms and hands reaching to form a living bridge. When Leslie drove under, it always felt like the trees sighed and hugged her. She couldn't explain it any more clearly. She just felt an overwhelming sense of love and comfort from the canopy, and she envied the people living in the house next to it, believing their dreams soothed them with fragrant blossoms and soft breezes of content. The bough wouldn't break beneath them as it did in her dreams nightly.

The Void

Her dad would joke about her great-great-aunt, Josephine Starr, unmarried nag hag who scared everyone in town with her troops of ghosts. Doors would open for her and chairs would slide out to accept her large derriere without a seen human hand to guide them. She was labeled a witch. Among the town's folk, a rumor circulated about Josephine's prophesy of a tornado that would wipe out the tobacco fields. Half feared for their livelihood if such a thing should happen; the others scoffed.

In 1913, in the hottest summer on record, a violent tornado touched down, roaring winds twisting so fast that the grass was torn up from the earth. Most of the farmers lost their crops. Josephine was then sought after by folks, to tell their fortune, or contact the dead. She acquired enough money to purchase the Gothic mansion on Main Street. She had had her eye on the Queen Anne on North Adams, but the owners wouldn't sell to her. The neighboring church paid a fine sum to the family to keep it out of the hands of a she-devil.

The grand white house had gone through a few owners after Josephine died, before the bank finally owned it. When she was younger, it was the house the braver boys would put dares on to sneak into and spend the night. No one, as far as she knew, ever made it beyond a couple of hours. Most of the kids would stand across the street, eating pizza, drinking their colas, watching the flashlight's beam bob up and down in the house for fifteen minutes until darkness blinked on. After that, the kids who watched from outside listened to the yells and the crashes, nearly wetting their pants but feeling safe enough across the street not to consider running away. The boys who'd accepted the dare would sprint from the house, eyes wide on plaster-white faces.

They would never say what really happened, but their arms had scratches and their cheeks had ruby kiss prints. The next day everyone would laugh about the boys being frightened by the Cootie Monster.

Still, the house stood forlorn on the top of the hill, its paint peeling away like dry skin flaking off. Its foundation began to crumble under the weight of its rotting beams. Honeysuckle grew tall and wild around the grounds, permeating the area with a sickly sweet scent like a woman's perfume. Leslie's dad used to say it reminded him of lilac instead, the *eau de toilette* Josephine supposedly wore.

Leslie considered driving by the house, but she pulled into the K&L Inn, a simple ranch-style motel with eight rooms. During the hunting season, it would have no vacancy. She walked into the office, and Peggy Johnson, a tall woman with brittle yellow hair, cigarette-stained teeth, and heavy-lidded brown eyes, greeted her with indifference until Leslie signed the register.

"Lordie! I can't believe it's you. How long's it been? Since high school I think. Did you come back for Charlotte's funeral? I'm sorry about that, dear. Bonnie's all shook up over it too." Mrs. Johnson handed her the key. "How abouts I give her a call? She'd love to hear from you. We've missed you coming around. How's your mom?"

"Fine," she said, knowing Peggy loved to gossip. Bonnie and Leslie would play Scrabble in the office just to hear her mom dish out the dirt on everyone. They'd heard the funniest and the raunchiest stuff.

"Good; I worry about that woman sometimes all alone in the woods." She clucked her sympathy.

Leslie's brow pinched together. *Mom's alone? What happened to Jake? Did I abandon my family for nothing?*

"What's wrong, dear?" Peggy asked as she pushed a broom around a spotless tiled floor.

"Nothing. I have to call my mom about the funeral. Excuse me, please." Leslie hurried out of the office before she got drawn into a lengthy discussion with Peggy.

After she settled into her room, ignoring the stale stench of mold and sweat, she called her mom. Moon curled in her lap, possibly to avoid napping on the less-than-fresh sheets. Leslie frowned at the large wet-looking stain on the white chenille spread.

"Mom, it's me. I'm in town."

The decor was sparse. One cheap painting of a buck standing in a clearing of wood, its twelve-point rack covered with moss hung above the bed, and a cross and Bible were displayed at the desk.

"Where are you? Why didn't you come home first? I filled out a pass for you at the gate," her mom said.

"Is Jake there?" Leslie nibbled on her thumbnail.

"No, he's away on a hunting trip down south. Won't be back for a week."

Leslie breathed in relief.

"Leslie, I know before you left you thought something bad happened, but it didn't. You hadn't dealt with your father's death very well, and he had filled your head with all sorts of crazy notions. It was only natural for you to lash out at Jake. You thought he was trying to replace your father."

"Mom, that's not it at all. You know that isn't true." Anger welled in the pit of her stomach.

"I just wanted to speak my peace. I'm done with the subject. We have other things to worry about, like Sam," she said.

"I'll be over soon." Leslie hung up the phone, feeling as empty as the room.

She set out Moon's food near the window and put his litter box near the toilet. Black spores clung to the shower curtain and rings of rust circled the sink and tub drains. Her old room beckoned her, but she couldn't go back, not yet anyhow.

Gray clouds accompanied her to Elk Lake, darkening the area like a mammoth vulture soaring over decay. Nostalgic memories invaded her mind. Times of cruising the curvy road with gusto but nowhere to go except the Dairy Queen parking lot or back to the lake to spy on the summer boys showing off on water skis. Mornings of birdsong and golden sunrises, lazy days of fishing and hiking, and quiet nights of fireflies and crickets. All of it was dead. Just tall weeds hiding the copperhead.

Her happy memories were the greatest illusion of the goodness surrounding her life. Her dad had known something seethed beneath the thin crust of soil and had burrowed up, like maggots from a bloated carcass, in search of fresher meat. He had tried to warn her. Seven years ago. She wished she had trusted him earlier.

After turning into the entrance, she stopped at the gate and gave her name to the guard. He brought out a pink pass for her to sign. He was new, a squat older man making extra dough to supplement his Social Security checks. A sign to her right read GIVE US A BRAKE. SLOW DOWN. KIDS AND PETS. As she drove down the gravel road, she noticed they had installed street signs. She turned right onto Lakeshore Drive.

They must've smoothed out the ruts, because her Jetta had no trouble navigating the hills. She remembered how after heavy rains the gravel washed away and the tires sank into the sandy dirt and left huge tracks. The truck would bounce, and she would hit her head against the roof, laughing.

She slowed down the hill, veering to the left, gawking to her right to check the level of the reservoir. It was a habit. Wind rippled the army-green water, and the stark trees bent their crooked branches like old lady fingers knotted with arthritis grasping at thin air.

At the fork, she ventured straight, her dust trail coating the firs with an extra layer on already powdered needles. Gravel clanged in her spinning tires. Her old home, a clapboard ranch cabin painted white with blue trim, showed through the clearing. A Kentucky Wildcats flag flapped against the gutter. As she pulled into the driveway, Roseanne Starr walked out the door, wearing Leslie's dad's cargo pants and a sweatshirt.

Middle age had crept upon her weather-beaten face, deep wrinkles at her eyes and mouth, uneven ruddy complexion, broken capillaries on her nose. Telltale signs that her mom binged on the bottle again. She'd rounded out in seven years, losing her square shape in favor of softer curves on her shoulders and hips. But she kept her auburn hair styled the same, straight-cut bangs and shoulder-length spirals, glamorous hair on a country frau.

Leslie stepped from the car and faced her mom, unsure what to say or do. She felt like a stranger around the woman who'd carried her in her womb for nine months and raised her through happier times, times before the drinks, before the shadows. Without warning, her mom hugged her, crushing Leslie's skinny body into her ample, cushioned bust. Leslie stiffened. The comfort she'd known as a child, rocked against her bosom when ill, had vanished, and guilt gnawed her gut. She shouldn't have drifted from her mother, who loved her.

"Oh, Leslie! I keep thinking about Charlotte and how it could have been you. I thought about you every night, wondering if you were safe, or happy, or in need." Rose wept, her tears spilling down her face and wetting Leslie's brow. "For seven years, I mourned for my daughter who was alive."

Leslie choked on her building tears and whispered, "I'm sorry."

"I should've been there for you more after your father died, but I had to support you and your brothers. I should've sat down and discussed my relationship with Jake before we got married. Maybe you would've handled it differently and things would be better now." Rose brushed the hair out of Leslie's eyes and kissed her forehead with thin, hard lips.

"It's not your fault. I don't blame you." She scooted out of her mom's embrace and took a step toward the house, reconsidered, and walked up the drive. "I'm not ready to go inside. Let's walk, and you can tell me about Charlotte and how Sam's involved."

Gravel crunched underfoot, and the crows cawed periodically. The odor of decomposing leaves wafted up from the ground, mingling with the bitter scent of pine. She shrugged off the creeping dullness of winter as it tried to settle in her bones, a gray film spreading inertia in her marrow. Winter made her sullen. During the late spring, Leslie loved her long walks through the woods, jade green bursting in new leaf shoots, wildflowers blanketing the ground in sporadic patterns of color, grasshoppers whirring in the disturbing wake of her feet. Life renewed. Yet the tall grasses only hid the snakes and bloodsucking ticks.

"The neighbors called the police the minute they heard her screams. When they arrived, they had to break down the door. All the windows and doors were locked with no sign of a break-in, but someone came in, smothered Charlotte in her sleep, cut out her eyes, and left without a trace," her mom began. "Buddy was out of town. He left after he found out Charlotte had an affair with Sam. She had promised him that she would end it with Sam if Buddy forgave her. Buddy broke down, ranting that Sam must've killed his wife."

"Sam had an affair with Charlotte?" As much in denial as she was that her oldest friend was murdered, this news was unbelievable.

"Yes, for over a year." Rose kicked a rock in front of her. "Buddy and Charlotte had their share of loud fights, and her neighbor said that she used to sit on the porch after the arguments. Sam happened by one night, and they talked for hours. Next thing they knew, Sam's truck was seen parked out front every Thursday night when Buddy played poker."

"Sam and Charlotte?" Sam had never paid much attention to Charlotte when they all hung out together, although he did make it a habit to date her friends. Robin was his high-school sweetheart. "If it's true, and they were lovers, why do the cops suspect him? Sam's the gentlest guy I've ever known."

"Well, the army does strange things to a man."

She recalled the letter from Sam, explaining why he'd enlisted. Robin had gotten pregnant with another guy's baby, an older guy, a summertimer. He'd split with his heart broken. He'd lost everyone he ever loved—his uncle, his cousin, and his girl—and needed an escape. He figured dying in a war was more honorable than suicide. At the time, she empathized with him; she'd run away herself.

She and Sam were more like brother and sister than cousins. Her brothers were three, five, and eight years younger (the youngest born after their father had died), but Sam was her age. He probably ate more food from their refrigerator than she did. Since both his parents drank, he'd skip out of his plate-throwing, wall-smashing, angry, shrieking home and sleep over at Leslie's. They'd stroll the shoreline in the dark, frog-gigging, cat fishing, talking. Sometimes they'd sit silently side-by-side, understanding each other's pain and easing it with their accepting company. It was like they shared the same heart.

"What's going on with Sam?" Leslie asked.

"Seems Sam's army records shed an ugly light on him. Army officers came to find him after Charlotte's death, telling us he had violent seizures, acted aggressively, and jeopardized a top-secret mission with his mental instability." Rose twisted her gold wedding band, the one Jake bought her at

Roger's Jewelers. Her parents hadn't had enough money for rings. "The police suspect he had an outburst when Charlotte ended their affair."

"Do they have any evidence?"

"None so far. Sam told me, though, that he had nothing to do with it, and that Charlotte had never broken it off with him. He didn't make it to her house that night because he was documenting what he saw during a training session. He's afraid the government's after him. He almost doesn't believe Charlotte's dead, that they're concocting this scheme to get rid of him."

Leslie shifted her attention to the spindly dogwoods. Cocoons of spider eggs clung to the branches in huge white clumps.

Eerie, she thought. Aloud she said, "Did he tell you what he was documenting? It sounds like he's being paranoid. Is it true he's unstable?"

"He worked on something called remote viewing. The army was trying to create what Sam called psychic spies."

"Psychic spies?"

"Yeah, something to do with ESP," Rose said, picking a spiderweb off her cheek. "He said they could spy on the enemy with their minds, like invisible spirits watching."

Chapter Five

Take her to Xibalba and hand her over to the Bat-God.

Coatl snuffed the burning sage and paced the brittle, creaking floor, wondering why Camazotz would demand a living sacrifice. The Bat-God was not a deity to show mercy. Instead he decapitated unwary travelers in the dark of his caverns with his mighty swordlike claws, the same that severed the hero Hunhun-Apu's head from his body.

As his feet connected with solid ground, after so long detached from this reality, pain issued from the balls of his feet and coursed through his calves and thighs, pinching and prickling nerves with pins and needles. The back of his neck burned from the stiff position he'd held for hours. Coatl wondered where he would find the strength to carry on through the labyrinth cavern of bats, especially dragging an unwilling traveler along.

The thought of the trials that lay ahead tapped his reserves, and sweat beaded on his brow as the demon within churned his anxious guts. He suffered this dark sickness, knowing the only cure was to do as the dreaded gods commanded of him.

He recalled the balmy winds, heady with hibiscus fragrance, that breezed through the caves. An illusion, all of it, because the whispers in the tunnels led wanderers into a dead end. Literally a dead end, with the path pitted with stalagmite-filled wells, with red-crusted points waiting for fresh bodies to fall and impale themselves. Beyond, huge bats hung sleeping, and, if a figure walked upright instead of crawling upon the shale fragments and bony pebbles, skinning palms and knees, the bats would swoop down and tear into them. Coatl had seen numerous headless bodies still standing, their feet cemented with bat guano.

Those who survived and reached the end of the craggy tunnels met with the most horrible sight, of the Bat-God perched upon his throne of bones, sniffing for blood with his convoluted snout. His eyes glowed crimson upon his black bat face, and his blood-worm gaze bored into the mind as if extracting thoughts and dreams and every last bit of sanity.

And then the horrible god would greet his visitor by wrapping his giant leathery wings around him and goring into his soft sides with his bone hook tips. With fetid, blood-curdling breath, he would relay his message.

Coatl had heard, "Warriors slay, and you have yet to shed flesh and blood. Slay or be slain." Deeper the bone hooks sank into his side, and the Bat-God pressed his twisted mouth against his side and sucked Coatl's blood until he collapsed, near drained of spirit. He'd woke back in his body, with no memory of how he got there, with an ache in his core but with a vile intent to be a warrior.

He wished he'd experienced the man-flaying festival for Xipe, when the red god's devotees removed and wore the skins of their victims, in order to keep his ritual on a par with what Xipe expected. Any mistake would result in his own skin torn from his body, his bones crushed, and his blood devoured.

"I can't imagine the agony of my flesh being torn from my bones," he said aloud.

Groans from the corner seemed to sympathize with the sentiment.

He addressed the figure bound in the corner. "But then I'll have an idea tonight, won't I? Vicariously felt, of course. I'm not such a monster that I can't feel empathy for your pain as I strip your skin from your parasite-infested body. Think of it as my way of showing you mercy—a quick death rather than a long, insufferable death as your heart fails because of the parasites multiplying within it."

The figure kicked both feet against the floorboards, stomping up dust but unable to break free.

Coatl grabbed a glass specimen jar from the step. Turning it in his hands, he dissected the kissing bug with his eyes, noting the long sharp proboscis in which the insect pierced the sleeper's skin, mostly near the corner of the mouth, and fed. The beetle-like bug came from Central America, a gift from the man who once performed priestly rituals in the temples of Mitla and who still practiced sacrifices in secret in this small town.

While the kissing bug fed, it defecated, and the parasites in its feces would flow in the blood until they reached the heart. There, the parasites would feed and breed. Eventually the parasites would inhabit the entire heart muscle, destroying the organ little by little as they filled the reddest spaces. Their host would never know of his infected state, would never know of his slow death until his heart finally stopped. A seemingly natural death. Coatl grinned at the warrior bug.

Years ago, he had placed the insect upon his victim during a wild turkey hunting trip and watched the bug kiss him to death. He had done it for Leslie. But what he intended for tonight, he'd do for the gods.

"Too bad Leslie won't witness your screaming death. Do you think she'd enjoy watching you die after what you did to her?"

Unable to answer, Leslie's stepfather Jake struggled with the ropes and gagged on muffled curses.

*   *   *

Coatl worked his way through the woods, frozen moss crinkling beneath his feet, tangles of dead weeds and limbs snagging his ankles, pine branches scratching at him. Through the web of trees he spied the neighboring farm in the clearing, its fields empty, its double-wide trailer home dark. He knew the owners weren't home and would never return, but it wasn't unusual in the country to abandon homes, leaving them to rot like the fields. Rot like their bodies, even.

The couple had fallen victim several years ago, the first of his attempts at bringing souls to Xibalba. Though he couldn't recall the husband's name, he'd worked with him in the tobacco fields, watching the man's cancer show upon his face, in the way his flesh coated his skull like gray paste, and the way his sulfurous breath tainted his lips.

He'd crept into the man's dreams over the course of three nights. At first, Coatl had shifted the mindscape, warping the design of the man's river-dream where the waters rippled in the formation of steps, of stairwells that spiraled into the earth, where fish-headed gods waited in the depths and sharpened their hook-mouths for the bite.

The second night he had entered the stairwell, ascending from the darkness with the changes he'd wrought upon himself, the skull face, the shadowy cloak, the wounds. He'd met the frightened man at the shore. He'd whispered in the man's ear, the demon slipping its arrow-tongue into his skull and licking his brain, and the man screamed himself awake, leaving Coatl still lurking within his mind.

Disturbed by the presence of something he couldn't describe, the man had ranted and periodically smacked his head as he hung the harvested tobacco in the drying barn. He'd ripped a broad leaf and chewed the nasty bitter plant-flesh, mumbling about devouring demons. The field manager had approached him, in an attempt to coerce him into taking the rest of the day off, but the man had spit on the manager and tore his hair from his scalp, screaming insanely about the Dark Man gnawing at his brain.

Coatl had enjoyed playing with the man, tormenting him until he had passed out in fear, and then he had gripped his spirit and pushed him down the flight of nightmare stairs onto the Xibalban landing, beginning his death journey a bit earlier than nature had intended.

That night Coatl had taken the dead man's heartbroken wife. Simple enough to lead her into Xibalba, wearing the face of her dead husband.

As he'd returned to the laboring fields, he'd spotted an omen, of two obsidian butterflies fluttering among the honeysuckle growing at the edge of the farm. Black butterflies were considered the dead souls, and he saw how beautiful the two he had delivered to the dead abode had become. It had pleased him.

Between his dark deeds and the shadows, Owenton had swarmed with black butterflies.

And then Leslie had upset the balance by fleeing like a fickle butterfly to another flowering state. His efforts to show off his metamorphosis powers had failed to attract her attention, and so he had stopped the unnecessary killing in order to concentrate his powerful eye on her.

Take her to Xibalba and hand her to the Bat-God.

Years of watching her life would end when he watched her death.

Reaching the creek that bordered Elk Lake, Coatl stopped and squatted at its bank. An injured bat floundered in the winter grass, its left wing shattered at the shoulder bone and its wing fibers torn, as if it had been mauled by another animal, a dog perhaps. A bad omen.

Bats represented change, death, and rebirth, of facing fears and darkness, and this dying symbol could only mean Coatl would face his darkest transition with the possibility of not coming through it.

He placed his fingers upon the bat and crushed its neck.

Or better yet, it possibly foretold his defeating his fears and death forever.

Demons bubbled in black gurgling crude from the creek and slipped murky tendrils around his ankles.

"Come into Tlillan," they growled.

Tlillan, blackness, a Tenochtitlan chamber of perpetual darkness where the stone image of the female deity Chiuacoatl was kept, and the only entrance was through a small crawlspace. The

Woman Snake, with her large mouth and horrible teeth, demanded the sacrifice of war victims and a great feast in her honor, the blood and hearts of slaves.

"Why?" Coatl asked, wary of the demons.

"Share the feast of the gods. Will you refuse again?" Blackness grinned silver and chortled metallic laughter.

Share the leftover bodies half-roasted on coals and sip blood that has dripped from slit throats, an honor he couldn't refuse.

"I will, but Tenochtitlan does not lie beneath the water."

"We did not mention Tenochtitlan. We spoke of Tlillan," a demon said, rippling the waters with a talon.

"But isn't Tlillan in Tenochtitlan?" Coatl tried taking a step from the bank, but the demons held him firm.

The shadows rose from the waters, black corruptions smudging the air and blocking all the day's gray light, dim red eyes slick and revolting like blood-pus sores.

"Come into blackness, we said." They enveloped him then with their coal-dark, choking ether. "Eat our flesh and drink our blood."

Dark tendrils wormed into his mouth and fished down his throat, and Coatl's gag reflex spasmed and his stomach acid burned up his pharynx. Bloody ectoplasm seeped into his mouth and gurgled slow and thick down his esophagus and into his agitated gut, tasting of tar and corpses.

The demon within him made terrible sucking sounds and sighs as it fed intravenously. The others hissed like dangerous gas leaking from corroded pipes and suicide ovens.

With this slime running down his throat, Coatl shuddered and endured the revolting ingestion, even as it choked through his body and stiffened his muscles and softened his bones. He stood flaccid in their embrace, feasting on blackness.

Take her to Xibalba and hand her over to the Bat-God. He felt the strength he would need filter through his marrow and enrich his blood. The strength of demons made of gods.

He crossed the creek, sloughing off the demons along the way, grinning as he headed toward the boundary of Elk Lake. The cut in the wire fence was easy to make, and he trespassed onto the private property, picking her scent off the chilly breeze with his enhanced sense of smell. Indeed, he caught the odors of the frozen earth and the cold itself, sharp and fresh and slightly ionic. He breathed deeply all the interesting and subtle tinctures of life and death. He felt extraordinarily renewed after feasting on god-children.

The dead bat still hung limp in his palm. A good omen after all, he thought, and let it drop with a soft plop onto the brambling pile of twigs and leaves.

In the woods no trails existed, and he forced his way through overlapping branches, fallen timber, and various degrees of organic rot. His footfall snapped in places and sank quietly elsewhere. Birds and rabbits darted from his noisy presence, creating even more racket, and he slowed his pace, taking more care where he stepped as he neared the road. Though he couldn't see her, he heard her voice drift and echo upon the whistling wind, a warbling of fear as she questioned psychic spying.

Not very psychic now, the demon within joked.

Coatl's grin widened. *Certainly not.*

But then his grin vanished as he smelled something altogether unnatural in the woods, an odor of rancid demons darkening the ground, of the acrid sweat of someone else hiding in the shadows and walking through the formless paths.

Chapter Six

Leslie stopped walking. Sky and earth deepened in gray shades, and the temperature dropped down with a weighty cold thud. In the wood's darkness, things unseen moved. She sensed the Dark Man in there, could almost feel his warm breath against her nape, could almost hear his laughter as he watched her. Twigs crackled a warning, and Leslie swayed in dizzy fear.

Images reeled in her mind, of Charlotte, eyeless, chalk white in dark death; of the Dark Man's hands clasped upon her mouth, stifling screams and breath; of the Dark Man watching her, surrounded by shadows, lurking, a shadow himself in her dreams and mind, blackening her soul with terror; of Sam with his emerald eyes dimming in their sparkling light and with blood covering his hands.

Images of utter blackness. Images of disembodied eyes spying.

The Dark Man was coming.

Staggering into her mother, she sucked hard for shallow breaths, and her mom clutched her arm to steady her, her concern evident in the wide eyes and the lips parted with unspeakable questions.

The Dark Man was coming, she tried to say, but only a whimper escaped.

Leaves rustled and a woodsy symphony of footfalls breaking undergrowth was conducted by shadows. Leslie screamed as the pine boughs parted and a snorting figure trampled into the road.

Leslie picked up the nearest rock and flung it at the charging figure.

"What are you doing?" her mother yelled, holding her arm back. "Why are you throwing rocks at a deer?"

The deer's white tail flipped as it loped across the road and into the woods again, and Leslie shrank to her knees, embarrassed by the echo of her screams and her apparent disorientation. The sounds of the deer's departure dwindled away.

"I thought . . ."

The wind carried her thoughts in gentle eerie tones. Somewhere in there, he still waited.

"You thought what? Thought you saw something that wasn't there? Like the shadows that frightened you so much when you were little?" Rose crouched beside Leslie and kneaded her shoulder. "I never wanted to admit that I failed you as a mother, that it was my lack of intervention that ruined you."

A brisk gale zinged icy drizzle against them, and her mother's face seemed pearled with tears, such was the sadness of her pale blue eyes.

Leslie struggled with a rebuttal, some comforting words that would alleviate a mother's guilt, but she couldn't, not with the gravel gleaming like rounded bits of bone in the ruddy dirt. Not with the stick cross of her father's death site pointing at her.

Rose stood again and folded her arms across her chest, staring beyond the road at the cross. "I should've realized how traumatic it was for you to watch your father die, especially after he filled your head with ghost stories, family witches, and maddening prophesies of doom and darkness.

"I should've sought medical help for you when you suffered the night terrors, the fainting spells, and those visions. When you accused Jake of doing such a heinous thing." She paused, as if waiting for Leslie to admit she'd made a mistake, but she got angry silence from Leslie and howling wind from the world.

She continued, "They might have missed a slow-growing tumor or something when we first took you to the doctors. I should've pressed the issue. But I was afraid of the county thinking me an unfit mother because I had a disturbed child. They might've taken you away from me."

The calm surface of the lake billowed with the storm winds and darkened beneath the gathering clouds. Ozone in the air, the drizzle quickened in the wind, coming faster, building up more icy moisture. The woods came alive with noise, and Leslie started to return to the house. She couldn't shake the cold, not of the slight rain but of the Dark Man's nearing vibe.

"But then you took yourself away from me, and all my fears came true. I had lost my daughter," Rose said. She kept pace with Leslie and frowned whenever Leslie glanced behind them.

"You didn't lose me."

"I did. Seven years you've been gone without a word or phone call, without a care for the family you left behind." Rose's cold, wet fingers encircled Leslie's wrist and motioned her still. "The last of my babies at home cries out in his sleep every night like a little boy for his sister to save him from the shadows, and I'm worried I'll lose him too."

Their tension seemed to bring the rains down harder, but they stood, locked in their own misery and anxiety, each daring the other to break their silence and the years of separation. They waited for the freezing rains to dampen their bitter hearts.

Leslie wiped the rain from her face, swiping away her tears as well. Her jaws tightened with the screw of her emotions.

"Andy cries in his sleep about the shadows?" Leslie asked, never considering that the dreadful legacy that followed her would have tortured anyone else in the family. But she should've known, should've understood that being a Starr meant exactly what her father said, that they couldn't escape the darkness.

"Yes, a perfect repeat of everything you'd gone through, and it confuses me. What should I do to help him? And are you and Sam beyond my help?"

Pale blue eyes less bright in the sodden gray background begged for the possibility.

"I don't know," Leslie answered quietly, barely audible over the pattering rain, thinking about witchery and prophesy, thinking about her father and the shadows.

The day flooded back into her memory, her dad flailing, struggling with the unknown, falling, dying in brambles, in confusion. Shadows of the honeysuckle branches etched his face like arms and talons tearing him apart for the blackness to flow into him, and then the blood spit from his gaping mouth.

"Can I at least get you out of the freezing rain?" her mom asked.

Leslie shook her head, knowing no matter where she went she couldn't warm the chill from her soul and preferring to drench her sorrows in the open for once.

Rose squeezed her daughter's hand, defeat in her gentle smile, saying, "So much like your father, always avoiding the warmth and comfort of home. But I'll have some hot chocolate waiting for when you decide to get out of the rain. Come home, please, before you catch pneumonia and your death."

Then Rose threw her jacket over her head and ran down the road, splashing through the same puddles she'd always told Leslie and her brothers to steer clear of. She stood for a moment, fearing that death would catch her, listening to the droning rain scatter the quiet from the lake and woods, listening for something other than rain to hit the ground.

The wind numbed her skin with its winter sadness but not her heart. Years of suffering nightmares and heartache in secret flooded out, and she wailed into the wind, begging for eternal silence, where wounds never howled, where every terrible thing she'd experienced didn't scream into her mind. But in that same silent darkness, the terrible things lived and hungered and taunted her. She had no escape, not even in death, and her tears stung hot on her cold face. *Infinite misery*, Leslie thought, and she yelled her curses to the Hell that surrounded her.

A crow cawed an answer.

Long ago, while she helped her father search the fields for heather and lavender, he had taught her to note the differences of the crows' voices to figure out their screeching language. This crow was a sentinel, and he warned of danger. It was the same caw she'd heard on the day Jake attacked her.

The woods crackled and thrashed with abrupt movement. Fright paralyzed her tingling spine. Another sharp caw, and the crow took to the air, startled from his sentry, floundering in the gray sky like a torn kite, unable to catch wind and fly.

Dark clouds descended and ravaged the crow, raining shreds of black feathers and blood down upon her. Dark clouds hovered before her with red glowing eyes.

The shadows, her mind screamed over and over to her unmoving body.

Winds blew the clouds apart.

But all around her she sensed shadows and a shadowy man, menacing eyes watching and gnashing mouths hungering, and, in the building confusion, she turned shaken and scared to find them hiding in the dark of the woods, sensing them coming into the gray light.

Closer, getting closer, the wind hissed with the chorus of slithering tongues. With the voices Jake had spoken with when he had lumbered behind her and pressed his gun and cantankerous lips against her cheek.

"We got the wrong Starr when we took your dad, and we're here to amend our mistakes. We will devour you entirely," Jake had growled and slavered in her ear, *his breath like fumes, burning, sickening her with its butane odor.*

"We want you, Leslie." His voice slithered; his hands roamed along her neck and down into her shirt, his fingers creepy crawling like worms across her chest.

The seven-year-old memory twisted vile in her gut, and she cried for it to stop. Her head swelled with pressure and pain as winds and memories continued to bombard her with voices and horrible faces . . .

. . . shifting from his grasp, she had faced her stepfather and screamed as she saw what eyes looked back upon her.

Veins had squirmed like black cobras upon his waxy cornea, and his eyes had spit oily, venomous tears.

Laughter and swollen blue tongue wiggling from his mouth, he had pushed her to the ground and pinned her with his hefty body, straddling her hips. His eyes turned completely black.

She had kept thinking, *this can't be real. This isn't happening.*

"But truth, Leslie, your life is the illusion. Even after your father's death, how could you doubt us? We are your reality, and that reality is death." Blue tongue had licked bleeding lips. "Daddy's dearest will taste so sweet."

The man who had married her mother and taught her how to drive ripped off her New Order T-shirt and ran the slime of his tongue around her nipple. Black bone barbs broke through his tongue and cut into her breast.

Screaming, she had fought to find the darkness to escape the pain, but her mind refused to fall into a void. Her hands were held, and she couldn't even take the gun to blow herself away because she didn't want to live this, didn't even want to live through it.

Jake had moved his tongue down her sternum, down the softness of her belly, and down to the waistband of her jeans, tracing a bloody belt at her waist.

Talons had sprung from his hands, and Jake had yelped, then howled, and then grinned with wolfen teeth. He had worked the denim to tatters in furious slashes, while the blackness from his eyes had oozed about her and held her immobile on the ground.

Whipping her head from side to side, she had only seen a blur of laughing darkness as it mounted her and thrust hard, pushing deep brutal inhuman bone within her. The pain had radiated from her insides, around her hips, down her legs into her curled toes, and up along her spine into her head, where it pounded relentlessly. She had felt Death in every shrieking cell.

She screamed, realizing with the one rational bit of her mind that she didn't fear death itself but the pain of dying.

The darkness had sung, "Can't get no . . . satisfaction."

Those guttural voices of the things that had killed her father singing and enjoying themselves.

Leslie had puked in revulsion, and the stink of her half-digested pizza and acrid fear had made her throw up again until her stomach emptied air and her lungs filled with vomit.

Jake had collapsed upon her, ebon sweat dripping from his pores, shadows vanishing from his eyes and body, panting, "Now they'll leave me alone. I've done my part of the bargain."

Without explaining what that bargain had been, Jake had sauntered into the woods, whistling, and startled a family of rabbits from their burrow, and the shadows had jumped upon them, snatching them up into their large gruesome mouths, grinning at her as their barbed tongues licked the meaty crumbs off the ground. They had coalesced before her, a massive stretch of fanged darkness, and raged upon her to make her obsolete.

But something had happened. Something that she couldn't remember, because her next recollection was of fighting her way to the lake's surface and sputtering for air beneath a starry night. No shadows. Nothing but night songs of owls and frogs and crickets. In that blank period, something had occurred to vanquish the shadows and save her life.

Something she wished she remembered as the woods crackled with dark stirring.

Closer, getting closer, the wind whispered.

Iridescent wavy lines squiggled in her sight, and the piercing pressure behind her eyes blurred her vision. She strained to catch the lurkers pressing upon her, unseen but felt in her sinews, an ache of cold beyond the cold.

Take her . . .

The Dark Man's thoughts were upon the wind.

Pain split through her skull, seeming as if it separated the bone and a keen edge sliced into the springy furrows of her brain. Clasping hands to her head, Leslie winced and fought hard not to cry out, not to intensify the pain with loud noise. She trembled, weak with the crushing migraine. She clenched already tight muscles, waiting for the black blows of demons and Dark Man.

Minutes passed and only sleet blew upon her.

Even the icy numbness of her hands, feet, and face burned as extreme as the agony in her head, and Leslie wondered if their plan was to watch her freeze to death.

Go back home, came a faint thought. A thought not quite her own.

But the ache had increased to the point where her head seemed to weigh as much as a bowling ball atop a rubber neck, and she feared she would topple headfirst if she attempted to walk. It was difficult enough to remain standing.

I'm coming, the other voice in her head whispered.

With that shock, Leslie jolted into action, shuffling head-heavy and dizzy down the gravel road, kicking rocks from their dirt bed, cold air held within her lungs. Skeletal trees bent wicked in the wind. Rains bit her. Winter-dense clouds swirled around her, and she feared any second she would see the red blink of shadow eyes within.

Instead, on the road ahead, a figure in a hooded black slicker appeared.

Appeared almost as if he had dropped from the clouds, with the sky's shrouds drifting about him.

She slowed, afraid to completely stop, the sensation of being watched and followed still strong, and approached with caution. The minute it took to approach him by a few feet seemed to have stretched into a year. Shaking, she finally stopped, unwilling to step any closer to the man with the hidden face.

"I knew I'd find you here," he said. "I've been waiting for you to come home."

Quick, crackling rain upon the fallen leaves matched the pounding of her heart. Confused by the whispering wind, she thought his voice resembled Sam's. But it couldn't—something that threatening and gruff couldn't belong to Sam.

His hands dripping red and reaching . . .

"Sam?" she asked anyway, her head spinning, uncertain.

"Yes, but you don't sound very happy to see me." He closed the short distance between them and pulled down the hood, his face stark with pallor, his eyes gloomy with dark circles. "Don't be afraid of me, please. I couldn't bear it if you thought I had killed her too."

Jewel eyes dim and blood on his hands.

Take her . . . the echo of the Dark Man's thought.

Sam grabbed Leslie's hand and crushed her fingers together. A little squeak broke through her tight lips and her teeth chattered as she hitched in ragged breath.

"Believe me, Leslie, I didn't do it," he implored. "*Couldn't* do it. It's the reason I've had such problems with the army, for disobeying direct orders to kill."

He waited for a response and got none, then continued anyhow. His voice was barely audible.

"I loved Charlotte and I miss her so much I think I'm losing my mind. It's like someone's stolen my brain and locked it in a black room, where I can't see or hear a thing but I can sense something else in there with me. Something that wants to destroy me. And you."

His jaw popped as he ground his teeth in stress.

Grief-sunken eyes and broad shoulders sagging, Sam was the perfect picture of the forlorn, and, for a brief guilty moment, she wished she had her camera. But capturing an emotion, making the abstract concrete, was what she strove for, and here stood a masterpiece that she'd refused to acknowledge.

"I believe you, Sam." It was all that needed to be said for the two cousins to wrap their arms around each other and lock themselves in some impenetrable shield, to guard themselves against a hostile world, and to find what solace they could with the only other person who could understand.

Sam had been the only person she'd thought to go to after the shadow-tainted Jake raped her, and he was the only one who had believed her then. She owed him her trust now.

"Do we dare believe your dad, though? Can't you feel how everything he'd always warned us about is happening?"

Her cheek twitched as he rested his head against hers.

"I do," she mumbled, wondering why she decided not to elaborate on all that had been happening.

Maybe because the wind seemed to whistle the Rolling Stones song.

Sam heard it too as his body trembled, and his hold around her tightened.

"Do you guys want to die out here?"

They dropped their embrace and pushed away from each other, hands curled into fists, adrenaline-tense bodies turning toward the intruder. Leslie's sixteen-year-old brother aimed an umbrella at them and chuckled.

"Mom won't be too happy to see you," Andy told Sam. "Good thing she's left for the store. You'll have to wait for that hot cocoa though, Leslie."

Winds buffeted them, with rain, and Sam retrieved the umbrella and popped it open, leaning it a bit to cover Leslie as well. Already wet and cold, she thought it made little difference. She listened to the wind, listened for the shriek of shadows, but they seemed to have disappeared, or at least faded into the deep of the woods, to watch in silence and wait for a better time to take her.

Andy stared at her as they walked along, finally breaking the uncomfortable silence. "You haven't really changed much, you know? I thought I wouldn't recognize you."

"Well, you've changed. I don't remember such a tall, handsome brother." Amazing how he looked like their father, bone thin yet rugged, ungainly tall, curly brown hair flirting over his Mississippi blue eyes.

"Okay, you've changed. I don't remember you saying that many nice things to me. You used to pinch my cheeks all the time, call me 'big baby blue,' and force me to hide in the hamper whenever I played hide-and-seek with Dale and David." Andy scowled. "They'd never find me, and you wouldn't come tell me it was okay to get out. I stayed in that hamper for hours, I bet."

"Did you develop claustrophobia?" Sam joked.

"No, just Charley horses," Andy replied.

Leslie tried not to laugh, knowing what she'd done to him might've been considered cruel, but at least he'd escaped the pillow beatings she'd given Dale and David. Smother the brother, she had called that game, which her brothers hadn't found fun at all.

Nearing the house, she was gripped by an immense sadness, partly for abandoning her family. A rusted beast of a bulldozer sat in the adjacent lot, mud and clumps of tree roots and grass stuck in its metal teeth; exhaust and mildew and hibernating sleep blackened its window-eyes.

The lot showed the effects of its passing. Its land had been partially cleared, made barren, and the fallen pines reminded her of beached whales, of decaying stumps, with pine needles browned or missing to reveal the bark ribs. Nestled within, the carrion feeders stirred.

Eyes on the ruts, she distinctly saw the tooth grooves in the mud swirled into screaming mouths and heard their gurgling pain. Her stomach ached as if punched.

Leftovers of destruction, she thought. Like herself, and Andy, and Sam, all trying to deal with the wake of a dead man's haunting legacy.

Sam curled his hand around hers as if he had heard her thoughts and sympathized. Together they entered the home that neither had set foot in for years, and memories flooded them both.

Rose Starr didn't have the money to decorate with fancy knickknacks and instead lined the tables and mantels with photographs of her children. Some frames were of silver plate, but the majority boasted of a wood carver's craft. At night when her father couldn't sleep, he would make the frames for his beloved wife, the only thing he ever felt she appreciated.

The wooden frames fit the mood of the pictures, and Leslie smiled as she spied her favorite one on the end table, of wooden coils bordering a candid shot of Leslie and Sam blowing dandelion weeds at her father. His arms reached out to catch the seeds on their puffy flight. His lips reached from ear to ear; the sun caught bright in his smile.

With some pride, she recognized where her own talent stemmed from and wondered if, after all, she was her mother's daughter as much as her father's.

Her mother certainly displayed her love for her family—something Leslie never displayed. All her photographs were dark and creepy and devoid of anything remotely uplifting. Depressing, she supposed, and then wondered what those arrogant doctors would've said about that.

The warmth of the room touched her cold flesh, and she shivered violently.

"Here," Andy said, preempting their requests for towels and dry clothes.

As Leslie scrubbed the rain from her hair, she noticed her mother hadn't replaced any of the furniture she'd grown up with. The same beaten green-and-blue wool plaid couch pressed against the far tan wall and faced the same oak cabinet, with the same tiny television set with the same rabbit ears. She figured the TV still barely picked up the one channel, a Lexington station, as well.

Her Aunt Josephine's rockers flanked the couch. They had a unique design, with the rocker slats set upon chair feet instead of the floor, its rocking mechanism working on springs. Fine needlework fabric covered the walnut backs and seats, but no one but guests had ever sat in them, because at times the chairs would rock as if with a life of their own.

Perhaps with Josephine herself, unwilling to give up the Norwegian antique rockers.

The chairs creaked. Leslie shivered again, excusing herself as she rushed down the hallway and locked herself into the bathroom.

Although she hadn't shaken the cold, her face flushed and sweat broke out along her brow and neck. She braced herself on the ceramic counter, staring at her reflection in the mirror. A ghost-white mask with haunted eyes stared back.

Leslie wasn't ready to face the dead again any more than she was ready to tackle the shadows.

Stripping off her sweatshirt, she wrung it into the tub and threw it into the dryer. She did the same with her jeans and undergarments, picked the heat setting, and then hit the button to begin the drying cycle. If only it was that easy, to hit some button and turn on the light to combat the supernatural dark.

Her gym shoes banged in the tumble, sounding too much like the night the harrowing dead decided to knock on walls and windows.

Knock-knock on the bathroom door. Her heart knocked against her sternum.

"Leslie, coming out soon? I need to talk to you, but I have to leave in a bit," Sam called through the closed door.

"Sure, sure. Let me run through a hot shower and I'll be right out."

The knobs squeaked as she turned on the water, and the shower spray sputtered before the streams hissed steamy lake water. With the rains, the cistern must've gotten contaminated with runoff; the water ran murky in the tub. It smelled of fish too.

She didn't care, as long as the hot water washed away the chills.

Standing in the hard rush, Leslie allowed her mind to relax with her muscles and imagined crystal waterfalls cutting through a jade mountain rift. Volcanic springs steaming below. Fairies dancing on jasmine. Great billows of mist gracing the space between earth and sky like gossamer silk shades.

The steam formed into a woman's face before her. Hollow eyes and mouth. Solid commanding presence.

"Bring it to an end. Bring on the Void," the vaporous face hissed.

Leslie gulped, tasting terrible things hidden in her mind, and flew against the shower curtain, tangling herself in the folds, pulling the rod down with a clang and her scream.

Tumbling over the tub's side, she fell onto the plush plum rug and met Sam and Andy as they slammed the door from its hinges and burst into the room.

Vapors effervesced with a popping sigh and a hint of lavender.

"What's wrong?" Sam yelled.

But Andy gawked at the ceiling, the blood draining from his face, whispering, "You saw her, didn't you?"

Wrapping herself in a towel, more chilled than before, Leslie only nodded.

"Looks like we've all got things to discuss," Sam said, slowly backing out of the bathroom before he saw what they had seen, tugging Andy with him for company.

She pulled on Andy's Wildcats sweatshirt and stuffed herself into an old pair of jeans. The short trip down the hall proved quiet and uneventful, though the wind shuffling roof slates above did little to calm her fears.

She couldn't help but think of shadows peeling away the layers of the house to get to her.

"Feeling better?" Sam asked. He sat on the floor with his back against the couch, knees pulled up, arms crossed around his legs, fingers linked. His gaze drifted from her to the front door.

"No, and I'm beginning to wonder if any of this will get better."

Sam grumped and agreed with a hearty nod and a scowl.

Wind rattled the door, and Sam's eyes narrowed.

"What did you see in there?" he asked, eyes glued to the door.

"She saw our great-aunt's ghost," Andy interjected, chewing his nails as he leaned against the wall.

"How do you know?" both Leslie and Sam piped up.

"Ever since you left, Leslie, she's visited this house, speaking to me in the middle of the night about shadows and death. She speaks about you too, how you'll bring an end to it all."

"How? Why me?" she wondered aloud, recalling the face of steam and its command.

Andy shrugged.

"Mom says you've had nightmares."

Andy shrugged again. "Sometimes."

"You've mentioned these shadows, Leslie. And now Andy," Sam said. He stood and crossed over to the door, peering through its side lights into the winter gray beyond. "Your father mentioned an evil invading our town and bodies. The shadows, right?"

"I believe so," Leslie answered, goose bumps rising on her arms at their mention, with the innocent shadows crawling into the corners, beneath the furniture, and obscuring the faces in the photos. Dark opportunity presented itself in these places, providing cover for evil to materialize in secret. For the evil to shadow across their own faces and suffocate them.

"Okay, let's assume our imaginations haven't played nasty tricks on us. What do we know about them?"

Andy shrugged and chewed his nails as if he meant to gnaw them from the cuticles.

"Shapeless, tormenting, murderous, fiendish, hungry, black as death," Leslie rattled, and she would've gone on if her voice hadn't cracked with resentment. *Her father dying in brambles, slipknotted in shadows.*

"Right. How do we kill them?"

Ghost hissing bring an end to it all, bring on the Void.

It was Leslie's turn to shrug, and Sam tapped his fingers against the glass, lost in reverie.

The lights flickered and hummed with zapping electrical static, shifting the darkness here and there, creating a charged atmosphere in the room. Winter-dead branches talon-screeched on the house, like bodies splattering apart, of bones and blood gushing into the glass, rain sloshing against the windows in buckets.

Insane laughter was in the wind.

"I don't think we can," Andy groaned, rubbing a livid bruise on his arm. "We can't touch them, but they can touch us. How do you kill something like that?"

"Kill them on their terms, then." Sam moved away from the door and turned to face them, his eyes sparkling like lightning in a green tornado sky. "In the army, they tested the soldiers for higher brain functioning, trying to find those few gifted ones who could move things with their minds, or predict the future, or even start fires. They picked me and two others because we could remote view."

Flickering light changed the contours of his face into something less than human, simianlike yet non-mammalian.

Blood on his hands. Instinctively, she watched his hands, his fist beating into his open palm for emphasis. Clean.

He continued. "They trained us to spy with our minds. Eventually, they taught us to kill with our minds."

Leslie jumped at this, and her blood rushed into her head, drowning the sounds coming into her ears. His mouth moved and formed silent words. His hands gripped and ungripped, fisted and unfisted, *bloodied and unbloodied.*

Moments passed in still panic, *the Dark Man's hands upon Charlotte, upon her,* before his voice reached within her again.

"But it was after that night we found out that the man we picked was one of our own. Our commanders had us practice on an American grunt. I couldn't contain my rage."

"Your troubles with the army then?" Leslie asked. Her voice was thick, as if someone had stuffed cotton down her throat.

"Yeah, and because of my unique battle skills they were frightened of me and wanted to put me down like a mad dog."

"You weren't discharged, were you?"

Sparkly eyes went dull. "No."

"You AWOL, cuz?" Andy's mouth tweaked into a lopsided grin. "Cool."

"Oh, yeah, that coming from a guy who wears his pants backward." Sam folded his arms across his chest and returned to the front door, his attention once more on the side windows.

"I still don't see how this remote viewing will help us against the shadows," Leslie said, ignoring all her skittering doubts.

"The Starrs are the watchers and keepers of darkness," Andy interrupted in monotone, speaking almost as if by rote.

Leslie turned toward him riveted. His eyes were clouded with confusion, and he shrugged his slumped shoulders, as if trying to shrug off the wraith that clung to him and whispered in his ear.

Lavender and shiny dust infused the space around him.

Dust particles pulled apart in a smile and then separated completely in the blinking light.

Her sigh lingered, though.

No one breathed, and the room became quiet enough for them to hear the dust settle onto the floor. In the distance, winds disrupted power lines and knocked out the lights in the house.

"Fight fire with fire," Sam muttered. "Fight spirit with spirit."

The crunch of tires on gravel and headlights circling the room sent Sam on jitters, and he spun from the door and hugged Leslie fiercely, whispering in her ear, "Someone will die tonight."

Then he fled through the sliding doors in the kitchen, into the wind-laughing darkness.

Chapter Seven

Wind gusted against the wood siding. The old house moaned and creaked like a shuddering, unsteady old man ready to fall down a flight of cellar stairs. Indeed, a cellar's pitch pressed against the windows as the things with the flesh of night and the glowing eyes of harvest moons looked within.

Sitting before a tarnished mirror, Coatl applied red paint to his face and smeared on the mask of Xipe Totec in preparation for the ritual. *The Red Mirror*. He liked this reflection, his face crimson as if with blood, as if he had stripped his own flesh from his skull and stared at the image of the god hidden behind human flesh.

He laughed that anyone could think the Xipe mask was a symbol of agricultural fertility. In the mirror, the blood-faced god laughed back.

Actually, he thought it was silly that historians proposed that the ritual stemmed from a culture's need to appease the god of spring, as though the yellow-dyed skins represented the husks of corn, the new skins of the earth, as though the flowing blood made the ground fettle and simulated rains.

The god of suffering wanted none of that.

"The awesome and terrible lord who fills with dread" desired war trophies, severed skulls of slain enemies with stone and shell eyes and tongues, of leather masks made from the flesh of flayed faces, of golden clothes tailored from the defeated captives' yellow-dyed skins. A god attired in victory. A god uninterested in the arrival of spring if that season didn't come with suffering.

With two fingers, he dipped into the ochre paint and carefully lined his face with jaundiced stripes. He grinned at his reflection, red mouth filled with white teeth.

"All wrong," he told the grinning god.

Coatl picked up an arrow and walked over to Jake, who hung inverted on a wooden cross frame.

"Maybe the rites do have some small part in vegetation, because your face looks like a turnip." Coatl bent to the side and looked at Jake upside down. He ripped the duct tape off Jake's mouth, a satisfying *rrriiiippp* and yelp.

"You fucking assho—"

Coatl's fist hit below his jaw, snapping his teeth together with a sharp crack, cutting off his curses.

102

"Quiet. Else the shadows will fuck *your* asshole." Coatl pointed at his lips and the ceiling with the arrow.

With wide eyes, Jake watched the darkness swirling on the ceiling drift down like charcoal smoke before him, and Coatl waved the arrow like a wand, calling forth more shadows.

"What's a sacrifice without worshipers, eh?" he asked, running the arrow point along Jake's chest.

"They promised to leave me alone," Jake whimpered. He shirked on the frame as the shadows crept beside him and clicked their talons along the wood.

Coatl stuck the arrow into Jake's navel, and he howled. Twisting the arrow deeper, Jake's blood dribbling down in rich ruby streams, he asked, "Since when can you trust demons?"

He yanked the arrow from Jake's abdomen and sucked the blood from the tip, mingling it with his spit, spreading the red froth with his tongue along his porcelain grin. *Mirror, mirror on the wall . . .*

The copper-gold ambrosia intoxicated him.

"Do you think the followers of Christ ever drank real blood? Did they assume pagan rituals, as they assumed all things pagan as their own, of sipping blood from cranium bowls and eating the flesh of the sacrificed? Or did they fake it, since they had a false god anyway?" Coatl pondered this while chewing the tip of the arrow.

"Nooo," Jake wailed.

Blood rolled down from his belly to his sternum, and the demons surrounded Jake, wisps of blackness curling around his heaving torso, talons glinting orange in the light of the fire. Sharp tongues stabbed into his navel. Beneath Jake's guttural gasps and choking sobs, the wet sounds of demons lapping the primal offering were heard. Dark ropes of shadows wriggled into his abdomen, creating a bizarre ebon umbilical cord from the womb of death to the screaming fetus.

A fetus waiting to be delivered from his flesh.

"Think of it anyway—the Christians believe if they partake of the Eucharist, the symbolic flesh and blood of their God, that they seek redemption and will find salvation," Coatl said as he worked the arrow into Jake again. He waited for Jake's shrieks to dwindle to quiet dripping before he continued. "They *pretend* to consume their God. I guess their God will pretend to show them the eternal kingdom."

Five punctures, the last centered through the vena cava, waited like rosebuds to bloom in blood, an apt image Leslie had described of her photograph of a gunshot victim, *bullet holes reminding her of roses budding open.* How he enjoyed her visions.

"My gods, though, won't pretend to devour their God," he whispered in Jake's bleeding ear. "Nor will I."

Out of Jake's body, the shadows dropped onto the blood-saturated floor and chugged the body's wine, fanatical in their communion, snarling in the tongues of fallen angels.

A deep rumbling and roar shook the walls and toppled fiery logs from the fireplace onto the hearth. As the ground trembled, the blood ran in rivulets away from the pools beneath Jake. Some of the blood fell into cracks. The floor moaned its gluttonous thanks. Other trails hissed upon sparking embers with gasoline effects and lit the faint orange glows into red pulsars, star-blinding-bright.

Blood Gatherer exploded on the scene. Floorboards splintered and cracked as he crashed up from beneath the house.

Dust and smoke obscured Coatl's view of the elder lord, but the silhouette stood nine feet tall, with the body of a hulking man and the head of a giant vulture. With a snarl, the dreaded lord crashed to the ground like a mountain laid asunder in an earthquake and buried his beastly face within the congealing puddles with the *slurp, slurp, slurp* of an embalmer's sucking tubes.

Vast wings snapped open from the bony ridges of Blood Gatherer's back, shielding him and the blood from poaching shadow creatures. Dust fanned by his wings, the air cleared and the light shuddered upon the awesome god.

Crocodile hide covered the bony architecture of his wings, and his black flesh crawled with shiny mucous, moving like leeches, sucking in blood; mucous turning from clear to red until the dreaded lord crouched the deepest scarlet instead of black.

105

Terrifying to think, this was just the phantasm of the god.

Blood Gatherer eyed him, and his bowels constricted and threatened to loosen onto the floor. Black iris and white pupil stoked his fear that perhaps he wasn't godlike at all in his Xipe mask, but masked instead as food for the gods.

Blood Gatherer's gray-purple tongue syphoned up the crimson liquid.

Talons and demons' breath scratched at the back of Coatl's neck. "Yessss, a very hungry god. Do you think that one body will satisfy him?"

"Can't get no . . ." they belched.

Pain whipped into his skull as a vision lashed into his mind, of wind-strewn ash stinging his eyes, burning into his windpipe and lungs, and burying him like the people of Pompeii.

The shadows circled him, hungry eyes bright red. Blood Gatherer growled, pulled himself to full height, and towered before Coatl, bloody raw hunger in his eyes as well.

Another vision wrestled his mind, pinning strange sights to his eyes. He couldn't move, anchored by the horror in his mind.

Of his flesh breaking into an itchy rash and blisters forming beneath his nails as he scratched.

Of boils and festers of sores growing until they burst pus and rot.

Of flies and gnats buzzing upon him and feeding off him.

Of parasites squirming in their shit and burrowing into his body.

Of tumors swelling behind his eyes and spilling bloody tears down his face.

Of eternal agony if he refused the god, Xipe-Totec-Tllatlauhquitezcatl.

No gentle prodding from the god of suffering, Coatl thought as he picked up the flaying knife and walked in front of Blood Gatherer with trepidation.

In his mind, the dreaded god spoke. "Tlatlauhqui Tezcatlipoca demands the sacrifice. Will you stand a warrior in the teocuitlaquemitl? Or do you offer yourself instead?"

Coatl dragged the curved blade against his arm, cutting through the layer of skin but stopping before he reached a vein. "I will stand a warrior, but I offer the blood of the battle for you."

"Wise." The word hissed into his skull, inflating painful pressure within.

Blood Gatherer's livid tongue forked into the small wound and sucked until Coatl swooned. Images of vultures and crocodiles thrashed in his mind, hungry beasts feasting. Floating skulls appeared in the darkness, terrible grins upon them.

"I am the poison in your blood."

And then the phantasm of the dreaded lord vanished, but his blood flowed like fire in his veins and filled his heart with fury.

On the framework, Jake stirred with the last of his fading life, with very little blood pumping through the gaping wounds, and Coatl approached him, waving the flaying knife before his weary, pained eyes.

"Interesting design, don't you think?" he asked, but Jake only grunted weakly. "The copper vajra handle has wrathful vajras. See the splayed ends of the spokes? Personally, I think it's just a fancy number eight."

Jake's eyes wobbled in their sockets.

"I found it at a flea market in Burlington, if you can believe that. They sold it as an antique weapon, thinking it something the Hindu army used against the British."

He fingered the crescent-shaped blade and the iron hook at its tip. "Really it's an ancient butcher knife from India, called a gri-gug. They used it to flay or scrape off animal hides."

He placed the blade against Jake's chin.

"Sometimes they used the gri-gug in ceremonial khandroma dances because of its large size. In their right hand, the hooked flaying knife was a symbol of compassion. Remember the mercy I said I would show you . . . ?"

Coatl grinned as he cut along the curve of Jake's chin, bringing it around his jaw and up along his face and across his brow, moving behind the other ear and meeting the cut at its start. The hook had caught the skin and pulled it apart from the muscles. Placing the gri-gug on the ground, he used his hands to pry the rest of the skin from the face. *Like peeling peaches or pulling off gum*, he thought.

As his face came off, Jake screamed with every ounce of remaining strength.

Coatl slashed the skin at the mouth, the final attachment, and Jake's screams were more blood than sound.

Wet with blood, the mask of Jake's face stuck to Coatl's. Coatl wore the mask of Jake, and Jake wore the mask of Xipe with his red gleaming face. A good omen, the sacrificial victim representing the god; such was the Aztec way. He fought the urge to glance at himself in the mirror, to find the other likeness of Xipe Totec. The Teotihuacan culture referred to Xipe as the "God with a mask," since his idols always showed the eagle-headed god wearing the leathered masks of human faces.

But then, the gods all wore masks and changed them at will.

He thought of the hideous sight of the Bat-God and of Blood Gatherer, and how awful it must be to look upon their true faces.

In the distance, sirens sang like wolves in search of blood, setting him on edge even though the sirens were fading because he sensed trouble coming, an irritating vibration along his spine that the presence from the woods earlier was in search of him.

Jake gurgled on blood as he tried to beg for his life.

"No, no can do," Coatl said, shaking off the irritation, reminding himself to keep his mind on the pressing matter at hand. "My dad taught me never to do a half-ass job, and I'm not done with you yet, my friend."

Retrieving the hooked knife, he set about performing something else he learned from his dad—skinning a carcass.

He made the first cut at the groin, slicing toward the chin. *Much messier than rabbits*, he thought as he dragged the knife from the center cut down the limbs to the feet and wet his hands with copious blood. All those capillaries keenly split . . .

Much noisier too, with Jake's screaming like that of pigs being slaughtered, the high-pitched, insane squeals of agony and terror.

The demons thumped their darksome tails on the floor like ravenous dogs anticipating table scraps. They circled the room, shadows of shadows slinking along the floors and walls, jaws unhinged for the feast.

"Soon," Coatl crooned.

After he separated the skin from the ankles, wrists, and neck with the blade, he was able to pull the skin right off, as easy as stripping off a soaked shirt. He cringed, though, at the sounds of skin tearing away. Flesh, though woven armor, was as delicate as lace, and he groaned to think of his between the sharp shears of the dreaded gods' hands. He stepped away, skins draped over his arms, and shrank from the hungry brew that raged upon the skinned pulp of Jake in black smoke and gory flames.

The shadows chanted, "Devour, devour, devour . . ."

And Jake was skewered on the frame, a bloody mass of throbbing muscle and gristle burning in the demon-fire.

"Chest and nuts roasting on an open fire," they shriek-sang, greedily picking the medium-rare meat from his ribs and groin.

"Feed," they hissed and pushed Coatl back.

Talons snared through his hair and ripped his head down against the charred remains, and the reek of burnt human flesh stung his nostrils. Tears spilled down his greasy Jake-face.

Trying to avoid their wrath, he slipped his tongue through the slit of the supple mask and tentatively touched the sacrificial offering. Jake, who had raped Leslie and hosted parasites, tasted rotten like the man he was. Worse than he imagined days'-old 'possum roadkill half-fresh from the tarry asphalt would taste.

"Feed," they insisted with snarly sniggers.

He loathed the first bite. And the second. And the third. And every one thereafter.

After the initial chewy hunk, he swallowed the pieces whole and tried not to pay attention to the way they crawled down his throat instead of slid. He appeased his revolting mind by believing that along with the man's flesh, he ingested the man's strengths. Like the Wendigo.

But that was another dark god . . . another spirit world in which he didn't belong.

The demons laughed as he swallowed his vomit as well.

"Xipe awaits," they said.

Without hesitation, Coatl rushed outside away from the funeral feast and, beneath a bruise-colored night, he stripped off his human clothes and slipped on the human skins.

Xipe's rumbling voice was in the wind.

"Dark will battle starlight, and you will bring me her skins. Else I make you a war trophy instead."

"Yes," Coatl said to the brisk winds, unnerved once more by the irritating sensation of an unwanted presence. He'd have to deal harshly with the nuisance.

Which one disturbed him more, though, bringing Leslie to the slaughter or hunting the unknown?

Or were they one and the same?

Chapter Eight

Leslie tossed in her old bed, unable to sleep. Too many images skirted upon the moonlit ceiling, of hands dripping with black blood, of eyeless faces peering, of the shades of the dead congregating.

Curse this secret sight...

But Moon had no trouble sacking on her pillow, his bushy tail flicking on her face as he dreamed of anything but bad things. His purrs weren't even muffled by the pillow. She had a mind to wake him the way he always did her, the master rat-cat deciding the hour before dawn was quite appropriate to scratch and meow for a can of shredded chicken.

But he needed his rest after what happened at the motel.

Something more to keep her awake and relive the moment.

*   *   *

Someone will die tonight. The thought churned anxiously in her stomach, and Leslie picked at her mom's spinach lasagna, usually a favorite for her. No one spoke at the dinner table. The crackle of the hearth fire kept them company enough on this oppressive night, all of them only too aware that the next day they would attend Charlotte's funeral and that the law might doom another beloved.

Like phantoms, the damp winds rattled the roof tiles and whistled against the windows. Leslie scraped her fork onto the plate absentmindedly as she stared into the darkness beyond for any hint of red-glowing eyes or silver-haired wraiths.

Only dark waves rolled onto the rocky shore of their property. *From the deep, dark waters . . .*

Sharp pain struck behind her eyes, and she squeezed them shut, blood-orange fireworks spotting against her lids. Acid rose in her throat. She tasted fishy water again.

Putting down her fork and pushing away from the table, she said, "I should go now. Moon needs his dinner too, and I don't feel well."

Her mother nodded and wiped her lips with a paper napkin, *the crinkling of leaves crushed by the stalking hungry.*

Leslie pressed her index fingers against her temples.

"Won't you bring your things back here and stay?" Rose asked. "No sense paying for a room when you have a free one here."

"I already paid for the room."

"Peggy will refund your money, but I don't want to argue with you. If you don't want to stay, you don't want to stay." Rose stood and started to clear the table, clanging flatware onto the plate, stacking plates without scraping them.

Flames in the fireplace popped and snapped fiery ash into the air, and the sparks landed like tiny meteors onto the hearth, where they sizzled harmlessly. The house always took on her mother's anger. Rose Starr might not be a born Starr, but she had a bit of the witch in her at times, and Leslie smiled for once this evening.

"Okay, as long as we won't be an imposition," she replied.

Rose laughed. "The definition of children reads imposition, disorderly disruption, and chaos, no matter what age the child, but parents don't mind. Gives us something to hope for."

"Yeah, like will he ever clean his room," Andy added.

"Speaking of which . . ."

"Homework; did I mention I haven't done my homework?" Andy twiddled his fingers at Leslie and smiled, their father glowing in that grin. " 'Night."

"G'night, Big Baby Blue."

His lanky form disappeared into his room, and the door screeched shut.

"He has a phobia against oil, the strangest thing." Rose sighed. Frowning, she squirted dishwasher soap into the sink and ran the water.

Not strange at all, Leslie thought as she heard the lock click. *Oily things could slip anywhere, even through cracks of doors and windows, even through the holes in your head and into your mind.*

"I'll be back soon then, Mom." Leslie grabbed her keys and walked out into the damp night, anxious that *someone will die tonight.*

The rain had left its glistening imprint on the trees and ground, and, in the wind-hissing dark, it contained none of the romantic qualities of diamonds. She hurried to her car, wary of the glimmer all around. *Where there were diamonds, there were coal and caves and eyeless life watching.*

Slamming the car door, she sat inside the Jetta, and her breath drifted in the cold air, billowing upward like smoke, like ghosts rising to heaven. The windshield fogged with round, wispy faces.

Faces without eyes.

"Hang on," she whispered, blowing more ghostly faces upon the windshield, remembering a ghost story from years ago.

On another cold damp night, her father had hosted the Halloween Haunts in the parking lot of the old jailhouse. Cardboard silhouettes of hanged men had filled the barred windows on the second floor, and the adult chaperones, dressed in jailbird stripes and with cyanic blue painted faces, had handed out miniature nooses to the attending children. When they laughed, black tongues showed in the open mouths.

A perfect celebration for the dead, her father had decided.

All the children had gathered in tight bunches near the hay bales on which her father had sat, waiting for the story time, waiting like the witches, goblins, fairies, skeletons, and superheroes he would tell about.

He had worn a black robe, his face hidden within the dark folds of the hood, his gray-white painted fingers holding the scythe, which lay upon his lap. Try as it did, the wind had failed to reveal his face, even though the robe had whipped about with a frightening sense of movement, as if he really were the Grim Reaper floating on the wind in search of victims.

"Listen," he had whispered, his voice eerier than the rumble of faraway thunder, and the children had listened.

The United States flag had fluttered with the sound of a vampire's cape as its wearer flew through the night, thirsting for the blood of children.

The flag's ropes had banged against the metal pole, echoing funeral bells.

Fallen orange and russet leaves had scattered along the concrete with the scritch-scritch of rats' nails as the black plague crept ever closer.

Through the narrow passages of the century-old buildings, the wind had howled, and the children had huddled closer, scared that the wind might turn into the dead spirits that were supposed to walk out of their graves on Halloween night.

"Listen to the ghost of Denmark, how his voice sounds like waves hitting the shore. Whoosh, whoosh, whoosh . . ." He motioned his arm, mimicking the roll of the ocean.

Some of the children in the audience had bobbed their heads as if they were buoys adrift. Then the rest of the children had followed along, caught in the exciting current of her father's *whooshing* wave.

"His voice, heavy with the ocean's mists, dampens our air. Can you feel his voice murmur against your skin?"

Nervous giggles and furious nods had answered him.

"Can you hear what he says?"

A collective shake of heads.

"Listen, then . . ." And her father had stood, tall and ominous in his Death's cloak, and leaned conspiratorially on the scythe.

"The ghost of Denmark whispers about the Sunday Children."

For effect, her father had rattled off several names of Owenton children, who indeed had been born on Sunday.

"The Sunday Children, born during the chime hours of midnight, had the power to see hidden things that no one else could see. Hidden things like ghosts and invisible hearses that traveled on their way toward the dying."

He struck the ground with the scythe, and the front row screamed and then screamed with laughter. When the noise died down, he continued.

"The ghost of Denmark whispers of a Sunday Child named Faye, how the poor girl could not attend church because of the specters and hearses passing into the nearby graveyard, and how the priest called upon the parents to question them about her absence in the pews.

"When he learned of her grim sight, he advised her to cry, 'Go to Heaven!' whenever she saw a specter, and the specter would rise into Heaven. Whenever a hearse crossed her path, she should shout, 'Hang on!' and the hearse would do exactly so.

"Faye, who had difficulties with her memory, scrambled up the priest's advice. A hearse crept by, and she cried, 'Go to Heaven!' And the hearse rose into the sky and vanished forever into the kingdom of God.

"The next moment she saw a horrible specter and shouted, 'Hang on!' And the spirit wrapped its terrible arms about her and hung on, even as it dragged her into Death's realm. What do you think happened to poor Faye?"

Silence as he had circled the children. Saucer-eyes were riveted to him.

"For three days, the town heard Faye's screams, until her wretched life ended and she was heard no more. But the Sunday Children still see her haunting the world, and they never say a word for fear of misspeaking."

An unnatural quiescence had settled upon the children, and, in the silence, they had heard strange laughter in the wind. Laughter that crawled and crept up their spines.

The jailhouse chimney, long ago stuffed by birds' nests, had coughed sooty smoke into the dusk, and a black powder had drifted down on the crowd. It had burned through their costumes and singed their skins. In seconds, chaos had erupted in the courtyard, and everyone had hurried about, stripping their smoking clothes and brushing the acrid powder off themselves. The air, thick with black clouds, had choked off the screams.

Then, as soon as it had begun, the smoke had dissipated, along with any trace of the black powder, and the blisters had popped and gone away as well.

Only the laughter had remained.

"Go to Hell," her father had whispered, and the laughter had faded into crackling leaves that flurried at his feet.

Leslie had never seen anyone frightened of leaves until that cold damp night. But she happily crushed them beneath her feet every time she came upon them after that. Her father's champion.

"Hang on," she muttered, a perverse dare for the ghostly watchers in the woods. She sensed them there, crouched, the black voids upon their faces sucking in the foggy sight of her. Darkness all around, within and without, and things darker sensed.

Wraith of yellow skins hanging on to the Dark Man . . .

Fingers upon her temples, Leslie pinched away the startling vision. "Hang on to sanity . . ."

The chortle of the car's engine grounded her as she turned the ignition key and, shaking off the creeps, stomped on the clutch and jiggled the gearshift into reverse. Lights on, CD player on, she put the car in first and drove toward the lake's exit. She sang along with the stereo and kept the panic at bay, even as she rounded the curve around the reservoir, the water shining black beneath the pole light and near overflowing. *From deep, dark waters . . .*

She sang louder in response, the chorus becoming some kind of mantra.

The car bucked in the ruts and slid in the muddy grooves, and she gripped the steering wheel tighter, determined to keep control of the Jetta even if she couldn't control her own mind.

Gray-blue needles of the pines were luminescent in the sallow span of the headlights, in contrast to the midnight blue of the sky and the blue-black darkness of the woods. *Almost phosphorescent*, she thought. *Glowing like ghosts themselves*. The furry boughs waved, and, whether they bid her farewell or begged her not to venture into the flat darkness beyond, Leslie didn't know. But she had the urge to pull over and crouch beneath the pines and borrow their luminescence.

If only to chase the dark sight of empty skins from her mind.

Pressure built behind her eyes and in the middle of her forehead until it collapsed along her jaw and settled in her molars. Red flashes wavered in the air before her. The road dipped out of sight.

At the guard's gate, she stopped and cradled her aching head in her hands.

Tap, tap at her window. In the dark of her palms, she saw Poe's raven tapping, gently rapping upon a chamber door, and Poe in madness staring at the floor. At the raven's floating shadow from which the poet's *soul shall be lifted nevermore.*

Tap, tap once more.

"Okay in there?" asked a muffled voice.

Lifting her pain-heavy head, she glanced at the elderly guard and nodded. He tipped his *I'd rather be fishing* cap, grinned a mouthful of false pearls, and sauntered off to open the gate. Inside the guardhouse, the television showed blue light and snow.

"Have a good evening," he called, waving her on.

Pulling away, she swore the TV's static had formed a face without eyes. The wheels spun the last of the gravel from its hub spokes as she sped away from the property of Elk Lake and whatever else claimed it as home.

Her speed reached fifty. Despite tight curves ahead, she pushed the speedometer to sixty, and the tires squealed around the bend. The rear end barely hugged the road. She pressed the accelerator to the floor and raced down the middle of the winding lanes, with her car shuddering and screeching in protest on this seeming suicide mission. Running high on adrenaline, she handled the car perfectly and with a possessed grin glued to her lips. Her daddy's champion.

Take her, the Dark Man said, but he would have to catch her first.

Leslie soared past the stop sign, cutting across the path of another car coming into the intersection. The driver cursed her with his brights and horn, and her head felt every blaring pitch of light and sound. By the time she reached K&L's parking lot, she was shaking with pain and anxiety.

She paused at her room's door.

Metallic pings echoed within, like ball bearings dropping into tin bucket.

"What in the . . ."

She had the key poised in the lock when Moon let out a strangled howl and the door buckled outward and cracked with the force of something hitting it.

"Oh my God!" she cried, jumping away from the door.

Moon howled again, a drawn-out caterwaul that curled her insides.

Twisting the key, she threw open the door. The bang came from deeper in the room.

Moon yowled in the farthest corner.

Leslie flipped the light switch, and the room was illuminated for a brief moment before the light bulb shattered with a spark and a pop. She flinched at what she had seen.

In the corner of the room, a strange man sat in the chair, with Moon thrashing in his clutches.

"Who are you?" she demanded with bravado. "And let go of my cat."

"Always a price to pay for what you want," the man said, his voice deep and hoarse from years of smoking. "Even your father understood that."

"My father?"

Moon hissed and growled, and she could hear his claws raking the man's denim jacket. In her mind, a short inventory of suitable weapons ticked by— hair dryer, duffle bag, ceramic cat food bowls, and camera.

"But he paid more than he ever bargained for." The man laughed, and other things in the dark joined him.

As the light from the parking lot filtered into the room, the rumpled bed and dresser came into view, but the man in the corner remained in the dark. Shadows surrounded him.

"I can sense your confusion, Leslie. Someday you'll recover your lost memory, but until then you must decide what you will surrender for your precious Moon." He thrust his arm through the shapeless sable clouds, and Moon was gripped by the loose fur around his nape and hanging amid the crimson-hungry eyes. "Unheard of, to have stars in the night but not a moon."

His round eyes filled with dim streetlight and bright terror.

"Please don't hurt him," she whimpered, taking one step into the room, one step closer to the man and the shadows. Her head throbbed with their presence because their thoughts crackled in her mind.

Black noise threatened her, *devour you, devour you.*

"We won't, if you give us the Void," he declared.

"Give you the Void?"

"Yesss," the black mass hissed as it floated toward her, grinding teeth, like bone scraping on a steel file, and noisily licking lips.

"Drink this," the man said. His other hand reached beyond the shadows and offered her a skull bowl filled with scarlet-black liquid.

The Dark Man dancing with yellowed skin costume, crescent-bladed knife in his right hand, skull bowl in his left. The grinning corpse skinless and skull-less.

It felt like someone hammered her face with a chisel and dumped fire ants into her cerebrum. Instinct and premonition struck her hard, and she gasped, "No."

"Very well. You'll drink it to raise your cat from the dead then."

Snap of fingers and jaws, and the shadows' talons streaked flash-pan silver through the air toward Moon.

Leslie screamed and rushed into the formless howling black.

And then she found herself in her old bed with Moon curled atop her head and worried that she had imagined it all. The lake's loon. Except that her clothes lay in a wet heap beside the door, a definite sign that something she didn't remember had happened. Again.

The pain in her head weighed down her eyelids, and the visions on the ceiling sank into her exhausted mind and transformed.

Bloody hands splayed their fingers into wings, and bats without faces flew in her fitful sleep.

The dead milled around her dreaming self, intestinal nooses around their necks and their hands chopped off, chanting in tongues, Moyohualihtoatzin.

"Night Visitor," explained the unknown man from the motel, present in a disembodied voice and smoke. "Metaphor for sleeping. The link to the land of the dead."

"Moyohualihtoatzin," they sang, and the bats' wings drummed the rhythm in their flight.

Throwing her astral arms above her head, Leslie tried to shield herself from the bats as they bombarded her and attempted to tangle in her hair and in the furrows of her brain. There was a subtle shift in the images. She saw herself then, an ethereal cocoon, and the mammalian flyers crawled upon her, wing-arms bent like knees. They hooked syphoning fangs into the woven spider-silk sac that covered her.

Her blood dripped out golden and thick as honey.

Emitting a black noise, the bats metamorphosed into buzzing wasps, with sleek ebon bodies and crescent-curved stingers. Buzzing, buzzing darkness, and she fell through the darkest channel.

The hint of another world lay beyond.

"Moyohualihtoatzin," the dead chanted still, their voices drifting from the beyond.

Night Visitor to the land of the dead.

Another voice drew her back, through the dark channel, through the swarms of wasps.

"Mind your father," the voice clicked, like locks bolting gates. "Don't play with shadows. Else they devour you entirely."

The Dark Man.

He stood behind the hive, knocking it with his fist, sending the wasps in a fury toward her. A mask of flesh covered his skull face, and Leslie narrowed her eyes, frowning, suspicious, because it resembled the face of her stepfather.

"Yes, Jake," the Dark Man said as he thumbed the chin's loose skin. "I doubt you'll miss him."

"Moyohualihtoatzin," growled the dead gathering behind Leslie.

Winds and wasps swirled in buzzing symphony upon the dead, and their stinging music made the dead dance. The Dark Man joined them, dancing in his yellow skins, swan songs coming from his gaping mouth.

Like arrows, sable feathers flew through the air and dropped down upon Leslie. The points pierced her, needling through the skull bone and into her brain, and soon she wore a morbid headdress of oily and bloody plumes and a mask of wasps as the insects covered her face.

"Come dance with me, and Death will take you away." The Dark Man pulled his cowl over his head, darkness obscuring his face, and red eyes peered at her. "Else we devour you entirely."

"Go to Hell," she whispered, and the wasps slipped through the slit of her mouth and crawled down her throat.

"Been there, done that."

He hummed, and his voice seemed to caress her beyond the dream, his breath warm upon her sleeping body, inciting shivers upon her and the wasps within her.

Whirring madly inside her mouth and throat, the wasps stung the trachea's cartilage and the back of her tongue. Frenzied, they stung each other as well, and one burrowed into the soft palate of her mouth to escape the spearing tirade.

"Moyohualihtoatzin," the Dark Man chanted, laughing. "I'm your Night Visitor and your link to the land of the dead. Honored?"

But she couldn't answer, not even when she jolted awake. The stings had swelled her air passages, suffocating her.

Terrified, she struggled for breath. She opened and closed her mouth like a fish out of its tank, unable to breath, sides heaving, eyes bulging with the sight of death. Dark and awful, the face of the Dark Man was in the mirror.

If she had her breath, his image would've taken it away.

His face faded from the mirror, and Leslie tumbled out of bed, chest burning and throat aching, and rummaged through her dresser, hoping her mother hadn't cleaned out her belongings. Long ago, L.W. had given her something to ward off the allergic reaction to bee stings.

There, beneath her sweaters, his old medicine bag. She pulled it of the drawer and untwisted the horsehair cord. The bear teeth dangling from it clacked together as she opened the animal skin sack. Inside, the potion lay untouched. She withdrew it, anticipating its vile scent. Noxious odors of milkweed, cat mint, and mystery herbs accosted her, but it cleared her sinuses. Leslie breathed deeply, savoring the potion's lifesaving piquancy.

Above the dresser, the mirror once again reflected her own face. She opened her mouth and, in the faint morning light, she saw no sign of wasp, sting, or hive. The dream stayed within the dream for the most part.

The nightmare suddenly dawned on her—he had killed Charlotte through her dreams. Dreams she could never wake from because he had taken her . . . taken her away forever through the dead land links.

"Oh, God!" she moaned into her hands. *How close had he come to taking her?*

Her alarm buzzed, and she jumped, shaken by its reminder of wasps. Shaken as well because it was time to get ready for the funeral.

Charlotte's funeral. Charlotte, the prettiest girl in their high school, the most optimistic person Leslie had ever known, without a shadow at all smudging her happiness, her dearest girlfriend who always gave a smile and a hug and ultimately the encouragement for Leslie to pursue her photography. The one who believed in good dreams.

Was she really going to that girl's funeral?

Not a girl anymore, Leslie realized, since it had been seven years since she had last seen or spoken with the deceased. Charlotte, reduced to "the deceased." Not a real person without her soul.

Take her . . . the Dark Man's hands upon her.

Riddled with guilt, as though she were responsible for Charlotte's death, as if she could've stopped it somehow, she scratched at her own eyes, digging through her brows and into her soft lids. The pain only sharpened her guilt. Charlotte had suffered worse than this.

She has no eyes, only shadowy pits, but she is not blind to hell.

Been there, done that.

Tears burned over the hot pink scratches. Ironic that some men found her pretty when she cried. Dewy eyes and plump lips. But she never felt uglier than when she wept.

After showering and dressing quickly before the rest of the house awoke, Leslie grabbed a muffin from the table and her camera and headed out the door.

She reminisced about that last summer she and Charlotte spent together, flirting with the summertime boys, ogling their taut, tan bodies as they skied barefoot on the lake. Charlotte had dared Leslie to take their pictures. She had gotten the nerve to attract their attention and called them over. At first, she had them pose on her dock with their skis. Stiff smiles or funny faces. Then, she had ordered them to act natural, to get back into their boats and do their thing, which was waterskiing.

But do it close to the dock, she had said. *My lens can't go the distance.*

They laughed as they showed off for her and the camera, and she was pleased with herself and the photos after she had them developed. She had framed her best one, of the cutest fellow spinning in the air, water spray like crystalline wings at his back. Definitely a hot angel to her. On another of Charlotte's dares, she had given the guy the picture as a gift and had asked him out on a date. A good summer.

Then the summer changed into fall and strange things began to happen, and her life began to fall apart.

She had two hours before Charlotte's funeral, but she wanted to visit her dad's grave. The cemetery was located next to the Scoopy Doo restaurant. No gate or sign greeted the mourners, just a bronze plaque honoring Jacob Hunter, a former Revolutionary War soldier and hero who had moved to Owen County in 1817 and stayed until he died in 1856. Leslie glanced to her left, at the newer section of the cemetery, where the grave diggers had already opened up Charlotte's plot. Turning to the right, the older section, she drove down the gravel road toward the back, toward the family plots.

An array of tombstones sprouted from the ground like weird stone plants. Obelisks, crosses, blocks, and spyres, even carved tree stumps, ornamented the graveyard. In spring, the rich, sweet peonies would grow and bloom around the tombstones, pink pom-pom flowers cheering the dead.

Many of the stones had an orange rust or fungus growing on them, obscuring the names and dates of those who lay beneath the ground. Leslie spotted her favorite marker, simple rounded slate with the dates 1796–1872. When she was a child, she liked to search for the earliest occupants. She'd found no other person in this section born before 1796, and she always wondered what it would've been like to have lived so far back in time, crossing one century line and almost making it to the next.

She passed the Slaughter family. Its huge rectangular block stood three feet high and two feet wide. Flat plaques of the family's dead made a square as they were lined back-to-back and side-by-side through the many years. With a name like Slaughter, it was no doubt a large gathering beneath the soil.

It was too quiet, she realized. Even the echo of the pebbles crunching under foot was deadened and flat. Neither the Masons, the Poes, or the Smiths could tell her why.

The crack of a tree bough cut through the near silence, as if someone had taken an ax and split it. Leslie saw no one else in the cemetery. An old saying of her father's crept in her mind, of omens he had memorized, "The third omen was that of the night ax cutting wood. So it was said that perhaps something will befall him."

Perfume was in the wind, with the stale scents of leaves and the sharp odor of decay. A hint of lavender wafted in between.

Dead voices carried on the wind. "Bring it to an end. . . ."

Leslie's heart bounced faster than her feet as she made her way to the two-hundred-year-old maple, the greatest marker of her father's grave, as well as all the dead Starrs buried within these hallowed grounds.

Dawn's golden veil draped over Josephine's plot, emblazoned upon the red-paint graffiti that dripped from her name like symbols of a black spell.

Sadness washed over her as she stood beneath the tree, wondering who would desecrate the grave. Sunlight streamed behind the tree and shaded her father's grave, and she didn't have to dwell long on the culprits.

133

Shadows burdened her family even after their deaths.

"Gloomy prophecy," she said, knocking the camera against her thigh.

Intrigued by the way the light refracted off the stone and the way the red screamed off the gray, she wound the film and readied the camera.

Ethereal faces showed through the viewfinder.

She brought the camera down. She saw nothing but the various shades of gray and light. Braced for the strange, she peered through the lens again.

Faces without eyes stared back through the lens. *Snap.*

"Bring it to an end . . ." Leslie breathed.

Something wet dropped on her cheek. Absentmindedly, she wiped it off, thinking perhaps it had rained during the night, but her fingertip had a brick red smudge. She stared at the color, terrified to look up. She imagined her father impaled upon the pointed limbs.

Slickness flapped above her, like sodden sheets dangling on a clothesline. With a deep breath held, she tilted her head back.

"Oh, my God," she gasped.

Yellowing pink skin danced in the wind like some fleshy vampiric cape.

Wraith of yellowing skins hanging on to the Dark Man . . .

She held the camera up steadier than she felt and

clicked away, not even using the viewfinder to frame her shot. It didn't matter, if only a portion of the skins showed, it would be enough.

Invisible eyes bore into her and sucked the courage right out, and she ran away screaming.

Chapter Nine

Stepping from the cemetery maintenance shed, Coatl watched the dust of the tires trail Leslie's retreat, *ashes and ashes*, and made his way to the maple.

"She frightens easy for someone who has a power the gods fear," he said to the demon within.

Talons raking on his ribs, the demon asked, "How do you know the gods fear it?"

"Because you always send a lackey in first to face the danger."

The demon grinned. Coatl could tell by the tickle in his throat, by the bubble of maniacal laughter on the verge of bursting out of his mouth. This confirmed his own fears that the gods were using him as a shield. *But why?*

Climbing up the tree fast, before anyone spied him, he retrieved the skins and slipped them on. Elastic silk upon his flesh, he sighed and rubbed it as though it were the finest material in the world. *Well, it was, wasn't it?* Or the gods wouldn't have dressed our bones in it, he thought.

He danced around Raymond Starr's grave in his gown of skins, the demon within him singing soprano, "Tra la la boom dee ay, I met a god today. He gave fifty cents to go behind the fence. He knocked me to the ground and pulled my panties down. He counted one, two, three and stuck it into me."

A man materialized beneath the tree. Coatl skidded to a stop, and his grinning lips turned down into a snarl. He knew visits from the dead were never good, and this one didn't look like one of the Bat-God's messengers. He was too intact.

The man tipped his soldier's cap and said, "You've a mite of trouble seeking you."

"Is that so?" Coatl scratched his neck where Jake's skin touched his own. The fluids had begun to dry and crust upon him.

"Aye, you've chosen the wrong side to fight with," he said, sucking on an empty pipe.

"Civil War's been over a long time, fella. Better crawl back into your bones before I show you the way to a real battle."

The man-spirit opened his coat and revealed his wounded torso. Between the man's armpits and hips, a black hole gaped at Coatl, and he took several steps away from the ghost. He was afraid if he touched the dark space he would fade away. It was the feeling that emptiness emitted, soul-sucking oblivion, the stuff of Leslie's mind. *But what was it?*

Sirens wailed in the distance, "Whoop you, whoop you."

"Battle scars run deep, as you can see. By the time this ends, there will be nothing left of you. I assure you of that," the man said.

"I should take your word as truth when you don't even have the guts to take me down?" Coatl chided.

The man laughed. "It's not me who's going to battle you."

"Who then?"

"Leslie Starr."

Before he could answer, the squad car, its siren now silent, pulled into the drive. Leslie followed close behind. Saluting the ghost soldier, Coatl sprinted off toward the cemetery keeper's shed to hide.

"Light always defeats the dark. Remember that," the specter called from behind him and vanished into the ground like dew dropping from grass blades.

Somehow every war was between the forces of light and dark, between good and evil, between right and wrong. Coatl wasn't so sure it was black and white. When factions charged, wars blended into grays, the color of the corpses left in the fields.

There are no absolutes in life, he thought. *Only in death.*

Squeezing in through the slightly open doors, he pressed his back against them, thrilled by the prospect of being caught. His heart did a jerky dance, and his breath whistled a fine tune through his nose, fast and thin.

Car doors thudded and gravel was kicked up by heavy shoes. Their voices carried in the morning wind, distant but clear.

"Ms. Starr, are you sure this was the correct spot?"

"Yes, it was hanging in the tree, above my father's grave."

Coatl smiled as he heard her voice waver. He would bet that ghost-soldier a new set of intestines that Leslie's mind would crack and all that unknown power would leak out. His fingers ached to take her into Xibalba and find out what that power was once the gods laid their dreaded hands upon her. Wrinkling his nose, he wondered why he felt such hatred toward her.

Maybe your heart senses her strength, and you know she may defeat you after all. You always hate what you fear, whispered a voice much like the ghost's husky drawl.

Other windy voices drawled.

"Well, something was here. Got some blood on the grass and some footprints. Probably some kids stirring up a prank, but I'll get the samples done."

"It's no prank."

"Well, in my twenty years, I've never come across any skins hung on trees. At least not human skins. Are you sure it wasn't a deer hide? Maybe the sun hit it just right and the sight fooled you. It's understandable, with you here for your friend's funeral and sitting at your father's grave. I might've gotten spooked myself."

"No, the skin belonged to Jake."

"Oh? And how can you be so sure?"

Coatl slipped from the shed and braved a peek around the corner. Sheriff Don, who always reminded him of Mark Twain, with his thick white hair and bushy mustache, leaned against the tree, supporting his slight weight with a bony hand. He picked off the bark as he stared at Leslie.

Leslie brushed her hair behind her ears, shrugging. "I can't explain it, but the man who killed Charlotte has killed Jake, and I think he's after me."

"Last I knew, Jake was off hunting and hasn't showed up dead. I hate to bring this up, Leslie, but your cousin is looking more like our man every day," Sheriff Don said. "It's only a matter of time before we have an official arrest. If you have information that you're withholding to protect Sam, then you'll be held as an accessory to murder."

"He didn't do it." Her eyes turned feral, slitlike beneath her furrowed brow.

Her family loyalty was endearing. Coatl wondered if she'd still revere her father if she knew the whole truth.

140

"Leslie, let's leave the law to me and the judgments to the judge and jury if it comes to that. I just do my job." The sheriff placed his hat on his head and patted his pockets for his cigarettes.

She stared at the sheriff; then her gaze shifted Coatl's way.

An owl hooted in the rafters of the roof, and he remembered the fourth omen, if the owl cries out on the edge of the roof terrace, it is said perhaps he will die in war or his son will die.

Light always defeats the dark . . . nothing will be left of you.

Her thoughts were in his head as well: *the Dark Man dancing in the skins . . .*

"Your job waits over there!" she cried, pointing in his direction.

"Damn," he muttered, turning and running back to the shed.

He slid the door open wide. Dumping an oil can, he dipped his palms into the puddle and smeared it over his face. Pounding steps rounded the shed.

"Why don't you come out and have a word with me, son?" Sheriff Don barked.

Silence in tense minutes until the safety clicked off.

Coatl jumped on the dirt bike and stepped hard on the throttle. The bike sputtered and coughed into life. A shadow stretched across the entrance. Darkness flew in.

Gunning the bike, he sped out of the door. The front wheel popped high and nearly collided with the sheriff's face. Don dove to the ground, rolling, leveling his gun.

A shot cracked off. A bullet whizzed above his head. As the front wheel bounced back to the ground, another shot was fired. The bullet struck his shoulder.

Falling forward hard, Coatl held on to the handle bars and kept low. He raced across the bumpy ground. His breath came even faster. The rim dinged.

He swerved in quick loops to vary the target. Glancing behind, he saw the distance spread farther, and he relaxed a bit. He stayed on the land instead of turning to the road. The dirt bike handled the terrain well, and he knew he'd make it to the back woods before Sheriff Don had a chance to radio in his location.

He'd make it to the house on the edge of the tobacco farm. Its occupant owed him a favor.

His vigilance had paid off. For the past week, he watched the early morning routine of the caretaker, his son, and any funeral processions. Eight sharp, when all other sixteen-year-olds attended school, Billy Hopkins would take a showboat ride for his audience of other class skippers.

He jumped small hills with the ramp he set up, and the girls would clap, cheer, and giggle. Billy wasn't a handsome guy, kind of gritty with his wiry hair, pencil-thin mustache, and cheeks full of popped pimples, but he had what Coatl never did—macho show-off potential. Girls seemed to dig the dripping testosterone thrills boys sought. He remembered even Leslie had a thing for the barefoot water-skier.

Brazen ego was what a girl fell for.

Billy was good with the bike, though, keeping it finely tuned, cleaned, and gassed. Coatl knew he'd have an escape if one was needed. It was too bad he didn't consider bronzing the skins like baby shoes as a bulletproof sheath.

Deep in his arm, a numbness throbbed, but his fingers tingled in pain. His shoulder burned.

"Feels sooo goood," the demon within moaned. Its black tongue snaked around the bleeding wound, licking from the inside out. "Sooo hungry."

Coatl bellowed as its tongue razored through the puncture wound and spit the bullet through the raw hole. He felt as if he had been shot again.

Eyes squeezed shut from the pain, he wrecked the bike into a tree with a sudden jerk and a deafening *bang-thwack*. The back end flipped him off. He flew, and the demon screamed, "Whee!"

Coatl landed hard on his shoulder. He wailed as he rolled in the dead leaves.

"Do it again!" The demon tugged on his esophagus like a child at his mother's skirt, making Coatl vomit.

"Shut the fuck up," he growled. He was seething in pain and anger. His hand shook, and the knife hitched to his belt beneath the skins sang for blood. He was tempted to plunge the blade into his own heart just to slaughter the fiend.

Its tongue coiled out of Coatl's mouth, choking him. It lapped up the vomit. In the light, the tongue was more blue-black, like the tongue of a strangled man. His throat spasmed and gagged on the protrusion. The demon withdrew.

Coatl gasped for breath.

The tree trunks swayed in his distorted vision. Brown skeletons stood tall, risen up from their graves, chattering insanity down to him.

"Bog gurgle black man . . ."

A hand lifted him up. Spinning images mocked him, and he struggled against the two strong callused hands.

" 'Bout time you came. I've been waiting here all morning, and the moisture in the air has settled in my joints. My old bones ache."

Coatl sighed in relief to see Jorge Chevas. He grinned despite his agony.

"You look ready for the Underworld," Jorge said, his weather-beaten face crinkling in odd joy.

"Speaking of Xibalba," he started as he leaned against Jorge. They walked off deeper in the woods to his house. "I found a later passage in the *Popol Vul* about the downfall of the princes of the Underworld."

"Yes, the brothers tricking the tricksters." A series of coughs racked his body. The aged Mexican was dying of lung cancer. None of his shaman medicine could save him. The white man's tobacco was far greater than the red man's herbs.

His house, a humble cabin fashioned of logs and mud, stood bleak in the clearing. The wood had long since bleached a whitish-gray in the sun, and the roof sagged a bit. Nothing, not even weeds, grew around the cabin, as if the land sensed Jorge's connection with the Dark Gods and the black magic he practiced.

It was here in these desolate surroundings that Coatl learned to live in dreams and kill. He'd watched Jorge do it first, sitting in a lotus position on a wolf-skin mat, his chest only rising for breath every five minutes, his eyes open but turned inward to see what lay in the world beyond the flesh. Even though Jorge had shape-shifted in spirit, the changes had showed upon his face, in the slight lengthening of his teeth, in the thickening skull bones that pushed against the skin. An hour later blood had spilled from his mouth. Coatl had thought the man had died. But Jorge's eyes had rolled forward, and the old man had grinned, licking his lips of the blood that wasn't his.

In return for his silence, Jorge had apprenticed him. Astral travel, shape-shifting, gathering souls were only a few of the lessons. Learning about sacrificial rituals and the dreaded gods and the ancient lore filled the years as well, and Coatl had become a master himself, a self-appointed high priest for the gods he'd feared.

Serve your fears and live as a wise man, Jorge had said once. *You will be greater than the one who lives as a dead man in the gods' minds. You will be rewarded, given absolution from everlasting darkness, if you further the gods' plots. Indebt yourself to the gods. It is the only way to escape death.*

What do the gods plot? he had asked.

Isn't it obvious? Great floods, plagues, catastrophes, war, civilizations wiped out since time began. The gods mean to eliminate us.

"How did the brothers resurrect themselves?" Coatl asked when they reached the door, thinking he might devise another plan to escape the all-consuming darkness of death. "How could the two sorcerers bring back their bones after they were ground to powder and shape them into men-fishes?"

Jorge opened the door, its hinges creaking as much as the owner's stiff joints. Motioning for him to sit on the bench, Jorge brought out his bone tools.

"It was all a trick. They never really died. They never burnt the palace and restored its splendor. They never killed the king's dog and brought it back to life." He gave Coatl a jug of homemade whiskey and then pulled out a pronged knife. "They gave the princes a drink that produced hallucinogens, and the Xibalban royalty only believed it happened. But only in their minds."

He took a hefty swig. His throat was afire, and his words hissed from his mouth like spit on a grill. "It made no mention of drugs."

"It doesn't mention a lot of things. You take the *Popol Vuh* as literally as fundamentalist Christians do the Bible."

"From my experience, the things and places it describes are very much real and true." He flinched and clenched his jaw when Jorge poked the prong into his shoulder, fishing for the bullet.

"At least in your mind," he said.

"Why so cynical now? You used to tell me fantastic things about the Xibalbans and the Mayans."

"Those fantastic things are called myths." He inserted a spoonlike instrument. "Each day brings me closer to the Lord of Mictlan and his dead abode, and I wish I believed in merciful gods because the fear of death runs deep in my veins instead of blood. As it did in all my ancestors."

Coatl shrieked and cursed as Jorge yanked out a red gleaming bullet, and he collapsed on the bench, trembling in cold sweat and pain.

Jorge sucked the blood from the bullet. "I taste the fear in you as well."

"What do you know?" Coatl growled, gritting his teeth as he pulled himself upright.

"I know that you will fail the dreaded lords unless . . ." The old Mexican drifted from the room, and the sounds of him rummaging through a trunk echoed.

In the hearth, the ashes smoked and cried.

Jorge returned with an obsidian knife and handed it to him. "Unless you kill Leslie Starr, you will fail."

The ashes fluttered onto the floor and scattered toward the bench with the weeping of the dead.

"The gods want her alive," he said, staring at the ashen floor, lifting his feet and tucking them beneath him.

"Then you will fail because you will never take her alive."

Rising, rising, the ashes were rising around him.

"How . . ." And the ashes cut him off as the slate clouds forced into his mouth, and Coatl collapsed again, doubled over from the burning in his belly.

Jorge dipped a green stone called chalchuititl into a water jar of tlilatl, black water, and pushed it into Coatl's mouth. Holding his jaws closed over the chalchuititl, Jorge exorcized the dead from him with the grimmest arcana, and Coatl and his demon screamed in the throes of the body being evacuated by fire and smoke.

The chalchuititl melted in his mouth. He swallowed it along with the pus of the popping blisters and the few remaining ashes, deciding he would prefer the dead flesh of men.

"Because this will never compare to what comes out of her body to consume you," Jorge said, and he curled Coatl's fingers around the obsidian knife, pleading with the eyes of a man who had seen his death.

Chapter Ten

Two hours gone, and Leslie hadn't crossed the street yet to join the funeral procession that crawled through the gates. The purple flags on the hearse and cars waved, as if greeting the unseen inhabitants this side of the road.

Not all unseen, thought Leslie as she watched the Confederate soldier pace between headstones.

Charles Somner wrung his hat in his hands and marched three steps before turning and repeating the rigid stride, all the while muttering about the Guardian of Spirits and war.

The wind pushed through the cemetery, chilling even the dead. Charles glinted in the sunlight like frost.

"Why do the dead have an interest in me?" Leslie asked, sensing them slink beneath the soil, a cold seeping through the ground into her soles.

"You are a Starr, and the dead have always come to the Starrs. They are the watchers in the night and the keepers of . . ." He stopped, crouched, and put his hand through the frozen ground.

"Keepers of what?"

Head cocked, he acted as if he listened to a distant voice.

"Keepers of what?" she asked again, feeling unsettled standing above the unquiet dead.

Images of their faces pressed against the thin soil layer snuck into her mind. The hollow eyes of their skulls filled with black light, and something ghastly became visible among them, something colder than ice and more deadly. Something seeing her with all their eyes.

Charles withdrew his hand, icicles in place of his missing digits. He nodded toward the ground, and Leslie understood she had her answer. She was very afraid to ask another.

"Bring it to an end. We've grown weary and will not have the energy to help you for long," he said.

Questions burned in her mouth. But the ground kept getting colder and colder as something drew nearer.

"We've held on for the sake of our families who have survived the first onslaught. We have waited for another Starr to shine our way into the darkness."

"I don't understand."

The last of the cars entered the other cemetery addition, and Leslie was torn between continuing this conversation and paying her final respects to someone she wished she hadn't abandoned.

"Beware of shadows," Charles whispered as he faded into the ground, taking away her choices.

Or dragged, she decided when the wails of the dead rumbled from the ground and lifted on the wind.

With quick steps, she walked across the cemetery, constantly glancing over her shoulder for shadows and at her feet for something unknown to tear through the earth. *Hadn't she had enough madness for one lifetime? Was there a cure for cursed genes?*

She hoped the sheriff had caught the man. The Dark Man, a living haunt of flesh and bone and monstrous spirit.

Riddled with confusion, she walked across the street without looking.

"Run," came an order in her mind, a vision of Sam urging her forward with bloody hands.

Leslie turned her head toward the roar of an engine.

Blue pickup truck. Full size. Speeding ahead. Toward her.

She didn't need another warning in her mind to book it across the street before the Ford flattened her and, as it barreled past her, she caught the face of its driver—an old Mexican man glaring at her with shadows in his eyes.

On wobbly legs, she walked toward the funeral. Her chest hurt from her furiously pumping heart and the cold air she had sucked in, and she worried, as everyone turned to watch her approach, that maybe she had screamed. And maybe she hadn't stopped, judging by their aghast faces.

Leslie spotted Robin right away in the crowd and a pang of regret struck her heart. She worked her way toward her old friend and tapped Robin on the shoulder, nervously holding her breath.

Robin turned, and the look in her eyes reflected seeing Leslie after seven years. Finally tears welled in Robin's eyes and her lips trembled into a sad smile, and the two old girl friends embraced each other, closing the gap of time.

"Don't think I'm not angry with you for running away like that," Robin whispered when they parted to wipe their tears. "But I'm glad you're here, even if the gang's been reunited under awful circumstances. Minus one of the gang too . . ." Her voice trailed off, and her saddened eyes wandered toward the pearl casket and the glum pallbearers.

"Mommy?" A little girl tugged on Robin's navy skirt.

Leslie smiled at the miniature carbon copy of her mommy, same chocolate silk hair, same cinnamon eyes. Same subtle beauty. Robin's little girl. The sight of her was almost enough to warm the cold sorrow. Somehow a child symbolized hope.

"Mallory, this is Mommy's old friend, Leslie."

Mallory grinned wide, porcelain whites spotted with two dark gaps of missing teeth. She giggled. "Hi."

"Well, hi. You're as pretty as your mommy." Leslie bent down to talk to her, hands on knees for balance.

"Mommy hates it when people call me pretty. She says everyone will forget I have a brain. But I don't know how they would know I have a brain. It's not like you can see it." Mallory shrugged.

Robin hid her laughter in her palm and shook her head.

"She's a doll," Leslie said to Robin. "Well, Mallory, I take pictures. So I tend to notice when something is pretty. How would you like to pose with my cat?"

"Oh, Mommy! Can I? We're not allowed kitties in our apartment." Mallory jumped up and down in her frilly dress.

"Yes. Now hush. We're supposed to be quiet, remember?" She gave her daughter a stern look, pursed lips, pinched brows. Leslie could tell it was an act, but Mallory stood still and solemn like a flower waiting for the clouds to pass so it could spread its petals for the sun.

Leslie leaned close and whispered, "I wish I hadn't missed her growing up."

"She's not grown yet. We have plenty of time to catch up." She grabbed Leslie's hand. "You're not getting away this time."

Robin pulled her through the crowd and presented her to Trisha and Bonnie. Neither looked as if the years had treated them kindly.

Trisha had aged beyond her twenty-four years, deep lines in her brow and around her mouth, dark circles beneath her eyes, sickly complexion. Her trademark lemon-blond pigtails had been chopped off, and the blunt cut she now sported framed her face with harsh edges. *Bitter* and *haggard* were good ways to describe her expression as she surveyed Leslie as well. A curt nod was all the acknowledgment she got from Trisha.

"Aren't you a little late to visit Charlotte?" Bonnie asked, propping her hands on her hips, which had expanded through the years, her ample waistline also a testament to the bulimia battle she had either lost or conquered, depending on the perspective.

"That's not fair," Robin interjected in a hushed snarl.

"Oh, sticking up for her when she decided long ago that she wanted nothing to do with us." Bonnie looked Leslie over with disdain. "What, she's just a small-time celebrity now, and she has to put on a show that she has any feelings whatsoever."

"Have some respect, please," Robin said.

"Bonnie, lay off. This isn't the time or place," Trisha added.

Is there any time or place to say hurtful things? Leslie thought. *They must really think I'm callous and cold to say such things to my face, without a care about my feelings.* Once she had overheard her mom tell another adult that her daughter wasn't sensitive at all and that she didn't think anything would bother her. But they were both wrong. On the contrary, she felt too much. She felt more than she could handle, and so she had to find measures to cope with her raging emotions—build a dam inside and stop the flow of tears. That's what happened when she grew up with monsters, whether alcoholic or inhuman.

"Girls," Charlotte's mother reprimanded, sending them on a time warp, back to those preteen years when they disrupted her classroom with their giggles.

"I'm sorry," was all Leslie muttered before the dam broke.

"God bless you, that's all that needs be said." The depth of sadness in Mrs. Schneider's eyes rivaled the Void's deep, dark well, and Leslie once again suffered the guilt, wishing with all her might that she *could* turn back the clock and do it over again.

With a squeeze on Leslie's shoulder, Mrs. Schneider returned to her husband's side, and together they bowed their heads for the preacher to bless their daughter into the life beyond.

Voices hissed upon the wind, seething beneath the preacher's prayers. Voices not belonging to anyone human.

"Where's Sam?"

"Fucking the dead girl . . ."

"Where is Jake?"

" 'Where oh where has our little dog gone? Oh where oh where can he be?' "

"Old Yeller . . . Old Yeller."

Eerie laughter hummed upon the sweet alto of "Amazing Grace" until it vanished into the thin air it was made of.

The choir sang on, oblivious to anything unusual.

Ever since her father's death, Leslie had hated the song. She had once found the lyrics uplifting, feeling almost as fervent as a reborn Christian, but no more. It haunted her, as if she were locked in a dark room, no Savior to be found.

She wanted to believe in Heaven, in everlasting life, in the promise of eternal love and goodness, but she was afraid. To have faith in the one meant to admit the existence of the other. She didn't want to believe in Hell.

The chorus heightened, vocal chords in ecstasy, souls in somber rapture. She wished at that moment to have a camera in her head, to record the images. *With white wings dripping blood, the Heavenly Choir stood around the grave. The black pit swelled and stretched, hungry to swallow the casket of human fodder. The angels wept. Ruby tears fell onto the ground, and the enriched soil sighed in graceful melody. Charlotte's withered flesh crumpled into dust. Skeletal remains and creeping shadows.* Leslie clasped her hand over her mouth so she wouldn't scream.

Her imagination made her a gifted photographer, but it sometimes tarnished her sanity.

Her body tingled with awareness. The preacher droned on, sermonizing about paradise and souls. Something felt odd, as if the real world had slipped behind a sheer curtain and left her standing alone in a strange realm.

Cold mists rose from the ground, evaporating almost immediately but leaving a fine wet film on her skin and everything else. Sunlight twinkled on the dew and chased shadows from those gathered around Charlotte's casket.

The preacher exalted, ". . . the people who sat in darkness have seen a great light, and for those who sat in the region and shadow of death light has dawned."

Leslie squinted at the distant chain-link fence, at the streaming darkness coming through, at the shadows stretching the wrong way. *The shadows of death*.

"The Kingdom of Heaven has come for Charlotte."

Laughter soft upon the wind.

The Dark Man has come, Leslie thought, stepping farther back into the crowd, thinking she could hide, thinking in desperate self-preservation that maybe he'd take the person in front of her.

Guilt made her step forward again, and Robin glanced at her quizzically.

Leslie wanted to warn her: *Beware the shadows*.

"But thanks be to God, who in Christ always leads us in triumphal procession, and through us spreads in every place the fragrance that comes from knowing him. For we are the aroma of Christ to God among those who are being saved and among those who are perishing; to the one a fragrance from death to death, to the other a fragrance from life to life . . ."

The preacher sprinkled sweet myrrh incense upon the casket.

Strange liturgy, she thought, but then she noticed the sweat upon the preacher's brow, dark beads rolling from his temples. He was frightened. He knew.

He smelled the encroaching rot as well.

And that made it all worse, because now Leslie knew she wasn't imagining it.

Beware the darkness coming from the region of death.

Chapter Eleven

Somber waves of black rolled toward those milled about Charlotte's gravesite, flowing over the ground like the shadow of a cloud passing in front of the sun.

Coatl inhaled the air stifled with impending rain and braced himself against the oak as the breath rankled through the gunshot wound. He ached too from anticipating the coming storm.

Not of rain but of demons.

Along the shaded paths of the tombstones and trees, the demons surged toward the funereal mass and, in their chilling wake, stained the grass with black frost. Their talons flashed silver and sharp in the shade. The demons were ready for a winter harvest.

Winds pushed dark mists of shadows upon the mourners, and the darkness descended with such oppression that it crushed away the air. But no one gasped for breath.

Everyone lay inert, curled in fetal balls on the ground, as the demons settled silent upon them.

Shadows stretching beyond the people's bodies seeped back into them, the shapeless black taking on shape at last, the shape of the man or woman or child it crawled into. The bodies rose one by one, almost like balloons filled with blackish air. Charcoal-pasted faces opened their eyes, and every socket stared with ebony orbs.

Only one body remained on the ground—Leslie's. She began to stir as Coatl moved from the trees and neared the gravesite.

When he reached the casket, Leslie opened her eyes, their blue irises disappearing amid widening pupils. Coatl approached Leslie and held out his hand. The sleeve of Jake's skin flapped against his own, and she scrambled on her hands and knees away from him, screaming.

Black eyes and black grins met her on her way.

"Don't waste your energy running, Leslie," they said, their voices whistling like bog wind through the reeds. "You'll need it later."

She stopped, stared at the shadow-infested crowd, and then sat back on her haunches, rocking in fear, hiding her face in her hands.

"We're all dead. We don't feel a thing. . . ."

"We're always dying. . . ."

"You're always dying. . . ."

"You're all dead. You won't feel a thing. . . ."

Laughter oozed from the hollows of the borrowed lips, and the laughing mourners closed their circle around Leslie, their cold hands reaching into her hair and tangling black-tipped fingers into the strands.

Nightmare bats, she cried in her mind.

Coatl grinned, loving the creative associations her mind made, and the mask of Jake's face slipped, its bloody gum less sticky after a night and day. He pressed the flesh in place again.

In a demon-distorted voice, Coatl said, "Leave her. We must make other sacrifices first."

The hands snatched away and left Leslie hysterical upon the ground.

"Charlotte caught me one day offering blood to the Lord of Mictlan," he said, rapping upon the casket. "She assumed the worst, seeing me with blood on my hands. But the blood was all mine, coming from the sloppy cuts I had made in the vessels under my tongue and behind my ears."

Leslie sat with rigid attention, and he turned back to the casket, running his finger along the worm-tight seal.

"From the look in her eyes, I knew I had lost her trust and could no longer trust her. Do you see why she had to die?"

"No," Leslie muttered.

"I couldn't have her spilling my secrets . . ." He walked away from the casket and stood in front of

Teri A. Jacobs

Bonnie, his hands pantomiming before her face as though he were ripping out her eyes. "But she told anyway, before I cut out her tongue and silenced her forever. Those who listened will die first. And then everyone else will follow into the eternal silence. Especially you."

The shadow within Bonnie uncoiled from her eye sockets and dangled down like licorice strings, and the thin ropes wrapped around her throat, squeezing. Her face reddened, and her eyes jiggled wildly with awareness and fright. Tighter, the tendril wound.

Bonnie's face went black, not with shadows but with death.

Her body slumped to the ground, and the demon slithered away, spreading behind Bonnie's bulk in a murderous outline.

All the other demons flowed out of the bodies and stretched behind their recent hosts. Shadows.

Leslie screamed, and everyone turned toward her, aware once more, yet unaware of Bonnie, dead at their feet.

In the commotion, Coatl slipped away unnoticed, except by the one present in spirit only.

Chapter Twelve

Her screams rippled through the grieving masses, shocking them into attention. Then the others echoed her cries.

Several men and women milled around Bonnie, gloom glistening in their eyes as they drew closer for a ravening look at the dead body. Uncertainty ruffled them. Afraid to touch her. Afraid to turn and walk away.

Livid-cyanic flesh bruised the pink of Bonnie's face, and her eyes were wide with screams. An awful spectacle.

Children wept into their mothers' arms as their mothers guided them away from the grim sight, one that neither small children nor grown adults should ever witness. Bonnie's dead eyes bored right into the soul, and Leslie doubted anyone would ever shake that vision. Those eyes staring into death and utterly terrified of what she'd seen, terrified of what awaited them all on the unseen other side of life.

The ground turned glacial beneath Leslie's feet. Arctic cold seeped into her shoes, her toes went numb, and the icy floe traveled through her feet and all the way up to her shins before she jumped from the frigid spot.

From something colder than death . . .

Everywhere she stepped, white-hot ice.

"Leslie, what's wrong?" Robin asked, lifting Mallory to her hip, looking from Leslie's face to the ground and back up to Leslie's face, confused.

"Everything," she breathed, and rushed away from the things in the cemetery, running across the street and into the path of a car.

The car screeched to a halt in front of her, and she crashed into its fire-red hood, banging her hands against hot metal, thudding her knees, rolling down the bug-splattered grill onto the crumpling asphalt. Black road grit needled into her palms as she braced her fall. She cursed the chortling engine but thanked the warmth beneath her.

From the driver's side, a pair of rattlesnake-skin boots stepped out. "Are you hurt?"

"No," she grumbled, wiping the bits of asphalt from her palms.

In the glare of the sun, she made out only his wild sable hair and squinted at the hand he'd thrust out to hoist her up, at the familiar zigzag scar run-

ning ragged on his palm. Leslie took L.W.'s hand
and allowed herself to take his help.

"Leslie?" He clasped both hands tight around
hers and squeezed until she winced aloud. "I can't
believe I almost killed the person I came to save."

Pulling her close, he crushed her in a bear hug.

"Save me? Why?"

Walking her to the passenger door, he opened it
and waved her in. "Because I had a vision, of the
shadows walking among us and of you walking in
the Underworld."

"You'll save me from going into the Underworld,
then?" she asked, an uneasy feeling stirring in
her gut. *Those dark places and those darker things
within . . .*

"Oh, no. You have to walk in the Underworld to
play the Xibalbans and beat them at their game."
He gripped her elbow before she eased into the car.
"You might be the ultimate conclusion to the Xib-
alban tales, but too many forces will try to stop you.
I'm here to warn you, to be aware of the shadows."

Beware the shadows, echoed the haunting wind.

His silvery eyes, mysterious as the moon, pierced
her own and held her sway. Her body felt adrift on
ocean waves . . . down in the deep, dark waters.

"And stay away from the lake," he said.

"What's in the lake?"

"It's not what's in the lake. It's what's in you."

We're weary, whispered the wind.

In the near distance, moon-glow wraiths were
suspended in the limbs of the old maple, their

spirit-flesh twisting like the skins that had hung earlier, and their eyes and mouths were black spaces. But not empty, she sensed, and shivered.

The sheriff appeared from behind the maple. Something in his hand kept his attention as he headed for the road. He glanced up when he reached it.

"Just the person I'm looking for," he called, walking toward them, smiling. "I was going to catch you at the funeral, but I guess it's over."

"I doubt it, what with Bonnie . . ." She let the reasoning hang, like a dead man's skin, like ghosts.

The sheriff nodded, his smile fading quicker than moonlight in the flaming dawn. "Yeah, I heard the call on the radio. Terrible." Holding up a Ziplock Baggie, he asked, "Any ideas?"

Leslie shook her head as she looked at the small wooden figure. With its doglike head, large snout, long teeth, oxen hooves, and human body, it looked like a grinning demon.

"That's Xolotl's idol," L.W. said. "He's an ancient Mexican deity—the Dog-headed Monster or Lightning Beast, depending upon circumstances of sacrifice or war. In the myths, he was the twin of Quetzalcoatl, who went into hell to gather the bones to resurrect man and then nourished the bones into life. He also took the young goddess Xochiquetzal into the Underworld and raped her."

"Huh, lovely god." Sheriff Don rubbed the snout through the plastic. "Wonder what it's doing in Kentucky . . ."

"Where did you find it?"

"Jutting up from the ground near your father's headstone."

"I'd say that's a sign."

"What do you mean, L.W.? A sign of what?"

"Symbolism that Xolotl has gone back into Hell to retrieve his bones and resurrect him." L.W. closed his eyes, and his face creased with the pain of his thoughts. Pain that Leslie felt as well, a fast-and-furious fist well placed into her heart.

"Who?" asked the sheriff, shaking his head in confusion, wringing the Ziplock with the impatience.

"My dad." Leslie looked over her shoulder and stared hard at the maple for signs that his remains had not stayed in the ground. "He thinks some-one's trying to bring my father back from the grave."

Chapter Thirteen

The wind blew with angry force against the truck, and Coatl's heart skipped as the truck took sail and swerved onto the soft gravel shoulder, which dropped into a steep ravine. Jorge fought with the shuddering wheel to steer the truck back onto the pavement.

"The smell of rot is all over you, and they sense it," Jorge said, glancing through the rearview. "Her presence has opened the gates and already they begin to work against us."

Wind thumped hard against the passenger door, and Coatl leaned closer to Jorge, farther from the window with the ghostly torso pressed against it, farther from the spectral hand clawing to find its way in.

"But we have our own countermeasures. It should negate this onslaught," Coatl said, his shaky tone unable to conceal his wariness of the unseen trying hard to be seen; of the enemy watcher trying hard to see too much.

"Only if Xolotl concedes . . ." Jorge gritted his teeth and growled as he swerved sharply to the right, back onto the soft and crumbling shoulder.

In the middle of their lane, the monstrous god stood, holding spears of lightning in his hands.

Slamming on the brakes, Jorge braced his arms, elbows locked, onto the steering column as the truck failed to stop. The Ford skidded along the shoulder, the gravel and loose soil acting like ice. Dusty clouds exploded up from the tires, and the sounds of an angry god screeched above all the other noise and spider-cracked the back window. A trickle of blood ran from Jorge's ear.

The truck halted on the very edge in deafening silence.

Huffing in dust and fear, Coatl shifted in the seat and looked out the rear window. He saw glittering glass fissures and sandy air and a dog-headed man walking toward them on backward-turned feet.

Xolotl howled.

It cut through Coatl, ripping through his lungs and heart almost as if it meant to sever every bit of life from his body. He shrank in the seat, praying that the god didn't mean to take his soul to Mictlan.

As the howl reverberated through the truck's cab, the radio buzzed static and whipped through the FM stations, a mix of voices and music coming out garbled through the speakers. Or almost garbled, until he heard the god's throaty snarl.

The equalizer's spectrum lit up with red sine waves.

Hot breath steamed against his right arm. Coatl turned his head, cricking to the right a millimeter at a time.

Through the melted window, the glass turned back into sand, the Dog-headed Monster stared at Coatl with empty eye sockets. Hefty jaws gaped into a grin, large canine teeth stretching from inflamed gums and glistening from the bloody froth.

Xolotl opened his jaws wide.

He means to swallow me, Coatl thought-screamed.

Darkness and the dead wailed within the chasm of the dog-god's throat.

"For Mictlantecutli . . ." the stereo growled.

Viscous scarlet drool landed on Coatl's hand, a gift from the Giver of Misfortune, and Xolotl disappeared into the ashen winds.

"He came, but he did not bring Ray Starr back from the dead," Jorge whispered. "Are we doomed?"

In the red-pearl depth of the god's spit, an image of Ray Starr's face swirled, and her father's screams blasted through the speakers and blew them into smoke and silence.

"No, not us." Coatl laughed and his demon joined in, lending the laughter the madness of the moment and the future.

Chapter Fourteen

In the car, on the way to the potluck dinner and prayers for Charlotte's family at the First Methodist Church, Leslie listened to L.W.'s musical voice.

"One day—if day ever penetrated that gloomy and unwholesome place—a princess of Xibalba called Xquiq, meaning blood, came upon the tree in which Hunhun-Apu's head ripened with the fruits.

"You remember he was one of the brothers tricked into a game of ball and humiliated by the lords of Xibalba, then later tortured and killed. And it was forbidden to eat the gourds of that tree.

"But Xquiq plucked one of the desirable gourds, her feminine curiosity greater than the laws. In her palm, Hunhun-Apu's head spat, 'You will become the mother of my children.'

"He promised her safety when she returned home, but her noble father, Cuchumaquiq, doomed her to be slain for her trespass and misdeed and sent the Xibalban messengers, the owls, to bring her heart back to him in a vase.

"With splendid promises, she befriended the owls, and they substituted the sap of a bloodwort plant for her heart. She then sought the aged Xmucane, Hunhun-Apu's mother, for protection, but Xmucane did not believe the hero-god had bestowed favor upon Xquiq.

"Thus, Xquiq begged the gods to grant her a miracle of proof. And they did. She, being a princess of the Underworld and possessing extraordinary abilities, gathered maize where no maize ever grew, and when Xquiq presented the basket to her, Xmucane allowed her in her graces. The twin sons, Hun-Apu and Xbalanque, were born then.

"The divine children of the hero-god had many magical tools. While they played, these tools undertook their work in the fields. The boys would smear soil on the hands and faces to fool their grandmother, Xmucane. But the small animals replaced the roots and shrubs the magical tools cleared away overnight, so Hun-Apu and Xbalanque set out traps and caught all the animals, save the rat.

"The rat, upon being spared, told them their father's and uncle's brave tales and the trickery of the Xibalban court. And of the existence of some clubs and balls with which Hun-Apu and Xbalanque might play.

"Again, the lords of Xibalba challenged the brothers to a game of ball, thinking the sons and nephews of their first victims had no knowledge of the fates of Hunhun-Apu and Vukub-Hunapu. Xmucane, alarmed, sent a louse to warn her grandsons. The louse could not travel quick enough and allowed himself to be swallowed by a toad. In turn, the toad was swallowed by a serpent, the serpent by the bird Voc, the messenger of Hurakan. The bird released the serpent, the serpent the toad, but the toad could not rid himself of the louse. The louse had only hidden itself in the toad's gums and was never swallowed at all. At last the message was delivered.

"The twins returned to Xmucane and planted a cane, telling her that if the cane withered, then they had fallen to some ill fate like their father and uncle before them. And, with that, they accepted the challenge."

L.W. slowed the car before the church's drive.

Leslie shivered from the cold, which forced its way in through the seals and vents, and when she looked to L.W., he had covered his eyes with his hands. The hairs on the back of his hand and his wrist stood on end.

Drifting inward, the air pushed upon her and wrapped around her throat like a windy garrote. It squeezed into her neck and cut off her breath. However it wasn't air against her flesh but a myriad of invisible hands pressing harder and harder until she thought her neck would break.

The extra-long nails of those hands pinched into the hollow of her throat and seemed to dig deep into her, as if intending on shredding her esophagus. She struggled to scream, to breathe, but she was helpless.

With oppressive force, the wind rocked the car, whistle-singing . . .

Rock a bye, baby, on the tree top.
When the wind blows, the cradle will rock.
When the bough breaks, the cradle will fall
Down will come baby, cradle and all . . .

Then the brutal messengers released their hold upon Leslie and blew away, returning to the hell they'd come from. She massaged her neck and blinked back the burning tears before she sobbed instead of inhaled her breath.

The lullaby had begun as a way to pass a warning that the enemy was coming, and that warning had been resurrected from the past. The enemy was coming.

"You need to learn to fight them at their own game, to go into their world and defeat them as Hun-Apu and Xbalanque did. The twin brothers tricked the tricksters," L.W. said, dropping his hands from his eyes. Eyes as black as space. "You have to survive the ordeals of Xibalba and take down the dreaded lords."

"Oh my God," she wailed, thinking of Jake, of the harm he'd done to her, and of her proximity to someone with those same shadowy eyes.

"Leslie, don't fear me. The shadows taunt us all from time to time, but I'm better able to defend myself from their complete control. They can slip into my body but not my soul."

The shadow moved beneath his eyelid, a black bulging vein that squirmed snakelike, and blood ran from his flaring nostrils and hit the back of his balled hand in fat black droplets.

"Your father never meant to bring the shadows into our world," L.W. said, the blackness from his eyes receding slowly like dark clouds drifting away from the moon.

"What?" Leslie reached over and turned the key, shutting off the rumbling engine, hoping she'd heard him wrong. "What did my father do?"

"He did what any father would do to save his child, but he didn't realize the cost of his actions, that it would eventually put you at even greater risk." L.W. sighed as one does in grief, loud and wretched.

"What did he do?" she repeated, imagining her father setting a rabbit on a stone, its small body writhing as he tore its chest open with a stone knife, its beating heart laid upon the ground for the pitchy creatures crawling toward it.

L.W. sighed again. "He believed in a man who tricked us all."

"Who?"

"Jorge Chavaz. An old bastard from Mictlan, a village named after the Underworld, who served as a temple official in the Palace of the Living and the Dead, who prepared slaves and prisoners for secret sacrifices."

"But how can believing one man bring on this madness?" she asked.

"Because this man was a priest of Mictlantecutli and worshiped the darkness he falsely promised your father he would destroy." L.W. drummed his fingers against the dash, his rhythm for the story dance.

"One night, your father and I walked the cove, listening to our fears, which we could easily hear in the silence. The earth seemed to soak in the sounds of our footsteps, and the lake uttered nothing as we followed its shore. Every living creature had hidden, making not a peep nor a rustle, frightened of the things that waited one step beyond our world, that waited hungrily to break through the barriers.

"We had only heard stories about these dark spirits, how Josephine Starr channeled them into caverns of death and trapped them to rot away within the place you call the Void."

"How did you . . ." She was going to ask *how did you know about the Void?*

But his eyes filmed over like a starless night.

He continued in a voice not quite his own. "We met Jorge at the farthest bend. He stirred a boiling pot of guts and bones, his face greasy from wiping the slaughter from his hands, his grin bloody from tasting it.

"With a wooden spoon he dished out the entrails and bones and scattered them across the ground. The bones had fallen in a pattern of a five-pointed star. And the blood and guts had splattered inside it.

"Jorge had divined your death, Leslie, but he promised your father, if he followed Jorge's directions, that dead stars would still shine."

"I don't understand any of this," she groaned. Her head ached and heat flushed through her body as she tried to figure out the meaning of L.W.'s disturbing tale.

Opening the window, she let in a rush of aromatic air, of the chicken casseroles and fruit pies and spice breads carried by those passing by the car. Their heels clicked and clapped on the sidewalk as they headed toward the church's entrance.

"In time you will," L.W. said, closing his darkened eyes. "Hopefully before time expires for us all, though."

Captured within the indigo stained glass window at the front of the church, the crucified Christ stared down at her and accused her of His death and of every death hereafter. Each passing minute His pale glass-flesh reddened with the setting sun.

His eyes deepened, and the wind cursed her for the blood she'd let spill.

Charlotte, Bonnie . . . her father even.

"I don't understand what my father supposedly did, some pact or something with a pagan priest that would bring these shadows into existence, or how I'm supposed to reverse it." She hated to say it but had no other words. "Why me?"

"Because you're a Starr, with an ancient, potent bloodline between the darkness and the light." Eyes closed, he turned to her and gripped her arm, digging in his nails. "Bring the shadows into the Void and seal what your father had unsealed."

L.W. pushed her out of the car. Eyes wide, he stared at her from bottomless pits and black tears flowed upon his face.

"Save us," he moaned, then slammed the door and peeled into the street, driving away with dusk settling upon her, leaving her in shock and with many more questions.

The wind picked up, blowing the coldness of coming sleet, but it wasn't colder than the chill that had settled within her. Leslie stared at the church. In the tower, the bell tolled faintly, its copper body swinging with the windy hand of God. The day darkened in quick degrees, as if the sun was on a dimmer switch, and the church's facade glowed in a dreary sheen, its grayish paint lighter than the backdrop of the sky. Or maybe it shone because the ghosts that tried to throttle her had settled into the frames and waited for her to enter the lair once more.

"Leslie . . ."

Groaning wind and someone behind her. Leslie spun around, her hand raised in defense, a cry strangling in her twisted mouth.

Sam caught her arm. "Sorry, I didn't mean to frighten you. I guess I have a bad habit of sneaking up on you, especially during these strange times. Especially after what happened to Bonnie."

Winter's breath whistled, and the bell rang in metallic laughter. She felt dizzy, as if staggering through a carnival funhouse, tilted floors and weird angled mirrors, dry ice hissing, billowing in a whitish fog, and distorting her vision. *Sam. Sam, how did you know? You weren't even there. . . . Is her blood on your hands?*

Grabbing his hands, she checked his palms and underneath his nails, and the dizziness whirled in her. She swayed with a heavy head.

"What's wrong?" He steadied her with his arm. Her eyes rolled and she tried to keep her focus, but his face blurred and blended with the sky—storm clouds with green eyes, and they moved like a naval fleet across the sky, sailing toward her soul.

"Leslie? Hey, stay with me." The brisk concern in his voice sought to anchor her, but she was drowning in a sea of images.

The Dark Man on the mountain casting gruesome shade over the cliffs; Charlotte and Bonnie dead beneath an avalanche of blackness; her father rising from his grave with a dog-headed god on a leash of his entrails; her family, friends, and childhood neighbors gathering around her, morbid hunger in eyes blotted out with shadows.

Sam guided her, lumbering, to the church. As she glanced upward, the steeple of the bell tower seemed to curl downward, its pointed roof aiming to spear her, and, within the stained-glass procession in the arched windows along the side of the chapel, the lighted figures moved with life. She heard His screams as the spikes were pounded into His wrists and feet. The hammer of her heart clanged against her chest.

"Sam, help me . . ." she whimpered. "I can't stop the shadows. I can't stop the shadows."

"I'll help you. I'm here."

Yes, and you were at the funeral, not in body but in spirit, watching unseen. But did you do more than watch? I am so afraid for you. I think the shadows want you too, and I know you don't have blood on your hands. Yet.

She closed her eyes on the illusions and accepted the reality of darkness that crashed behind her lids. *Into those darkest tunnels*, she thought, and realized she believed in the mythical world that interested her father and in the ebon lunacy that finally brought her to her senses.

"Teach me to remote view," she said to Sam, opening her eyes at last.

"Not that simple, I'm afraid. Not something I can teach you in the short time I suspect we have."

"Then I'll never find the man behind the shadows." She hung her head, feeling the weight of her thoughts drag her down deeper into dejection and hopelessness.

"What if I told you that I have? Things have been happening to both of us, all of us, and I've taken it on myself to track Charlotte's killer. I've stumbled onto something frightening, the same as you. But I haven't seen you like this since..." Sam's voice trailed off, as if leaving it unspoken kept it far in the past and forgotten.

Not far enough, she thought and, with a tiny voice, asked, "You tracked him?"

"Yes."

They walked slowly up the steps into the church in silence, knowing they each understood the gravity of the situation and that they needed each other to pull through it. Together again to battle the darker sides of life. The muscles in her thighs quivered and ached from tension brought on by fear, the eerie glimmer of the church descending as she ascended.

"What else did you see at the funeral?" she asked, ignoring the way the light changed unnaturally as she stood under the awning.

"Glimpses here and there, nothing really besides you and Bonnie screaming. That's the problem with remote viewing—it's open to wide interpretation and skewed images. It's not exactly like using binoculars." Sam shrugged, gave a wry smile, and stopped before the door, his hand resting on the latch. He knew she wasn't ready to enter.

"I encountered a few more shocks than I wanted." Leslie waved him to go inside. "And I'm afraid Bonnie's death won't be such a fluke in Owenton."

Sam held the door, his mouth open nearly as wide.

"You didn't know?"

He shook his head. "I knew something happened, but nothing specific. How did she die?"

An attendant in the entrance hall placed a finger to his lips and ushered them to the lower level, giving Sam an extra long look of suspicion.

"Maybe you shouldn't be here, Sam," she whispered.

"I won't leave until I know you're okay." He clasped her hand, sliding more than gripping because of the clamminess. "Something terrible must be happening for you not to tell me the whole thing. I can tell by the way your eyes wander without really focusing."

As they headed down, the quiet was displaced by the static of conversation and the tinkling of china and silver. The different smells mingled together into a foul stew, competing odors of cottage ham and cabbage, baked beans, meat casseroles, potato salad, all sour in the warmth, unless it was the dankness of the basement coming full of life, of what life Leslie was unsure.

"Something terrible is happening and I don't know how to stop it," she said.

Sam halted before the last stair. "Then we'll need more than remote viewing to help us." He glanced at the wall, at the gold, gothic lettering of the Lord's Prayer stenciled on it. "Too bad I don't believe in God." He touched the word *Father*. "Or I'd be begging for His help."

Behind them, heavy footfalls thudded, and they both looked up to find Buddy, prodding down the stairs, his face stubbled and ashen. His eyes, cobalt like the Caribbean Sea, met hers for a moment, a glance that radiated a blue intensity of only her and him, a disconcerting intimacy, before he fixed a steely glare at Sam. Leslie tensed as their hatred became tangible around her. A crushing heat.

"Why are you fucking here? You belong in jail." Buddy stepped down, brushed by her, and stood almost nose-to-nose with Sam.

"Fuck you," Sam said, his jaw clenching.

"Didn't do enough of that, huh? Taking my wife, killing her . . ."

Sam whipped up his hand and gripped Buddy's throat, right beneath his chin. "How dare *you* accuse me of hurting Charlotte? You sick bastard! She told me all about 'poker' nights. Gambling with lives instead of money, eh?"

Buddy's face reddened, and he made weird sucking noises. Sam dug his fingers in deeper.

"Sam!" Leslie whispered harshly. Already they had caused a scene as the others milled at the bottom of the stairs, plates in hand, ready for their dinner entertainment.

With a shove, Sam released him, and Buddy hit the wall.

"You proved your guilt to me." Buddy massaged the swollen, tender tissue. Scarlet-stained impressions of Sam's fingers on his throat convicted Sam without trial among the witnesses.

Gasps and angry muttering sparked in their midst, crackling like a fire struggling to burn old, damp wood, hissing with the hint of an underlying rage. With a nudge, Leslie motioned Sam to leave. Sam seemed to weigh his options in glances, first to Leslie, then to the others, and finally settling on Buddy. Buddy's tight grin and cool sapphire eyes told Sam that he didn't have the luxury of support from anyone present, or the time to garner it.

"Wish upon a star tomorrow night for me," Sam said, invoking their secret code before he sprinted up the stairs, not waiting or looking back to assure himself that she had understood his meaning. He stamped away, echoing with eerie deadfall on the steps, and Leslie wished she didn't have to wait for tomorrow to meet him at the abandoned house on Main. The sense of bad omens chilled her. Whispering shadows celebrated along the wall, wavering in a quiet dance.

"Leslie, come down," they said. "Join us."

"Yes, we haven't had the pleasure of your company in over a hundred years, it seems." Buddy touched her elbow, cold fingers without a trace of his heated anger.

A dizzy spell threatened Leslie again, everyone closing in on her like walls, voices murmuring in discord, their psychic vibes emanating off their dark bodies in weird, irritating waves. Looping his arm through hers, Buddy led her down the stairs, and she went along, feeling lost anyway. Faces parted, the women's colored lips reminding her of the Red Sea. Maybe she only thought that because she was in a church, or maybe because at the end of the divided throngs stood Rod, coming to save her as Moses had his people. A man once troubled with identity and purpose.

Hidden behind Rod's legs, his daughter Jenelle giggled as Mallory crawled around on the floor, meowing, scratching at the air near Jenelle. They were a flash of life within the sepulchral basement. Leslie wondered why Rod came without calling, and why Jenelle had tagged along when she was supposed to be with her mom.

Fading, fading into a deaf-quiet, the voices stilled, but the mouths moved open, shut, open, shut, like gulping fish in a tank. The walls closed farther inward on Leslie. She was afraid she'd drown in the blackness that threatened to crush her.

"Can you just feel them eating us with their eyes, wondering about you, me, and Sam?" Buddy asked, his voice a soft wind in her ear.

Sounds broke over her like waves on a rocky shore.

"Yes." And she did—their piercing inquisitions gnawed at her with snappy judgment, making her wince as she walked past their roving, hard eyes. *As long as they don't turn black*, she thought, *I'm fine*.

"Buddy, I'm sorry about Charlotte . . . are you doing okay? . . . we missed you at the funeral . . . the nerve of Sam . . ."

Various voices merged as one collective tongue, womanly high lilt melding with manly pitch. White noise hissed within their words, and it sounded as if everyone spoke through a synthesizer, with electric reverb.

Nodding to those he passed, Buddy kept his arm on Leslie's and guided her to the left toward the buffet table, away from Rod. She craned her neck, swiveling her head back to Rod, imploring him with her eyes to come pull her from the quagmire because he was the only one who had ever kept her from slipping into oblivion.

Love is an anchor, her father once told her after explaining the meaning of one of his tales.

"Anchors," she said, half dreamy.

"Anchors? Feeling dragged down, huh? Give your mind a rest and just enjoy the company of an old friend," Buddy drawled. His hand slid down her arm and nested hers.

"Kind of hard to enjoy one friend when two have died." She eased her hand free and turned away from Buddy, feeling a bit guilty for leaving him when he probably needed a friend; but she owed it to Rod, who'd made a surprise trip to offer her the support she, more often than not, bickered for.

The people milling about seemed as insubstantial as clouds, and she ignored their every attempt to drift into conversation. Rod stayed to the back of the room, his eyes following her approach, his arms crossed over his chest.

Like sentries at a pharaoh's tomb, Robin and Trisha flanked him and watched the young children race beneath the tables with sullen eyes. At least seven kids had ganged together and played as usual, shrugging off the gloom that rested wearily on the adults. Their laughter rang within the reception hall. If only the children's resiliency would rub off and dust the depressing air; then she could breathe in vigorous and spirited life instead of death.

Leslie nearly collapsed into Rod's arms. She buried her face against his chest, and all the mingled scents of man and cologne calmed her. Pressing her hand against the muscles of his chest, she wished his presence were enough protection, but he too was only flesh and blood and vulnerable to the evil corroding their small town.

"Why'd you come?" she asked.

He chuckled low and soft. "Funny way to greet me after I drove two and a half hours to get here."

"It only takes an hour and a half . . ." She pulled away and glanced up at his hard-sculpted face and his tender eyes.

"We missed a crucial turn or we would've made it on time for the funeral. But Jenelle might've been too excited anyway. First time away from the city.

She's been mooing to every cow she's seen."

"Must've been a lot of moos," Robin said.

"Exactly." And Rod twisted a finger into his ear and exaggerated a painful expression.

"Really, we should quiet them down right now. They sound like bellowing cows," Trisha said, moving away and grabbing her eldest child. She pulled him aside and motioned for him to lower his voice and to tell the others.

It worked for about five minutes, and then the children raised their ruckus again.

"Maybe we should take them outside," Robin offered.

Stroking the hollow of her throat, Leslie worried about the outside, with its cruel and hungry darkness.

"No, keep them inside," she urged a bit too loud.

But was inside any better? Mildew speckled the cream walls as if with the spores of shadows, and the people sulked in one place like malignant growths, their eyes roving from corner to corner, spreading cancerous black despair. Suffering filled the basement, and it seemed able to reach into and infect everything. Beneath the suffering, fear festered.

The townsfolk sensed the coming slaughter and waited like listless cattle, unable to break from their pens, unable to see inside the slaughterhouse. But they smelled what was to become of them.

"Why do people bring food after funerals? I can't bear the thought of even eating," Buddy said as he joined them. His eyes lit upon Leslie, and she stirred uncomfortably beneath his unwavering gaze.

Rod tucked his arm around her waist and drew her against him.

"Maybe to take our minds off death." Robin shrugged her shoulders but smiled sadly at the untouched plate of bread and cheese in her hand.

"To celebrate the fact that we're still living," Trisha said. "Makes a bit of morbid sense, don't you think?"

"Maybe."

Trisha twisted her wedding band, her red vamp nails reflecting in the gold like tarnished blood. "My husband's act of comfort this morning was to tell me that the pain I felt reminded me that I was alive, and to be thankful that I had the pain instead of nothing. Nothing at all."

Stifling silence as they reflected on their pain.

Pain, a symptom of life. Death, the cure. Then why didn't everyone long for death? Sometimes, Leslie wondered, wouldn't it be better not to feel anything, especially when all that was left to feel was suffering? She didn't even understand her own drive for survival after the tragedies she'd endured. A sick sadistic perversion, this will to live, she mused.

But then the thought of what waited in the death realm quickened her heart. Something far worse than mortal coils in unraveling agony.

Along the far wall, an artist had rendered a mural in a melange of bright colors. Christ sat in the middle of a wildflower field, with children of every race circling Him, and the sun glorified the scene, brilliant golden rays in a rainbow sky.

The wall children sang inside her head.

Ring around the rosies, pocket full of posies, ashes, ashes, we all fall down.

We're only ashes, ashes.

Christ, the Shepherd. His Father, the Creator, in the faraway kingdom, holding a checklist of His flock within His hand, scanning the names and scratching out lives in random order, forever erasing them from the lists. The endless lists. And, as with all lists, there was the duty to cross off the items until every last one was gone.

Christ, the Shepherd, gathering the flock for His Father.

"But then the pain will only worsen, won't it, Leslie? Now that Sam has come back home." Trisha crossed her arms tight under her bosom, and her lips trembled into a grimace.

"What's that supposed to mean?" Leslie asked, her mind collapsing under the strain of Buddy's intense stare and Trisha's insinuations.

The wall children snickered and whispered wicked words.

"Sam has been here for less than a year and already the weird deaths have begun again. Or maybe you've conveniently disassociated him from Charlotte's murder. Or Bonnie's. Or even those that happened before the two of you left Owenton."

191

"Sam would never hurt anyone." Indignation burned in the pit of Leslie's stomach.

"He threatened me, Leslie," Trisha said. "Before Charlotte died, he threatened us to keep quiet about the things he'd told Charlotte. Because he knew she'd told Bonnie, Robin, and me. The look in his eyes scared me, and I have been afraid to talk to the police about what I know. But I can't keep it to myself after what happened to Bonnie. It seems he's picking us off one by one."

"You're overreacting and very wrong," Leslie spat out, stepping away from Rod as anger threatened to boil her from the inside out.

The hoary-ghoul pallor of Trisha's face argued with her. Fat tears had welled in her eyes, and the dark circles beneath deepened.

"He did threaten us," Robin interjected. "And we all have had the same nightmare . . ."

Black blood surging from the deepest well and a man cloaked in death stalking them.

Leslie frowned as she caught the way the corner of Buddy's mouth twitched into a slight grin. The room spinning, the red colors on the wall mural bleeding, she gripped Rod's hand and held herself upright. Invisible hands once more wrapped around her throat.

Sight darkening, she choked on her screams as Buddy drew near, his face shrouded, his eyes . . . his eyes.

And then she regained her senses. A split second of blackness and she had landed on her rear, sitting now with everyone crowding around her. Buddy's hand reached and helped her stand. She felt the warmth of his fingers, the concern in his eyes. She must've imagined it all.

Except for the slight grin that still tottered on the brink of his lips.

"I need to leave," she announced breathlessly.

"Come to my apartment," Robin said. "I'll make your favorite cocoa, with my decadent twist of honey and rum, and it'll make us all forget our worries. We'll catch up too. Rod, you're welcome as well. We don't have much room, but I like to think it's cozy."

"Sure, if that's what Leslie wants."

Stay away from the lake, L.W. had warned.

"Yes, sounds wonderful, thank you." Leslie looked around the room and found Andy standing with a friend, hands stuffed in his pockets, boredom stuffed in his eyes. Their mother sat at a table a few feet away, consoling Charlotte's mom. "Let me give my condolences to Mr. and Mrs. Schneider and tell my mom about my change of plans."

"Here's the address." Robin handed her a note card with her neat script. "I'd had it ready for your mom, for her to send it to you in Cincinnati. But I'm happy to deliver it personally."

Trisha's clammy hand rested on her wrist.

"If you're staying for a couple days, we should meet for lunch," Trisha said. "I have other things to tell you."

"Definitely."

As Rod walked away to pull Jenelle from under the table, Buddy whispered in her ear, "Too bad death's overshadowed your homecoming, but I enjoyed seeing you in the flesh again."

Dark glimmer in his eyes, he excused himself and mingled in the crowd, and the wall children sneered, *the shadows are coming, the shadows are coming.*

Reality's bridge is falling down. . . .

Chapter Fifteen

Anticipation for the night made his heart flutter, and Coatl had difficulty reaching the trance state. A field mouse scurried into the corner, further intruding upon his concentration. For a dreaded moment, Coatl thought he would have to postpone his Xibalban trip.

From the ceiling, the lurking shadows dropped down, and it reminded him of how rain showers looked in the distance as they streamed down in a blackish curtain from the clouds. The mouse squeaked as if squeezed, and then silence spread through the room, not even the old boards creaking with the shift of his weight.

The thrum of the pulse in his ears quieted his thoughts, and he let himself get carried into that steady rhythm, its low tone sinking him deeper and deeper into the black funnel. An orange aura undulated within the blackness, pulsing with his heart.

Other images intruded—the long dark night of starless sky and howling shadows; his father creeping into his room, candle held beneath his chin, eyes staring completely black; the slippery form of his mother crawling after, bright red blood trailing, pulsing, spurting out of her leg. With the candle, his father had dipped the orangish flame under the curtains, and the fabric took the fire along its length, wavering with flames and a feeding breeze. Coatl had escaped the burning house and stood watching the blaze, figuring his parents had probably already melted away.

Someone had wrapped a blanket around his shoulders and ushered him away from the giant, fiery claws reaching out of the house and to the midnight heavens.

"Don't worry, no harm will come to your family. It's only been a lesson for you—to see how some powers can control another," the someone had said.

Indeed, the firefighters had raced from around the back, carrying two figures. His parents, after they were laid on gurneys and stuffed with breathing tubes, looked about with confusion riddling their expressions. The whites of their eyes were star bright amid their smoke-blackened faces. At least he assumed it was smoke until the smudges slowly dripped to the ground and slunk into the darkness.

"What happened?" his mother had asked, and Coatl caught the firefighter rolling his eyes and felt shame in the wrongful assumption written on the man's frown. *Drunks and accidents.* But it sparked something inside him, that assumption, that something unreal and horrifying could be frowned upon as something ordinary. Without question.

He wanted, no, *needed* to learn more of those powers.

And he had turned to Jorge Chavaz and asked the old man to show him how to control the things that already dwelled within him.

Coatl had become lost in memory and hadn't realized he'd drifted into a zone. Great masses of blackish fog swirled about him, and within their density, the wraiths of the newly dead floated, smearing the blackness with a pasty blue-gray as the spectral bodies spun and stretched in the vortexes. In the distance, one funnel turned utter pitch. The dead had been blended away, as if an artist had mixed the colors together into one.

As he passed through the fog, a few wraiths reached out for him, looping long fingers into his flesh, pulling themselves free of the ghastly gyres. He shuddered with their touch, like the cold sting of hypodermic syringes. But he ripped himself free of their grappling—unless his intended victim had the fortuity to die before he visited her, these were not the souls he was about to take into the Abode of the Dead. They would have to find other means before they could vanish into the quagmire of the otherside.

Upon their faceless masks, fury whirled like convolutions on melting wax. They barraged him, striking with vapid fists. He brushed them away with his ebony skeletal hand, already his otherworldy guise adorning him. Sensing his change, the wraiths shied away from him and tried to avoid his demonic treble, which tingled their ether, which peeled them apart.

The mouth of the Xibalban cavern opened before him, its black maw hungry as an ogre. Seeping outward, its chilly draft enveloped him, and Coatl shivered, savoring the frigid breath of death along his hardened skin. It would numb him from any pain within.

Closing his eyes, he let himself fall into limbo before Xibalba and drift into deeper spaces. He turned his thoughts to his victim, her long brown hair, her maturing beauty, and something of a doorway presented itself, wavering edges and misting grays.

He entered her mind.

Within her dreams, she swam in turgid waters, the waves lapping over her face, the salty wash forcing away her breath, and she struggled to keep afloat, but the small body she carried in her arms had drowned.

The intensity of her emotions flooded Coatl. He buckled against the heart-wringing, never liking this union with the person, fighting her wracked feelings, so alien and terrifying. He was squeezed as if by a titanic octopus. Twisting and writhing, he dueled the emotive phantoms. Little by little, the blood and thunder of her nightmare faded from him, and he harbored only ill-intent within his heart.

He hated how his heart was wrought. *Black as rot*, he mused.

Diving in her dream sea, he swam beneath her and watched as she dropped the body, which had transformed into a pair of flippers. He spotted her as a lifetime sufferer of nightmares because those most habituated by terror had learned measures to change their dreams and mitigate the frightening aspects, something he himself knew well.

She treaded water, and he kicked upward, grinning as he drew near.

Too easy, he thought, and created a challenge before he snatched her feet and dragged her spirit out of her body and into the mouth of Xibalba.

The waters blackened and surged. A riptide forced against her, pulled her under, and turned her around in its strong current. As she streamed by, her eyes and mouth wide with fright—*certainly she wasn't used to her dreams turning on her*—Coatl hitched on to her, wrapping hideous limbs around her slight frame. She screamed bubbles.

The Xibalban threshold shimmered in the water, onyx glitter beckoning. Toward the black hole, they flowed swift and sure.

As unexplained as his intrusion, she disappeared with the pop of a bubble.

He entered the wavering doorway empty-handed.

Mystified, he channeled himself back into her dream, but he drifted in a blank space, choking on the nothingness about him. Trembling with an unbound fear of this unknown dark, he withdrew and redirected his plans. If not her, then another. It didn't matter the order.

Chapter Sixteen

The good feelings generated from spending time with Robin and her daughter in their cramped yet charming apartment slipped away, and the memories of the easy conversation between the three adults and the quiet playing of the two little girls faltered into a nightmare.

Leslie dreamed of nighttime beasts hunting them.

From the dark hallway came the hungry blink of reflective eyes, drawn by the scent of raw meat, drawn by the rotting dolls in Mallory's and Jenelle's hands. The girls dressed their foot-tall corpses in the flowing gowns of infant skins.

"Here comes Beast to dance with Beauty," Jenelle crooned.

Teri A. Jacobs

Mallory grinned, and bits of the doll's globular shoulder had filled the gaps between her teeth.

An uninvolved dreamer, Leslie watched the beasts sludge into the room, forms still hidden, eyes still shining with borrowed light. Creatures made of the night.

They enveloped the girls and their dolls within the span of their darkness. Robin clapped, and soon the sounds of smacking flesh changed into smacking lips as the beasts fed.

And then the nightmare beasts slunk back into the hall, leaving bright red trails behind them.

This can't be a dream, but it has to be a dream, she thought, sickened by the odd splash of color, by what that color represented. Something unnatural was happening in her dreams.

Someone tapped her dreaming self's shoulder, and she turned to find Bruce standing behind her. He wore his beastly mask and held torn black fur in one hand and her skinned cat in the other.

"Give us the Void or else . . ." he hissed.

Off went his mask, and the face beneath had been cut, the eyes and mouth carved into holes.

"Let's have your next show on the bottom of the lake, my drowned prima donna," Bruce said, taking her hand and dragging her deep into dark waters with darker things swimming toward her. . . .

Screams like she'd never heard before pierced the night, not echoing but stretching into and throughout every space. A living force unto its own.

She thought the screams were her own, which startled her awake. Leslie bolted upright, reached for Rod, and grabbed a handful of comforter instead. Somewhere in Robin's apartment, a glass shattered.

She fumbled her way out of the twisted blankets and ran toward the screams. The flickering streetlight blinked inside the hallway, and the shadows moved strobelike down the hall until they slipped inside Robin's bedroom. Pushing the door ajar, Leslie hesitated before she rushed in, the silence making her even more jittery.

The hall light was switched on, its golden-sick beams flooding from behind her, casting Leslie's shadow into Robin's room. It streamed across an empty bed, and it looked as if a funereal figure slept upon it.

"What's going on?" Rod asked in a hushed voice as he approached her down the hall with a plate of cookies in hand. She answered with a shaky shrug.

"Robin?" Leslie called, flipping on the light.

Cracked walls were awash in a muted blue, and Leslie shuddered as she thought of broken eggs in a robin's nest. From the corner, creepy sounds came alive in the eerie room, whimpers, mews, scratchings on shells, and Leslie found her friend huddled with Moon. Her face was stricken with a cadaverous pallor, and the strands of her hair lifted with the static force surrounding her. Moon stared at the ceiling, tracking the invisible force with roving intent and dug his claws into her shoulders as he clung in terror. If she felt his sharp claws, she gave no indication in her rag doll stance and unblinking stillness. Milky fear filled her eyes, but it was a fear of something she no longer saw.

Glancing over her shoulder, Leslie spotted Mallory rubbing the sleep from her eyes and motioned to Rod to take care of the little girl before she saw her mother in this distraught state. Moon hissed and spat at the growing shades in the room. As if the walls morphed into a living entity, it shed darkness like squamous skins. The dark scaling the walls was repitilian, slow and ancient, and Robin returned to screaming, spurring further cries from the hallway.

The light fixture dimmed, buzzed, and pulsed, creating strange effects within the room, of light slicing through shadows, of shadows engulfing light. Leslie reeled from these images, feeling like Alice falling through the looking glass into an imaginary world.

And she remembered the day she finished reading that book and excitedly explained Wonderland to her father, and he had commented sourly that when one thing could go into the extraordinary, that other things unnatural could come out.

Moon struggled in Robin's arms. Robin's whitened knuckles clutched him too tight, and his back legs pumped furiously for release. Narrow stripes of blood soaked through her yellow nightshirt. Thinking of his sharp claws, so thin they gouged flesh without tearing the fabric, Leslie scampered over to Robin and tried to uncurl her fingers from Moon's fur.

"Let him go, Robin," she whispered.

"No!" She squeezed him harder, and he yowled in pain.

"But you're hurting him." Leslie worked on prying Robin's steel-wire fingers from Moon, but her grip remained tight. "Please let him go before you crush him."

Robin tilted her head to the ceiling and surveyed the dark scuttling along the tiles and dropped her gaze to Moon, who hacked and struggled in her arms. She nodded her head. Then she loosened her fingers from around his chest but didn't release him.

Moon growled at the walls.

"He sees something, doesn't he?" Robin sobbed.

Leslie didn't know how to answer, but the raised hairs on her nape knew Moon did sense something in the room with them. Something hiding in the dark.

"I saw something," Robin said. "A shadowy face appeared on the wall. At first I thought it was my mind playing tricks on me after my nightmare, but Moon leapt against the wall and scratched at the face."

White streaks indeed marked the pale blue wall where Moon had clawed.

"Let me keep Moon in my room for the rest of the night. In case it returns." She swiveled her head, scanning the walls for any sign, but the shadows no longer seemed to move or to present any threat.

But Moon continued to growl.

"I'm afraid to sleep again, though," Robin said. "I'm afraid whatever I dreamed of will come back and stop me from ever waking up. Irrational, I know, but I can't shake that feeling."

Leslie patted her cat's head and ruffled Robin's hair, unable to offer comforting words because she knew she couldn't refute Robin. She sensed that the Dark Man had indeed come, and that he would keep coming until the dreamers could no longer dream.

Bring it to an end.

She had to bring his visits to an end for sure, before he brought all their lives to an end.

Chapter Seventeen

"You've been idle for too long," the shadows said, and the near-empty border that he had inhabited became filled with pithy beasts, their eyes glowing red as if pitted with their own fires.

"Unforeseen circumstances is all. I was on my way to retrieve another, and if you hadn't interfered, I'd already have my prey in hand." He was bolder when he wore a portion of their black-as-death skins.

"The Xibalban gods grow impatient." Slavering tongues dripped viscous hunger.

"Then let me be on my way," Coatl said, pushing though the swarms of reek and rot.

They ceased their approach, maybe contemplating his request, maybe devising some scheme to devour him without upsetting the Bat-God's designs of gaining control of a town. The Underworld would become the only world.

With eerie decidedness, the shadows slipped back into their umbral recesses, but Coatl could still hear their presence, the buzzing of insanity, the hiss of lunatics. He realized the constant static in the silence wasn't his ears ringing or the pressure of air within his skull but the shadows lurking ever present.

He allowed their black noise to guide him into a deeper trance, the sounds scattering his thoughts like dust disturbed, and he felt the last of his corporeality disintegrate into whorling motes. Drifting in the space that wasn't space, Coatl filtered into another's reality. As she breathed inward, he was sucked into her, and he spread like bacteria throughout her mind, attacking the furrows, snapping the synapses, gnawing away at the fibrous clusters, invading the nuclei. Fragments of images bombarded him. Her dreamworld broke upon him in pieces—snatches of a man's face, lips curved in a seductive smile; her hand brushed against his chest, coyly pushing him away, but she smiled as well.

Stolen arousal coursed through him. Pushing further into her dream, he slipped into the man, her dreamed lover no more substantial than a photographic image, and leered at her in his new skin. She wavered in her dream as if she sensed the change. A static charge of danger crackled about her. Coatl grabbed her hand, which was still poised upon the chest, yanking her toward him, crushing against her, flickering snake-tongue seductions in her ear.

Around them, the landscape faltered, the white haze of her mind giving way to blackness to twilight storms to blue sky. Ferocious mountains towered along the strange horizon. In the low-hung clouds, he spied the twin peaks, their clawlike tips flexing as if the rocks sensed an intruder.

The ground vibrated beneath his feet, rumbling with the Lord of Mictlan's immense hunger. Nine Hells below, in a place without light, waited the Lord of Darkness, and Coatl knew a shortcut, bypassing the lengthy trials.

As the earth shifted, rocking, tearing with brutal force, he held on to his victim and soaked in her screams. They jostled and tumbled like swing dancers in an epileptic fit. Cracks split under them, odiferous fumes escaping with eerie grumblings as if the Lord of Mictlan rested inches below the surface, his monstrous mouth open, his stomach gurgling and spewing gases.

Sands spilled downward into the chasm. Coatl and his hapless companion lost their footing on the flowing sands and fell into the downward currents, swept along for a chaotic ride. As they slid down, he couldn't help but think of a mouth, earthen lips, dusty spit, and the esophagal tube that swallowed them into the bowels of Hell.

They churned within, their skin grinding away along the rough walls of the hole, pain rubbing raw.

Though he had brought them to the desolate Underworld, she clung to him during their descent, and he had the urge to rip her away from him and bash her against the smoothed rock when they stopped.   .

She was the worst of their small group. Trashcan Trish.

As they plummeted, the air grew colder and denser, whorling upon them like leeches from a glacial pond, sucking their heat away. Yes, like leeches, he feared. The air was shrouded with their formless swarthy bodies, drawing in the light as well. Suitable atmosphere for the cadaverous, starved Lord of Darkness. Dead souls as dark and cold as the air.

With sheer speed they shot from the tunnel and catapulted weightless through the murk until they dropped feet-first onto a pile of bones, the calcified spears stabbing into their bodies. Coatl grunted as another death wound formed in his thigh. His astral flesh bubbled away as though acid was spilled onto him.

Trisha gurgled beside him, and she reached for him with a bloody hand. Feeling for her in the dark, he pouted as sharp rods of bone met his hand instead of her supple body. He traced one bone to her chest, fingered the gap where her breast would have been, and sighed.

The demon married to his soul slurred, "She's still whole below the waist."

Tap, tap, to his ribs. Hint, hint, to his groin.

In the back of the pit, the skeletal rattle of the Lord of Mictlan alerted him to the Lord's arrival.

He slid his hand farther down her body, enjoying the slickness dripping on her abdomen, cupping the fluids in his palm, smearing her womanly slit with a bloody lubricant.

A pinched squeak eeked out of her mouth, and she crossed her legs and twisted her hips to avoid his touch.

"Aw, Trisha, don't fight me." He placed his knee between her legs and forced them apart with his weight. "I like you better passive, like the night of the prom. Too much to drink."

He positioned himself against her, throbbing against the red wetness, pubescent urgency stirring.

"No, no," she groaned. The brush of hair along bones rasped as she shook her head.

"Yes, even with vomit leaking from your mouth, I stuck my tongue inside. Your mouth tasted like sour beer, but you were sweet as red peppers between your legs."

"It was a bad dream." She struggled with the words, her voice nearly liquid from her mouth.

"No, very much real, I'm pleased to say, but it wasn't exactly a dream come true either. We were so rudely interrupted. He just never got the chance to tell anyone."

He disgorged laughter, malevolent glee, and her frothy cries tugged him back into mucky pools of recollection. Darrel's face swam into his mind's eye. Trisha's ex-boyfriend and Owenton's ex–football star had raged into the classroom, high as a tidal wave, stopping in mid-stride when he caught Coatl lapping his dog-thirst in Trisha's lap. With a stormy roar, he had crashed into them and plunged a fist into Coatl's back, Coatl's left kidney catching the brutal blow.

But then Darrel hadn't known about the cesspool of terrors hunkered in the corners.

The violence had whet the lurkers' appetite for slaughter, and they had rushed upon Darrel like a pack of hammerheads hunting a giant squid. Coatl had escaped, leaving Trisha to sober herself up in the dead red sea.

"His body was never found," she whispered.

"Look no further than beneath you," he said, his tongue circling the edge of her wound.

Brittle pieces scraped his knees as he moved within her, but it merely heightened his pleasure. The bed of bones snapped and clitter-clacked. Within the cavernous pit, her wails rose like a crescendo of an opera, piercing, strident, cracking the mirror of her sanity. Her cries shattered into choking sobs, and she chattered mindless about baking recipes and talk show hosts, about her dislike of the voracious bee balm perennial, about lazy days of youth when she was pretty and fun. Losing interest, he withdrew from her and listened to her prattle with breathy hitches about the unfairness of long lines and the beauty of toadstools.

But then her talk switched to infidelity and anger and secret wars. Coherency smothered her words like glue, sticking the fragments of thought together in a sequence he began to understand and fear. Trisha knew what Charlotte had known, and Charlotte had known too much. Blinking fast, darting his eyes, he scanned his memory for times when Trisha might have spilled the toxic truth to Leslie. He couldn't be sure.

And he would have to step up the time.

When he rested his palm against her thigh, the coolness of her skin angered him. So soon, she slipped from his grasp, dying before he even took her life, robbing him once again of pleasure.

"The shadows, the shadows," she chanted, and her astral body twitched.

Indeed, if darkness could darken, then the room of the dead deepened in its black hue as though far space descended upon the earth, covering it completely in an utter void of sight. The Lord of Mictlan growled upon his throne, and the thwang of his sacrificial knife made every hair stand up on Coatl's body.

Something was terribly wrong.

The darkness spread thicker, muffling the sounds, stifling even his thoughts. His heart pumped deadened beats.

As though encased in ebon ice, he was frozen and numb, and only the tiniest part of his mind itched with awareness, his fingers too stiff to scratch out the sense of something deadlier than the Death-God approaching.

Chapter Eighteen

Instead of going away, the night shadows encroached upon Leslie, stealthy blackness whispering in her ears and slipping into her mind. Harsh, guttural whispers as though from a masked intruder. As frightening as him asking her to strip vulnerably nude and allow him to abuse her.

She traveled with the shadowed intruder, a hood over her head, senseless. As if the floor dropped from beneath her feet like the old Roter ride at King's Island, she spun suspended, plunging into a convoluted abyss. Even if she had sight, she would see nothing but rapid whirling blurs.

One word hissed round and round in her mind: shadows.

With a thud, she landed on the ground and opened her eyes, not realizing she'd had them shut

214

in the first place. A bleak landscape unfolded before her, barren mountain ranges, horizons of deserts and simmering, smoky sun. The atmosphere smelled stale, its clouds like stalled sailboats in the sky, no wind, no movement of any kind that she could discern.

It was a dead place.

Drawn to the left by some psychic magnetic force, a sort of pressure tingling in her nerves, Leslie walked into the alien territory, her footfalls scuttling in the sand, and from the corner of her eye she saw an obelisk twist upon its rocky pedestal and follow her movement, life within lifeless matter. She walked a bit faster away from the monolith.

The earth heaved, pitching up and down as though the soil was of the thinnest fabric with terrestrial fists punching upward beneath it, and Leslie tumbled and bounced along the ground, a floppy rag doll riding high and low in the tossing sheets.

Thunderous was the sound of subterranean layers quaking, grating and colliding.

A gape opened before her and swallowed her, and she sped in a spiral decline. She flailed about, searching for handholds to stop herself. Her fingers sank into something soft, as if this tunnel was the inside of a mullusk's shell.

Screams whizzed by her. The whistle of a blade. The shrill of it pained her ears.

Dream, her mind screamed, this was no dream. Her stomach turned more than her body when she realized she'd fallen into a realm as alien as Mars and as unimaginable.

The solidity of the land slammed into her.

With the impact, starbursts of pain shone before her eyes, brilliant displays of violet novas. The Dark Man was like a sunspot in its starry bright center.

They locked eyes in that shining moment.

The glint of the knife in his hand dimmed in the body beneath him.

Chapter Nineteen

A panic seized Coatl, throttling in his throat, clenching his knuckles. The Lord of Mictlan had no sooner heard the rumbling in the underground passage than he flung his knife toward Coatl, the blade singing for sweet meat. Trisha sang like a siren herself.

The knife had a peculiar light to it as it tumbled end over end in the air, like flashes of silver lightning sparkling in the storm-mantled sky. He had no trouble, because of its light, snatching it from the threatening air before it soared beyond him.

He brought the knife down but looked up from it, missing the wet explosion. His attention was snared by the new arrival—Leslie.

Her presence, if possible, created a rift within the seams of darkness and, like twilight settling over

217

the velvet land, illuminated the pit of the dead.

For the first time, he noticed the viscera splattered on the wall, chunks of liver, kidney, and heart threaded through the entrails, all of this driven with spikes into the granite. Blood stained in streams beneath in a rusty patina. Beside the Lord of Mictlan's throne, a reptlian hound licked at its own entrails, which spilled from it like coils of pink serpents.

Leslie lumbered into the creepy cavern, shock written on her face, her eyes as unreadable as ancient Arabic tomes, but he couldn't mistake the brutal hatred slashed across her red-lined mouth.

Stepping down from his throne, the Lord of Mictlan shattered the stillness with his clacking heels against hollow stones. Skull-faced, he looked at the two of them as if trying to decide which to slay. He pointed a bony finger at Coatl and motioned him to retrieve the bowl for the offering, the red pupils in his black eyes burning hungrily.

As Coatl scooped Trisha's blood with his cupped palm into the fossil-skull bowl, Leslie broke from her statuesque stance, picked up a broken femur, and rushed toward him. In the cold air, her rage steamed from her nostrils.

The Lord of Micltan yearned for the bloodshed, and he yanked another wicked silver knife from under the cavity of his ribs. He pitched it, straight as an arrow flying, at Leslie.

Coatl stuck his fingers down Trisha's breast wound, fished within the grisly tissue, and tore off

218

a piece of her smooth heart with his talons. Standing to face Leslie, he sucked the chunk off his talons' tips. The core energy of Trisha flowed through his veins, strengthening him, pulsing necrotic vigor into his muscles.

Gangrene shields and scabious armor plates grew upon his body.

But he didn't need the protection. The Lord of Mictlan's knife pierced her dead center in the stomach, and Leslie faltered in her charge, skidding in the coagulated puddles of blood, clutching the knife with both hands. The femur dropped chatter-clack-rattle to the ground.

When her hands gripped the knife, blue lightning forked outward in spiderweb sparks and wrapped her body in a garish cocoon. Coatl watched in complete shock as she fell in the dark scarlet slough and disappeared as if the puddle were a muckhole, taking her elsewhere.

The Lord of Mitlan's knife glimmered in the red pool like the reflection of a crescent moon.

What kind of omen was that? he wondered, retreating as the Lord of Mictlan approached the bowl.

The Lord's skeletal hands handled the bowl as reverently as a priest lifting a chalice of wine before he consecrated it into blood. The blood within the bowl bubbled black, and the Lord of Darkness drank it with a hearty thirst.

The blood flowed through his insides and smeared the bones black, and Coatl witnessed the way the blood dripped through the slats of his ribs and dropped to the floor, spreading into the shadow of the Death-God.

The shadow slunk along the piles of bones, sinuous black creeping as it found its way into the husk of Trisha's flesh. Her body ascended, murmuring in tones of a creaking tomb, "Lead me above, so that I can walk in the moonlight and feast on a harvest of souls."

Chapter Twenty

Leslie screamed in the blinding light, arcs of pain in her eyes, pins and needles through her brain. Across every nerve in her flesh, synapse-shredding sensations seared, and she felt fried by the electrical bites of copper-blood wires inserted in every pore. Copper filled her mouth as her teeth sank into raw gums.

Unlike before, she didn't fall into a new place; instead, she drifted as though upon black waves, the eerie-sad song of titanic sea beasts echoing through her screaming body, buoying her along with their deep tremorous voices. Her pain slowly subsided. Bright, translucent creatures swam on the surface before her, their amorphous and iridescent shapes beautiful, and she watched their jelly innards bloom pretty flowers of azure light.

The strangeness of her surroundings felt dreamy, but the ache in her belly bogged her down. Looking down upon herself, she gasped as her blood streamed out, and the puncture opened and closed like a mouth, spitting out the blood. Her blood formed tiny red spheres that hung suspended in the blackness.

Familiar voices carried on the current, calling her deeper into the ebony sea of her mind, and Leslie sank from this realm into her material body.

Sunlight flooded into her sight as she opened her eyes, and she squinted in the morning glare, her head groggy, her mouth briny, and her stomach swelling with agony.

"I had trouble waking you," Rod said, perched next to her on the bed, fully clothed in a muscle-hugging caramel sweater, a pair of wide-legged jeans, and tan workboots.

Leslie feigned a smile, but she couldn't hold it long when she spied a picture atop the dresser. It was the photo of all five girls, pre-teen sun goddesses in their bikinis, Trisha holding a papier-mâché trophy of a volleyball they had won during a summer fair.

"Trisha is dead," she said, turning away from the frame of smiles and the image of life.

"What? Don't you mean Charlotte?"

"And Bonnie and Trisha, and next Robin and me."

Rod pulled back the coverlet and hooked an arm beneath her, pulling her up for an embrace. Expecting to cry out in pain, Leslie sucked in her breath and cringed, but she felt no punch of pain in her gut as she sat up. She pulled away from Rod, excusing herself to use the bathroom. She could almost feel his quizzical gaze.

In the bathroom, she lifted her nightshirt. Her abdomen was smooth except for a small black mark above her belly button, looking as if a large, new mole had formed overnight. It was more than a dream, she was sure, but how could she heal?

"Leslie?" Rod knocked on the door, insistent.

She took one last look at the black mark, its oily sheen compelling her to touch it, and her fingertip disappeared within it. She snatched her hand back. As though a match had been taken to her nail, the end had been charred, and a sulfuric odor clung to it.

Her hands shook with fear—where had her flesh gone and what had she brought back with her?

He has her eyes.

Crumpling to the floor, Leslie hugged her knees and sobbed. Light strained against the frosted window, a cold white glow like a shining block of ice, and she felt the chill of the madness settle upon her skin. She was powerless, unlike her great-great-aunt, who had an entourage of spirits, the ability to predict the future, and the strength to channel the shadows into the Void. Her father had warned her, had wanted her to flee from this dark cancerous town, because he knew they would hunt her down as though she was the last star in the universe. They wanted total darkness to descend without any light, even the cold wintry morning's. Even a distant star.

"I can hear you crying. Open the door, please."

"No, I need to be alone, sort my thoughts, compose myself. I'm not prepared for all this death."

"Okay. I'm here if you need me." His shadow stayed beneath the door, stretching across the tiles. "I'm glad I got that phone call, telling me you shouldn't face this alone."

Little icy stabs of suspicion needled into her mind.

"What call?"

"The night after you left, I got a strange call. I could barely hear him over the static and the sounds of gunfire. Really freaked me out, hearing the crack and booms in the background, but he caught my attention when he mentioned the killing hadn't ended in Owenton. He told me you needed me, that you couldn't face the events by yourself, and if I couldn't be there by your side, you might never come back to me. Very cryptic, but it worked. I'm here."

"Did he say his name?" she asked, but she knew who called.

"Charles something."

She nodded and thanked the air around her, in case the dead happened to wait nearby, ready to help her again.

"I'm going to shower. Give me ten minutes and I'll be out," she said.

"You sound like we're in a hurry."

"We are." And she turned the shower handle, its rush of water drowning out whatever else he might have said.

When she stepped into the shower, the hot water pelted her tender flesh, its heat tempering the cold, the chill of fear, which had lingered upon her body for the last few days. She washed more than grime from her body—she was purifying herself for battle. If she succeeded with her plan, she would take the keys to victory from the hands of the ghosts— Charles's, Josephine's, her father's. Charles was a link, she knew, to helping her find the place of the dead again. As L.W. said, she had to go into the shadows' world to defeat them.

The scent of Robin's shampoo, a blend of mallow flowers and healing herbs, saturated the steamy air, and Leslie inhaled until her lungs threatened to burst and sprout blossoms. Spring's promise of new life was held within her. Exhaling, she vowed to find an end to this cold, dark winter.

She found strength in the fact that she had escaped the horrific cavern . . . alive and even relatively unscathed. If Leslie learned to navigate the nightmare realm, knowing which bend or hallow would lead her to safety, much the same as the twins knowing the traps beforehand, then she could provoke a chase, a pursuit that would end within the Void. A dangerous game was underway. But at least she had a grand slam play in mind.

Shutting off the water, she stood in the drifting steam and shivered as the warmth dissipated into the exhaust fan. Beads of water drizzled down goose-pimpled skin, and the black pock on her belly dripped oily pearls. Leslie watched in numb fascination until the pearls bled into rubies. From within her gut came the thin sounds of beasts in torment, excruciating cries with a shrill pitch and guttural reverb, almost imperceptible except that she could feel their resonance rumble and titter within every corded muscle and wet nerve. Doubled over with pain that was not quite hers, she tumbled into the sink counter.

Queasy gurgling knotted her intestines, and she heaved into the basin. Sighs within the pipes freaked her out. She screamed.

Loud banging on the door matched the banging of her heart. When she glanced up, she caught her hollow reflection in the mirror, ashen pallor, eyes gloomed over with dread, her pink-white lips like grave-hungry worms stretched gruesomely across her face.

"It's okay. I just slipped," she called to the other side of the door. It wasn't too much of a lie, considering the floor was slick from the shower and the sink.

"You're not hurt, are you?" Robin asked.

"No." She continued to stare into her eyes, into a world of pain.

The pipes moaned once more, the surge of waste flushing from above, and she felt silly for mistaking the quirky plumbing for some poltergeist. With a cotton ball, she dabbed her wound, blotting its ruddy stain into her skin. Leslie pulled at the area below it, tilting the puncture for her to see inside, scrutinizing the pink crater walls and the black center. It resembled a mutated belly button, and she wondered if the umbilical cord to the dark, dead place was severed completely.

A memory flickered behind her eyes, of Trisha sleeping the eternal sleep on a bed of bones, her viscera and blood taken from her body and spread like scarlet sheets. The Dark Man, with the half-moon bowl in his skeletal hand, turned from his victim, and she remembered the black-hearted rage had left his eyes. White-shock fear filled them instead. *What was it he feared about her presence?* She had to find out.

But first she had to pay a visit to another dead friend.

"We should all go," Robin said, the worry deepening the fatigue lines around her eyes. "I can get a neighbor to watch the girls."

"I feel like it's all my fault this is happening. It's just like that last summer all over again." Leslie wandered to the window, pulled back the curtain, and wallowed in the bleakness.

"Charlotte and I always figured you left because of that. Some misplaced guilt you felt." Robin laid a hand on her shoulder, her perfume titillatingly sweet on the air like the breath of a songbird. "But I didn't believe it for a second, and I plan on keeping you close to me so you don't run away again."

"You don't think it's weird that people die when I'm around?"

"Why should it be weird that folks died of heatstroke? Or heart attacks? And if you're worried about Bonnie, she ate a few too many Whoopie Pies that clogged her arteries with marshmallow. Trisha . . ." She paused and tapped Leslie's shoulder a few times. "It was probably a bad dream, just like mine."

"It didn't feel like a dream, and I had this type before, when Charlotte died." Leslie turned from the window, and the bright winter sun created auras floating around her field of vision. Rod sat like a shining silhouette.

"Truth be told, mine didn't feel very dreamy either, but I refuse to accept it as anything else. I mean, how can I?" Robin shrugged her shoulders.

Jenelle and Mallory huddled together on the couch, eating powdered doughnuts, angelic white dust in their laps, and Leslie cringed in dismay at their images, like orphan children feeding off crumbs. She couldn't shake the image and thought for the first time that she was making a terrible mistake by taking their parents with her on her hunt. Not every player made it to homeplate.

"Hey, why don't you guys take the girls to Dairy Queen while I go to Trisha's house?" Leslie proposed.

"I want to be with you in case she's, you know," Rod said, glancing at Jenelle as if he stopped himself from swearing in front of her.

228

Robin picked up the phone and walked into the kitchen. The wallpaper above the stove had browned like gravy over the original ivory and cast a dingy appearance even though Robin had tried to cheer it up with bright yellow pottery, which lined the counter below. As she talked, Robin flicked imaginary crusty spills from the counter. She was animated as a canary, waving her other arm like a wing flapping in flight, chirping in a singsongy voice, and Leslie smiled at her friend, once again chiding herself for her absence.

"It's settled," Robin said, coming back into the living room. "Girls, grab whatever toy you can't live without and hop on over to Dorothy's. She told me she's making chocolate chip cookies and needs four extra hands; then she needs two extra mouths for tasting them. Anyone we know who can assist?"

Both girls giggled and raised their hands. Mallory nudged Jenelle as she scooped a Barbie from beneath the couch.

"I've got a Barbie that looks dark like you. Her name is Christy. Do you want her?" Mallory asked, and Jenelle nodded vigorously, not at all disturbed by the skin color reference, and followed Mallory into her room.

Leslie couldn't remember a time when things were so simple and unassuming. It was sad how adulthood stripped innocent perceptions into tatters of suspicion and negativity.

"I hope you guys will stay the night again, but I do have to hit IGA for more food if you do. Any requests?" Robin asked as she wrote a few items on a pad. "We'll have to take Moon to your mom's, though. The landlord slipped a nasty note under the door, saying she better not find a cat in here when she does her maintenance visit this afternoon."

"Andy will take care of Moon, but I hate to be without him," Leslie said, and Robin gave a shivery nod of understanding.

"Anything's fine with us, but are you sure you want us here? Plenty of vacancy at the motel." Rod pulled on his black leather jacket, the one Leslie thought looked so *GQ*, its leather soft, supple, luxuriant. When he put on his Perry Ellis shades, he looked like a movie star.

A pang hit her heart. He had spoken of relocating to Los Angeles to get better parts and more work than the occasional theater or commercial stint. His role in *Moor Slaughter* happened by chance, a brief encounter at a dive bar with the female producer, who found Rod handsome. He had decided he wasn't an *artiste* but a money-hound for hire. Even though he hinted that she should follow him, knowing it couldn't hurt her exposure, she wasn't ready for that commitment. Still, the thought of life without him gave her that awful, crazy feeling.

But, in the wake of all this death, she was going to reconsider.

* * *

On Trisha's street, they encountered very little activity. Robin professed it was a good sign that no ambulances or police cars lined the block, their lights flashing like red-death beacons. Still, Leslie choked on the anxiety, thick in her throat. The Dark Man was close. She could almost smell the decay of that world seeping in through the windows, and every shadow stretching toward them consorted with demon-gods, bringing their evil darkness nearer.

Flat, vapid grayness sagged within a low cloud, an oppressive frown upon Trisha's duplex ranch, and the blinded windows offered no sight within. Leslie opened the car door, stepping onto the drive, her skin tingling in the scary-charged air. Doors slammed shut as everyone followed suit. Walking up the drive, they heard nothing but their heels clacking. Even the wintry wind was hushed.

Before they reached the door, Leslie's cell phone chirped, and she snatched it from her purse and answered it.

"Darling, it's Bruce. I wanted to commend you on the superb job you did at the Cemetery Masque."

"But I didn't have the film developed. I left the rolls in the refrigerator . . ." Leslie was confused. She'd left distraught and in haste, and there was no way she would've even bothered with the rolls beyond safekeeping them until she returned. *If she returned.*

Rod mouthed, "What's up?"

She shook her head as she listened to Bruce and watched the gray of the sky gravitate to the ground. She held her breath, keeping the death that scented the colorless air from entering her body.

"Nonsense. I have the pictures in my hands. Delivered about fifteen minutes ago by the guy in the pictures, the one dressed in the Confederate uniform. Funny thing, he just appeared outside my office and dropped off the package, then disappeared." Bruce made *poof* sounds through the phone. "The frame of him in front of the mausoleum is awesome; but then I've always liked men in uniform."

"Can you describe how the picture turned out?" Leslie asked, suspecting that the soldier-ghost needed to show her something in the photos. Something that might help her.

"Creepy as hell, and I haven't figured out how you captured the mist the way you have, the way the white vapors looked like claws reaching out of the ground and seizing his ankles."

Something colder and more frightening than death. No doubt Charles wanted to show her something, but she was no closer to knowing the enigma that was her madness. The puzzle merely increased in the number of its pieces, and most of them were blank.

The phone's reception crackled, and Bruce's voice broke apart in the static. But then other voices replaced his.

Gargling and sputtering voices. Wet-rot voices. The voice of her father above it all, screaming, "Beware of me . . ."

Upon the stale winds came that awful laughter.

Leslie dropped the palm-sized phone, and it snapped apart on the sidewalk, its electronic insides sparking, its receiver vibrating with his screams.

Stepping away from the phone, Leslie grabbed Rod's hand and pulled him back before he bent to pick the thing up.

"Get my camera," she said, her eyes glued to the black plastic on the ground and the smoke that curled from it.

With a grunt, he backed away to grant her request and, a minute later, returned with her camera. It felt warm in her hands.

The world looked different, less photogenic, but she knew the real picture wasn't in what she saw before her but in what she didn't. Rod and Robin exchanged perplexed glances as she clicked off a couple of shots.

"Must be an artist thing we can't understand," Rod whispered conspiratorially, and Robin chuckled.

Slinging the camera around her neck, her hands poised on the dials, she motioned for them to head for the door.

Robin knocked as Leslie stepped onto the front stoop. *Bang, bang* like executioner's hammers on gallows being erected.

Leslie shifted her weight, uneasy memories flooding in on a wave of blackness. Bones stuck out of Trisha's chest like giant erect nipples.

Again, Robin's dainty hand pounded on the door as she called Trisha's name.

On impulse, Leslie set her shutter speed and focused on the door, knowing in her heart that something was inside there. Her heart echoed like the door knocker, no one answering.

Trisha's blood had flowed through the bones, puddling along the black earth, looking more like crud than a scarlet rain.

Robin smiled back at them, her lips quavering in doubt, and pushed her fingers into her jeans' pocket, fishing out a key.

"We have the spares for each other's places for emergencies. Kids and such, you worry," she said.

As she slid the key into the lock, the door swung open.

Leslie snapped a picture in surprise.

In the doorway, Trisha stood without a trace of bloody wounds, a smile plastered on her cardboard face, but her eyes were as dead as Leslie remembered. Her eyes shifted in their sockets, robotic and unseeing. Veins like bloodworms crawled along the whites, coiling, nesting around the enlarged pupils, and Leslie looked away, feeling the death-aura of Trisha's gaze burrow within her. As she turned her attention from Trisha, she caught movement in the background, a figure slinking down the hallway.

"Trisha, everything okay?" Robin asked. Her face registered her worry, the squint of her eyes not disappearing even though Trisha stood in front of them seemingly unharmed. Even Robin could tell something was amiss.

Trisha's eyes rolled upward as she nodded. Blinking rapidly, she moved aside and motioned for them to enter. Creepy alarms skittered along Leslie's spine, and she tried to think of a way to get the others from going inside. She reached for Rod, but he already had a foot beyond the threshold, darkness swallowing him into its gullet.

With reluctance, Leslie followed. The family room had a reptilian odor, an earthy musk that nauseated and frightened her, as though she had stepped into the lair of a giant serpent. Besides the reptile smell, the air was cold, colder than the outside, nearly arctic she guessed by the way the moisture from her breath formed ice crystals on her lashes.

"Did your heat go out?" Rod asked, blowing into his hands. He leaned close to Leslie, whispering, "Looks like your dream picked up her troubles."

"Where are the kids?" Robin played with the light switch, clicking it up and down a few times before she gave up and opened the shades instead.

Gray light filtered inward, with their breath swirling within it like smoke, and Leslie wondered how long they could stay in the cold before they became frozen statues and their breath ceased to wisp from their mouths.

"They're around," Trisha mumbled, her tone sounding deeper than usual. Something sinister slithered on her tongue.

"Maybe we should go," Leslie said.

From the back of the house, the floors creaked with movement. *The Dark Man was coming.*

Robin screamed. Clasping her hands over her mouth, she muffled her screams, but the terror in her eyes was louder than anything she could've voiced. Leslie tore her eyes from the hallway, and glanced in the direction in which Robin was staring.

On the couch, Trisha's three children sat, blue-skinned, mouths stilled in frigid cries, icy tears welled in their wide eyes.

Something crashed to the floor, and Leslie snapped her attention back behind her. A figure lurched from the hallway, stumbling along the walls, bumping into furniture. Though the face had been destroyed, globular blood streaming from empty eye sockets, flesh raked and razed into greasy chars, she knew it was Danny, Trisha's husband, from his bulk.

"Devour you," he sneered, his wormholed tongue wiggling across blistered lips.

Leslie and Robin shrieked while Rod muttered, "Fuck."

All at once, pandemonium broke loose. The ceiling dropped shadows like cobwebs, their dark forms tangling against them, and their hideous screeching deafened them. Danny lunged for Rod.

Knocked to the floor, Rod wrestled with Danny's stinking mass, thick, grisly pieces of Danny's flesh coming off in his hands. Leslie fought the shadows, but they weren't doing much to her, only taunting her as though they were bully children dancing in circles around her, poking her with sticks and throwing pebbles. On the other side of the room, Trisha had Robin in a crushing embrace.

Trisha's face altered. It looked as if she were shedding that human face, and another more beastly one had been hidden behind it. It was a face of blackness.

Trisha's body dropped to the floor like a discarded robe and a monster stood in her place with Robin in its arms.

"Duck, duck, duck, duck, duck, duck, *goose!*" the shadows cried joyously, swatting Leslie on the head before they vanished into noxious fumes and flowed into the floor's cracks.

Leslie tottered on the brink of passing out, her brains surely rattling within her skull from their supernatural fists. Before she toppled in a spin, she witnessed the incredible—Robin's spirit, a shimmery blur, being pulled from her body.

As the demonic wraith possessed her and carried her away into the floor's cracks, a dark spot tore where her mouth would have been, and Leslie fell into the Void with Robin's screams piercing her mind.

Chapter Twenty-one

From the bedroom, Coatl listened to the symphonic chaos, shrills of hellish flutes and drumming of fists upon flesh. He wrung his hands in anticipation; his mouth watered for a taste of their blood. Strange addiction, the partaking of human flesh and blood, and that he had acquired it with such rapidity.

Curiosity piqued, he had trouble staying hidden. Coatl snuck down the hall and peeked around the corner, feeling like a child spying on Santa Claus as the jolly old man placed bright, sparkly packages beneath a tinseled tree.

He grinned at the dark-cheery sight—dead Santas and mutilated elves and packages of flesh being torn open.

The lover boy lay beneath Danny, wailing from the kidney-whipping. Blood spurted from his mouth and sprayed the camel carpet, and Danny stopped his pummeling to lick Rod's gory lips. Rod kicked his legs but failed to shift from beneath the hideous bulk.

Drawn by the salty-copper smell, a shadow encroached upon Danny's prey. Snarls and jaw-snaps and bony shards of claws erupted. Two feral hunters fighting over meat.

Rod pulled himself from the rabid-wrestle and crawled away on bloodied arms and legs, and neither Danny nor the demon noticed the loss of their quarry, with their mouths clamped onto each other, their teeth on the verge of tearing away the competition. Stirred by some testosterone instinct, Rod rose to his feet and reentered the scuffle. His battered face registered a wrath Coatl found amusing.

Fists and fangs flew, and spilled blood soaked through the carpet. It was a front-row seat at a knock-down-drag-out championship heavyweight fight, with no mercy in the ring, and the demon within Coatl applauded.

Within minutes Danny fell to the ground and the shadows vacated the room. Trisha was gone too as the stench of corrosion pervaded the area. The shell of Trisha decomposed rapidly into vapors as though her cadaver had lain in a bog, fermenting in its rot-muck, embalmed with its mucosal fluids, before being taken into an arid place. She dried into a stinking husk, then evaporated.

With the retreat of the shadows, warmth spread through the house, and the children's tears dripped as they melted. Coatl felt a twinge of regret, but, at least he thought, they would be spared from the torment when Blood Gatherer and the Bat-God would come to snatch up the living and devour them whole. In a sense, it was beautiful the way the crystalline drops rolled down their cold, blue faces, the way the faint light glistened upon them like a golden dawn upon icicles.

Coatl's heart did a double beat when he saw Leslie sprawled near Robin and Trisha. No blood pooled beneath her, and from this distance he couldn't tell if her chest rose and fell with breath or if her soul was still intact. The shadows were supposed to steal Robin's soul and meet him an hour before the Xibalban princes, but he wouldn't put it past them to take two for better bargaining power with the princes. He had no choice but to travel to Xibalba and wait for the proffering.

But first he needed to leave the house.

Rod finally ceased ramming his fists into the bloody waste of Danny, his mouth contorted in rage and grief, snot and tears wetting his dark face. Coatl shook his head, unable to comprehend how a man could not tolerate violence. On his hands and knees, Rod crawled toward Leslie, and scarlet tracks trailed him like tire marks smeared with roadkill. He pressed two large fingers against her neck, bobbed his head as he counted, and then withdrew his fingers to lift her eyelids.

"Leslie?" he whimpered. "Come to. You have to tell me what happened here."

Within the wall next to Coatl, the pipes moaned in a morbid answer. Leslie's boyfriend turned his head toward the hall, scowling. Coatl ducked back into the bedroom. Urgent, he unlocked the window, pushed the lower section up, and punched out the screen. As he hoisted himself out of the bedroom window, running foot steps pounded into the room behind him, and Coatl slipped onto the ground in a heap, pins and needles shooting through his shoulder and neck, honey locust thorns piercing his clothes and his skin.

"Hey!" came the shout.

Throwing his hood over his head, Coatl struggled to his feet and ran through the side yard toward the street behind the house, where he had parked his car. His sides hurt from the impact and the wind chill filling his lungs. He heard Rod's grunt as he shimmied through the window after him. Reaching deep, he pushed on faster.

Hurdling the low hedge, he crashed into the mail carrier. Envelopes flew into the street, flapping in the breeze like doves in scattered flight. His knee scraped against the sidewalk. Pain like birds pecking apart his flesh.

He untangled himself from the spindly limbs of the old man and told the man to run, a killer was on the loose. With egg-white eyes wide with yolky fear, the mailman gathered his bag against him as if it were a shield against evil. *Chicken*, Coatl thought, and almost howled with laughter.

With his right arm, he shoved off the man and continued down the street, feet thumping hard and fast on the asphalt, mindful of the rustling branches of the hedge and the mailman's cry.

"Help, help!"

Coatl heard the screech of brakes behind him, and someone shouting, "What's going on?"

"He's covered with blood. Call the police!"

Car doors slammed, and the sounds of a confrontation filtered through the neighborhood. By the different voices, he figured his pursuer was outnumbered and surrounded.

Coatl cut across the street and the other side yard, forgetting his car for the moment. First and foremost was getting to a secure place. Still, how fortuitous his escape! Within him, the demon made an exaggerated snore and picked at his ribs for fun, and Coatl grasped his side as the stitch slowed him down.

"Not now, you cur!" he barked.

The demon giggled.

Cheap, girly perfumes stung the back of his throat, and he coughed, choking on the demon's spit. Light-headed, he wobbled onto the next street and paused by a parked car, trying to catch his breath and shake the fuzziness from his head. Now he tasted formaldehyde as it was expelled from his throat into his mouth. His lungs burned.

Biology class memories spilled into his mind, of pig fetuses swimming in tawny liquid, their flesh like wet lace on their wrinkled, half-formed bodies. Their eyes were squeezed shut, as if they didn't dare open them and see the bright world peering at them, bright interest in the strange creatures' eyes as they prepared their shiny knives. Once, when a classmate bumped a jar, it had shattered on the floor. The crash of glass exploding, the splash, the sharp sting in his nostrils from the necrotic fluids, and the sick plop of the fetus, all imprinted a certain horror upon him.

From watery wombs to watery tombs.

He had been the first to cut one open, dragging the scalpel into soggy skin, pushing it through a thin sternum, hearing the crack like a piglet's grunt. A dead heart pumped out clear blood as he jabbed the point into it, and a drop hit him in the face. He had the taste of formaldehyde between his lips, on his tongue, and swallowed into his stomach. With that taste, he had felt one step closer to the grave.

"Death to us both if you don't quit your games," he said to the demon spinning in his gut.

The tumultuous assault stopped, and Coatl wiped the sweat from his brow, his fingers numb from the glacial cold of Trisha's house. Sometimes the shadows came with fire, other times with ice. Brimstone or ice—it was Hell either way.

At a quick pace but slower than before, he made his way north, toward Elk Lake. He had a choice among a few homes at this time of year, and he enjoyed the quiet of the stark woods and the gurgle of the gelid lake. It was the perfect ambience for astral travel to the Place of Phantoms, because Elk Lake was like a haunt itself, mists rising off the still gray water, broodish sky casting a pall over it all. In the harsh squawk of the Great Blue Heron, he could hear the somber dead cry.

As he stepped into the field, his foot sank into mud, and the squish and *plurp* of his walk made him giddy, the days of a messy childhood right on his heels. Nostalgia came over him. Lately, it seemed more often than not, those wistful longings for easier days and dreamier nights, for sleigh rides instead of dreamstalking, for snowball fights instead of soul slaying. How did he grow from that spunky youth into the dreaded man he'd become? How did evil shadow his good?

The demon slurped in his ear and smacked its slobbery lips together, pretending to feast upon his insides, but he realized it wasn't much of a make-believe. For years, the demon had snacked upon him and emptied him of most of his humanity.

Dogs barked in the woods ahead. Coon dogs or pets? he wondered. As he slipped through the fence's rend, a pack of mangy mutts encroached, burrs sticking from their fur as though they were covered with a spiny armor, and their muzzles were smeared with a dark substance, mud perhaps, blood more likely by the way their eyes narrowed and their tails straightened down. He might've interrupted their breakfast of giblets and bits.

His chest constricted with anxiety; his heart beat rapidly against his ribs. Within him, fear imprisoned his heart behind a calcified cage, and it struggled and faltered. Scenes played in his mind, of wild, ravenous dogs hunting lonesome people, of blond hair and tons of blood, and he yelled without thinking.

Digging their paws into the ground, they turned and ran from him. A black lab/shepherd mix stopped, stared for a brief moment, and barked a warning, and Coatl's fast-pumping heart crashed against his chest with each threatening woof. He sank his feet in the ground, no matter how he wanted to get moving, knowing if he ran away, the dogs would give chase and he would end up dead and devoured.

The demon howled as if calling the raid, but the dogs seemed to hear the inhuman wail and tucked in their tails, disappearing quicker than fleas off a dead dog.

With all the racket, he didn't wait until he was deeper in the resort before he broke into a deserted home. A blue-gray A-frame suited his purposes, even though it was close to the road, and he entered through the back door, smashing out the windowpane, reaching through the shards to turn the lock. The glass crunched under his boots as he walked into the kitchen. Cobwebs greeted him, planting sticky kisses on his lips and cheeks. Sneezing, he figured no one had been in this house for months from the amount of dust coating the counters, and worked his way to the darkest bedroom with no concern for the owners barging in on him.

He placed his medicine pouch on the dresser, opened it, and pulled out a stick of incense. The other contents in the bag gave an eerie sigh. With a quick twist of the string, sighs cut off as if strangled, and he closed the pouch and lit the wick.

Sitting on the bed, his back pressed against the headboard, he stared at the dresser and concentrated on the wooden knobs. The room faded into a black blur. A monotonous circle steering his sight round and round, the knob drew him in, and a vortex opened within his mind. His journey into Xibalba was a whorling ride in midnight's arms.

He found himself in a room much like a funeral chamber, the walls, the plinths, the ceilings painted blue. Frescoes, in vegetable water colors, lined the walls in sections, and the adventures of a feathered serpent were depicted on the scenes. Along the ornamented base of the frescoes, hieroglyphs told the tale of the winged serpent and his battle with the boar, but Coatl could not discern their meaning from the golden symbols, and kept to the pictures that clearly had a better "tongue" for the catastrophe.

The boar held three spears in his hands and crept up behind the unarmed serpent. In the next fresco, the serpent had fallen, three wounds in his back, and, though Coatl didn't understand their argument, he felt angry at the treacherous injustice.

At the end of the pictures, an urn was set in an alcove, the charred remains of the dead serpent's heart and viscera inside. He wondered who the serpent symbolized.

He tipped the urn to peek within, but a feculent odor shied him away. As he backed away from the alcove, he bumped into a body, the scaly feel of the breastplates rough against his spine. He swiveled around. Three Xibalban princes stood, their owl-like faces painted black and white, elaborate headdresses atop their shaved skulls, feathered shields in one hand, swords in the other.

The door sealed shut with a hiss, and two six-foot-tall, beakless owls guarded the exit. Tales of how their beaks were chopped off flitted through his memory—the anger of the princes when the brothers tricked them.

"State your business," they demanded in loud, wrathful tones that shook the walls and sent dust crumbling down from the ceiling.

"I've come to strike a deal. For your help in a battle, I will deliver a prisoner for your . . ." He paused, trying to settle on the right word for the eager-eyed princes. "Amusement."

The princes glanced at one another, silence golden on their lips, their eyes rich in conversation as they discussed his proposition with bright squints and shifty pupils.

"Does he play ball?" the one with the crooked nose and scabious chin asked.

"Perhaps she does, but you'll want to wait for another to begin that game."

"We don't want women," they spat.

"Oh, you'll want this one." Coatl circled the princes, admiring their reptilian breastplates and snakeskin boots. "She shares qualities with the disobedient princess and plans on making fools of you once again."

"What qualities? We do not like guessing games."

"Magical qualities, and she snuck into the Lord of Mictlan's cavern and escaped without harm."

"She escaped the Lord of Mictlan?" Incredulous gasps came from their twisted mouths.

From the center of the room, embers sparkled in the fire pit, smoldering in copper glows among the burnt wood and ashen coals, and the smell of ozone lingered with the smoke. The ground rumbled with thunder. A figure rose from the flames, drifting outward in a blackish haze, more an apparition than a man, but when the wispy form flowed into the corner near the alcove, a man stepped out of the smoke. He wore an owl mask over his face, blue and yellow feathers fanned in royal elegance. By the colors, Coatl recognized him as an h-man, a wise man.

The h-man sat before the fire, legs crossed beneath his gaunt frame, and raised his arms. In his dark eyes, the light danced, and his tongue drummed the rhythm with an ancient saying: "Itz en caan, itz en muyal."

Throwing teeth, crimson pulp still fresh on the pearly enamel, into the fire, he hummed. The copper flames burned brassy, then violet, then scarlet.

"The fire talks to us, says the night will be soon. Says the night will not be dark as midnight, but not as light as dawn. Says the night will be painted indigo as twilight, with no moon but bright stars. Says it is the dead stars burning."

He stirred the teeth. Ashes snapped and spit from the pit.

"The fire talks to us, says the dead stars will fall from the night sky. Says the dead stars will light her way. Says she will find her way through the dark."

With a handful of ocher powder sifted onto the flames, he rolled his eyes and breathed in the thick sulfur fumes that wafted to the ceiling and created an ominous spectacle, like pus oozing from giant black wounds.

"The fire talks to us, says the last star is a shooting star. Says she will strike the target of darkness. Says darkness will fall upon her, the only star, and it will be as dark as midnight, as light as dawn."

"But what does that mean?" Coatl asked, and the princes shot him dangerous looks.

Digging into the sandy floor, the h-man revealed a buried armadillo shell and blew the grains from the lines. The dust cloud scattered outward and rolled like a turgid wave of dirty water. Within the dusty particles, an image of Leslie's face appeared, mouth grim, eyes determined, a halo of light around her. The h-man blew again. Her image dissipated with his breath, and the filmy mouth twisted into a snarl, banshee shrieks emitting and echoing through the funeral chamber as she faded away.

The h-man ran his fingers over the lines of the shell, reading it as if it were braille. In the air, the scent of rotting apples pervaded, and he caught a whiff of something else—of corpses fermenting with maggots, the saccharine odor of the grave. Mysterious winds gusted and stole the sands, creating dunes against the fresco wall. Mummified bodies beneath the sands were exposed. In the winds, their dry flesh peeled away and their bones clattered. Their tongues slithered from unhinged jaws like fat snakes, and they hissed, their sibilations rising in a crescendo of white noise. The static of demons.

Along his skin, Coatl felt the jitters as though fire ants crawled upon him, thousands and thousands of bristly legs creeping, hundreds and hundreds of mandibles biting. Panic scathed him. Something terrible was happening.

"The past is present, and the future is war," the h-man said. "And she . . ."

As his finger grazed the last line, his eyes shriveled in their sockets, drying like the dead around them.

"*She is the Void!*" he cried.

250

Chapter Twenty-two

Sucked into the Void, Leslie was cast into the nothingness, into the obscure darkness but, for the first time, her mind wasn't empty of thought, almost as though the chaos that dragged her within had disrupted the Void's intricate structure and allowed her to hold on to a piece of herself instead of falling victim to it. The darkness held a glimmer of light as her thoughts developed, and she felt her direction—toward the light. In that instant, she was there. In a different place.

Walls of clear ice surrounded her, and she spied her pale complexion within the icy mirror. She looked older, wizened, dark circles around her eyes, tightness around her mouth. Her image vanished as crystals covered the walls like frosty lace.

Her breath froze as it left her mouth, tinkling to the ground in glassy slivers. Turning from the wall, she slid across the floor and searched for a way out, but the shimmery lights reflected on the ceiling stopped her, mesmerizing her with their other-worldly beauty. Colors she'd never seen wavered in shattered rainbows.

The longer she remained still, the farther the cold reached into her limbs.

Soon she was fixed to her spot, like an ice sculpture, icicles dripping from her nose, through her hair, from her fingers.

Only when the light threw shadows onto the crystalline floor, and those shadows rose with red glowing eyes, did Leslie realize the extent of her predicament.

"Let's take her to the House of Gloom," they whispered, and steam flowed out with their hushed voices.

They circled Leslie, talons scraping upon ice encasing her, and she cringed with the raking screeches, fearful that they wouldn't stop after they broke through the frozen sheet upon her. Their silver talons would be the final nails in her coffin.

As a set of talons cut across her face, she screamed. The shadow pressed its black face against hers, its hot breath melting the ice, its scarlet fervor bright in its eyes. Her entire body convulsed with terror. Her own breath was rapid and shallow, and her mind threatened to black out.

The shadow opened its mouth. Rows of fangs, clear as ice and as deadly, snapped at her and grinned.

She screamed and screamed until not only her voice but the walls cracked. And the demons howled with laughter. With a swiftness much like the wind, they ushered her out of the glacial place and into the House of Gloom.

In the bleak light, she could barely make out the features of the room, but she knew it all the same. Its low ceiling crushed her, making the air oppressive. In every breath despondency was taken in; in every blink of an eye hopelessness was in sight. She struggled with sluggish limbs to move away from the shadows.

They whipped their tails at her, and she cried out in agony as their steel tips stabbed her in the side. In her pain, they found mirth. They leapt over her when she fell flat to the ground and giggled when she wept. Here she felt every melancholy emotion she'd ever known tenfold, and the wretched ghost of her father sank from the dark ceiling and plumbed into the grim depths before her, reaching languidly for her. Misery wrenched his face. Despair, darker than the shadows, filled his eyes.

And he crumpled into nothing when she touched him. Spiritless was this House of Gloom.

"We will devour you entirely," the demons hissed.

Dropping to all fours, they charged her like the hounds from Hell.

"Leslie, hurry! There's a crack straight ahead of you, only four feet!" an unknown entity directed, sounding so much like Sam.

She pushed herself forward, heavy legs pumping fast, shadows tearing into her thighs, her shins, but she scrambled away like a psychotic on crack, incapable of feeling the damage. And escaped through the rend. She ended up outside, near a garden.

Nothing like the abrupt, scary need to run for your life, she thought, trying to catch her breath, to slow her heart.

But it wasn't the time to relax. Several Xibalbans, she guessed from their skull-like countenances, surrounded her, clubs and swords in hands.

"We challenge you to a game of ball!" they shouted.

Someone tossed a ball to her, and she caught it. Cheers heralded the start of the game.

Chapter Twenty-three

With the h-man's cry, the walls shook and whispered in dusty sighs. The air turned grainy as dust fell from the ceiling, obscuring the mummies' movement but not their awakening groans. Coatl watched the h-man crumple into the fire, like soot dumped from a bag, and the smoke blackened once again, choking the room with ghoulish malice.

Things risen chortled within the blackness. Other things outside the room pounded on the door with echoic bangs and creepy scratchings.

"What is happening?" the princes whined.

The door burst open, and Coatl entered the room, of combustible winds roaring inward with fiery demons and a terror-ignited girl. Robin shrieked in the arms of a demon. Her face was streaked with dirty tears, and her hair was matted with demonic drool. Along her bare arms, several bite marks pocked the skin.

Daylight filtered into the open doorway, and the mummies shrank into the recesses of the room, growling. They were eyeless shrugs of brittle flesh and dripping maws, but when the light touched their dry rot, their skin began to smoke.

Stepping toward the door, Coatl kept his back to the exit and his eyes on the slavoring mummies and the perturbed princes. Too many volatile elements were crammed into the tiny funereal space. And he couldn't tell if it was a trick of the light, or if the serpent and boar frescoes on the wall swayed with life.

"This is my gift if you agree to help me," Coatl told the princes as he pushed Robin forward. She fell to her knees, and the mummies snarled and sniffed, their convoluted nostrils flaring like lips smacking. They inched forward, leery of the light streaming on the floor.

"What do we need to do?"

"Nothing more than allow a woman named Leslie Starr to pass through the various tests of Xibalba unscathed and even help her if you must. At least until she reaches the Cavern of Bats." Coatl ran a hand across the bones protruding in his altered face, thinking about the daunting future. "Then the Bat-God will decide her fate."

"Easy enough."

The prince with the hanging jowls approached Robin and grabbed her by the hair before she scrambled away. Pulling her to a standing position, he poked her abdomen. She jerked away from his jab as though he had thrust a sword into her.

"She's not meaty enough for roasting, but I can fatten her up with carrion. We've an abundance of that," he said, grinning. His gray teeth hung loose in his whitish gums.

"Fresh meat," went the whispers and sniggering among the rest of the excited princes.

The prince placed his fatty lips upon one of her wounds and sucked noisily. When he removed his mouth, the skin surrounding the bite mark bubbled away into a peachy froth, and she cried out in pain. Sallow flesh and blood dripped from her arm.

"We are pleased to eat your acquaintance." He coughed phlegmatic giggles.

Crawling on their bellies, tongues leading the way, the mummies followed the scent of blood, but the princes drew their swords and struck off their tongues. The tongues continued on like worms. Although the bodies whithered away into organic compost clumps.

The prince dragged Robin farther away, but she left a trail for the tongue-grubs, dribbling a long liquid meal for them. Her face paled, and Coatl didn't know if it was from lack of blood or fear of the advancing vermiform army.

"She doesn't have much constitution either," complained another prince, throwing his owl mask on the ground. Scars like tawny gristle covered his face, and his eyes were full of jaundiced hate. "Why do we have to help you? Doesn't seem like a fair deal."

"Because the Bat-God wants her, and I cannot protect her. She won't allow it." Coatl watched in fascination as the painted boar bowed its head and cracked the wall of frescoes.

"We need to hold counsel. The gods have schemed behind our backs and have left us out of the loop. Maybe we shouldn't help him. Maybe we should take this Starr ourselves and make the gods come to us and beg!" The prince spat onto a flopping tongue, and the taste buds reddened and popped from the sizzling spittle.

The boar broke through the wall. Unlike the painted version, this boar had coiled tusks, like corkscrews coming through its skull, and was a swarthy beast devoid of rich colors. It snuffled along the ground and snarled. Foam leaked from the corners of its mouth, and Coatl could tell it was immensely hungry, as though it had faced an eon of starvation within the wall. The boar charged around the room, hunger wet within its muddy eyes.

As if it were gorging on Parisian truffles, the boar chomped up the rolling tongues and swallowed them, mostly whole. The demons squealed as the boar approached them, and they taunted the hairy creature with their talons, scraping its hard tusks, tugging on its bristly tail. The boar grunted and struggled away from the demons, retreating back into the wall.

No one had noticed that the serpent was missing from the picture.

At least not until the petulant prince who conspired to trick the gods gasped when his bones crunched. The serpent had wrapped around him.

It hissed, "For the insinuation of your insurrection, release the girly specimen to us."

Coatl recognized the dark gods now in their disguises, Blood-Gatherer and Bone-Crusher, and shook with fear, knowing they had been listening and watching unsuspected within the frescoes. The dreaded lords would not be happy that he had involved the princes. And their moods would be more foul after the h-man's prophecy—that Leslie was the Void. He only understood enough of it to know she was the barrier that kept the dark gods and their shadows contained in the Otherworld. How she was that, he had no clue.

"My lord, I have bargained this girl for the safety of another. If the other doesn't make it to the Bat-God, I fear all is doomed. May we keep the bargain?" Coatl tipped his head down, awaiting a blow for speaking out against the god.

The serpent's tongue flickered on his neck, and he steeled himself from cringing, a surefire way to get himself killed.

"Yesssss . . ."

The demons hissed with approval, and Robin sobbed as the serpent sealed her death sentence.

Winds whistled through the open door and, in its breezy voice, they all heard the cheers. Beyond this room, a game of ball had commenced. A servent rushed into the room, breathless, red-faced, panting, "My lords. A princess was challenged. They want to know the stakes. She asks for a robin."

"Leslie," Coatl breathed in amazement.

"She is the one?" the serpent asked, and he nodded.

The serpent shed its scales, and Bone-Crusher, a hideous, corpse-blue giant, stood and towered over them all.

"Her surrender!" the dreaded lord thundered, and the servent raced away, grinning ear-to-ear, lusting for the mayhem of her loss.

Chapter Twenty-four

With trembling hands, Leslie accepted a club, shaped like a hockey stick, and hefted it in her hands. Heavy, as if made from stone instead of wood, the club weighted her heart with dread as she tried to swing it and failed with aching muscles.

Her opponent sauntered onto the field. Ogre-faced and fleshless, he brandished the club with expert skill, and his red-corded muscles flexed with each easy stroke. Flies buzzed about his seeping-reek spittled, grinning mouth.

The club slipped from Leslie's slick hands.

How the hell could she save Robin? She couldn't even save herself.

A judge stepped onto the field, his black skins flowing like robes about his bronzed skeleton, and announced the new conditions of the game: no rules, no fair play, no mercy.

"Do you surrender to Yuzan now?" the judge asked her.

Picking up her club, gripping it tight with white knuckles, she glanced at Yuzan, at the newborn flies erupting from his rank muscle sheaths, at the unborn maggots wriggling within him, and shook her head. Damn it all, she would play the game.

Yuzan grinned rabid-canine glee.

The judge nodded and dropped the ball between the two players.

"Yuzan, the ball!" the hideous crowd cheered.

With a quick stride and a weapon strike of his club, he swatted the ball toward his goal—a wailing hollow within the stone wall. Leslie struggled to carry her club along with her as she ran to reach the spinning ball. Beside her, Yuzan sneered and kept her pace by skipping, mocking her while he twirled his baton; then he stopped before the ball and waved his arm for her to approach first. Maggots slipped out with his drool.

She swung her club. His elbow whipped up and cracked her in the jaw. Bone shaft in her cheek, teeth-snapping pain, red breath dripping down her throat, she fell to the ground. The crowd whooped, and the dreaded thunk of the ball hitting into the goal sounded.

"Yuzan, one," the judge called over the triumphant noise.

The judge placed the ball into her hand, whispering, "Your ball," and stepped aside as Yuzan obliterated her sight with his flesh-stripped hulk. With his club raised above his head, he dashed all of her hopes that she could even compete in this game. Menace was in his every breath and viscous was his sweat. The club wooshed down, its wind cutting across her face, its blade slicing apart her clasped hands, and her broken fingers had no hold on the ball, which flew away from her once again. Leslie cried out, a damaged cry even.

Something strange happened to the air around her. Her voice shattered the threshold holding back worlds. Shimmering, rippling air, translucent whirlpools, and black-sky formed in its vortex, bringing things dark and light forth.

The crowd had yet to notice the manifestations and applauded another goal scored by Yuzan.

On her knees and elbows, Leslie watched in horror and wonder as anamorphic spirits walked onto the field with their own clubs and menace. Yuzan turned and faced the new parade of frightening players. The muscles of his face slacked, and the tendons slipped their sticky knots, causing the meaty structure of his face to fall and slide in a gruesome yawn of fear.

The only recognizable form among the new players was Charles. He had his wartime coat opened, and the unknown dead entered the Underworld through him, through his black core. *A voided space . . .*

Leslie thought these were the creatures that inspired mere humans to call them gods. Their spectral flesh ranged in an awesome array of colors, colors beyond the spectrum of earthly light and with an eerie brilliance blended with the primeval darkness, and the forms they assumed astounded her. Bestial-headed, contorted, sinew-threaded torsos carved open with screaming mouths and amphibian-murky eyes, and these were the more familiar.

Others had bizarre body puzzle parts arranged in disgusting and shocking manners. She shuddered. How would they have appeared if in flesh and bone instead of as ghosts?

Carnage. They would look like carnage.

Wind whistling through them, they rushed upon a stunned Yuzan, stole the ball, and scored one for Leslie. With no rules to break, they pressed onward to even the score, taking Yuzan down with their sticks and feeding on the scarlet strings of his body. Shrieks, steaming hisses, and the squelchy smack of ravening beasts silenced the roaring crowd.

The ball rolled from the pile and stopped at her feet. Grue painted the ball, chunks and bits of texture added.

"The Guardian of Spirits has sent you this team, but, though you may win on this field, the battle has just begun," Charles told Leslie as the darkness within him sucked him away.

Vise-grip cold flowed beneath Leslie. White mists of claws reached from the ground, reached for her, and she needed no push from those colder-than-death hands to spring to her feet and finish this game. *Bring it to an end.*

Straining through the pain and weakness, she raised her club and tried a shot for her goal before the mob that had filed onto the field destroyed her and her chances. The head of the stick connected sharply and soundly with the ball. Blood splattered on her face, its crisp ozone and metallic liquid on her lips, as the ball rocketed toward her goal.

A score, but a frail victory.

Yuzan's blood had formed a glutinous film across her mouth and nostrils and continued to spread over her face like some colloidal mask without holes. She tried to suck in air, but the membrane merely collapsed inward. Tight, tight throat squeezing for a single breath. With burning chest and suffocating terror, Leslie tore at the membrane, the second-skin substance sticking to her fingers, her nails unable to break its tenacious, sick-soft hold.

Instead, the gluey mask coiled into her mouth and wormed its way down her throat.

Scream-gagged, oxygen-choked, she tottered in dark dementia, and, in her bloodcurdling sight, something gigantic stepped before her, something that scared the fierce Xibalbans off the grassy court. Crimson sunlight bled around the silhouette. Almost man-shaped. *Almost.*

But not close enough to keep Leslie from strangling on her tongue and the bleeding tendrils as the thing neared her and breathed upon her.

Teri A. Jacobs

White-hot breath melted the red mask off her face. Clots in her mouth and esophagus de-emulsified into a gruel pool of slime, and she vomited the stuff from her throat.

"Bone-Crusher," her terrifying teammates murmured in fright. "Beware one of the makers of shadows . . ."

Leslie gazed into Bone-Crusher's cadaverous eyes, livid wounds upon his bestial face, and knew of a deeper darkness than the Void. A greater terror. And she longed to suffer with the red mask instead of his awful, unnerving stare. She would rather die than be this close.

His mountainous hands upon her, though, couldn't crush off her screams.

Chapter Twenty-five

Through the broken section of the wall, faint light streamed inward, casting sick glows on the princes, who sulked in the corner, and the ashy dust drifted gloomy in the bile-hued air. Coatl shifted the blackened remains of the h-man with a gnawed bone.

She is the Void. He couldn't get the thought from his mind, probably because he didn't understand the implications of the h-man's words, probably because he guessed it was not something he wanted to know. He remembered the grave depths of her black mind.

"We should kill you for the trouble you've brought upon us," a fat prince snarled. The flesh beneath his feathered mask was fringed.

Darkness oozed from the walls, ceiling, and floor as the shadows, darkness solidified, gathered around the prince, giving warnings with the malignant clicks of their talons. Intense, dense, the demons took malicious form.

"Somehow I doubt you'll get the chance," Coatl retorted. "Unlike you lousy things, I am needed."

"Why would the dreaded lords need you, a mere mortal?"

"Even you should know that power comes from those who give it to them." He avoided the true answer, that the dreaded lords were powerless to break down the boundaries between worlds without him, the husk of his body their host, his spirit their alchemeric key—as the demon within him cut its teeth on his intestines, making the perfect grooves to fit into the slick-scarred lock of another's soul. Souls for fodder, souls for power. Especially Leslie's.

The princes chortled. "You give the gods their power?" asked one.

"No, but without the likes of a servant, what good is power?"

"Who serves you, then?" the fat prince asked, fingering the frayed flesh beneath his chin. "Because without power you would never have made it through Xibalba, or lived through a bargain with any lord."

"Symbiosis," cut in a demon who had crept beside Coatl. Its talon sheared through his cloak, and from his vivisected gut came the wicked squeal of a giddy demon. Its intestinal tongue slipped between Coatl's fingers.

Skin-shreds of the bloated prince's chin swayed with his shaking fear as he realized what other bargains Coatl must have made, and didn't envy his protected situation at all. Bending before the demons, the prince cowered and recanted his threat, and the demons bared their metallic-glinted fangs, mouths dripping long mercury-beaded streams of saliva onto the prince until his entire back was shiny and wet.

The demons rushed greedily upon the prince. Demonic cocks, lengthy black-barbed shafts and arrowed heads, pierced his reflective back, tarnishing the flesh with oil-black wounds, splotching the perfect surface with slug-tar-slime ejaculate. One of the demons dragged Robin into the reekish orgy, the skunkish piquancy of their semen rousing her aware, and they forced her to lick off the inky crud.

Her tears couldn't wash away the grim stains on her lips and tongue.

The prince writhed in nightmarish bliss, hissing as phallic spears thrust into his sides and spine, gasping orgasmicly as more of his skin was left hanging in reddish strings. Spurred by the briny scent in the room, the other princes crawled toward the shadowy pile. Gangrenous tongues stretched out from the slits of their masks and added their poisonous spit to the brew. Hands of decay fondled Robin, pulling her closer, smearing her face across the bubbling spit and sperm. Her cheeks boiled.

Shadows crossed her face and fed upon her dripping flesh, and the princes broke other skin barriers with their masks, their beaks pecking deep into her shoulders and ass.

Gleeful pandemonium erupted.

But Coatl reacted with violence, slamming fists into brittle skulls, impaling soft underbellies with burnt wood, slaughtering Xibalban royalty because Robin was Bone-Crusher's prize, and he had to stop them before they left nothing for the dark god. *Else he devour Coatl entirely.* The demons turned their ferocity toward the fresh ruined meat, setting a battered Robin free of their torment. Scavenging, hunting, either way, the shadows feasted.

Princes already dead were consumed by the time Bone-Crusher entered the tomb. In his massive arms, Leslie squirmed, a grimace on her bluish lips, fear in her bulging eyes, but she quieted when she spotted Robin on the floor. Narrow eyes belied the plots within her mind. Coatl swore he heard her thoughts, like the cranking of machinery axles, of greased parts moving.

"Quate ta chi gecumarchic," the Dreaded Lord hissed as he looked around the splattered den.

Again the darkness appeared.

Smoke of charcoal rose from the fire pit, twisting, dancing with the shadows, filling the chamber with wavering darkness. Little flashes of light came from the demons' grins, and Coatl shielded himself with Robin's body, offering her warm, wet wounds to the building storm instead of his insipid self.

In the darkness sounds of bones cindering into dust echoed. Lightning mouths opened.

And a different sort of feeding began.

Bone-Crusher had transmogrified once more— purplish scales covered his body as though with bruises, limbs shrank into spindley coils, and his jaws widened to swallow the horde of bloated demons sceping along the ground. Appetite aroused, Bone-Crusher sucked in the shadows and the partially digested princes. Other demons, safe from his maw, watched with seething eyes.

"Quate ta chi gecumarchic," said the smoke with the h-man's voice. *And the darkness is the Void.*

While Bone-Crusher devoured the remains of his disobedient servants and the dark guts that housed them, Leslie snuck away. Coatl hadn't noticed until now, though he should've guessed, what with the Dreaded Lord's lack of arms to hold her. The morbid scene before him had held him in sway. Never had he seen the shadows conquered, hadn't even thought it was possible. But her absence now spiked anxiety within him.

Coatl walked the perimeter of the room, searching for her with his mind, his eyes, his hands, and even corralled a couple of stray, bored demons into the search. The room felt empty, save for smoke and shadows.

Then he felt eyes upon him, eyes not in this world but the other, where his body lay vulnerable.

Heart palpitating, Coatl stayed in the Underworld, even though his whole body quaked with the urge to flee as Leslie had, to travel through the darkest channels, to save himself before his enemy forever trapped him in this dead abode.

Red-fire eyes of the serpent god brightened the room, like sunrises burning the walls and chasing away the nightshades of demons. With blood-rimmed sight, Coatl saw emptiness. Emptiness that screamed.

Leslie was gone, and she had stolen Robin along for the abysmal ride.

Chapter Twenty-six

Instruments with their mournful tunes and singers with their ghastly ballads filled the great hall to which Leslie had escaped. At every turn, her fears increased because she was lost in this Palace of the Living and the Dead, in this village called Mictlan, otherwise known as Hell.

She knew this place from one of her father's stories—the temple of the evil spirit and the living rooms for his demonical servants. Stone comprised the hall's ornamented panels, as it did the grand pillars and high, wide doors, but the remarkable designs on the walls struck Leslie the most, not that the great size of the pillars, rounder than the arm clasp of two men, didn't awe her. But the carvings humbled her.

She ran her hand over the delicate woven lace and leafy patterns and marveled at the painstaking care and sheer artistry it must have taken to create such fluid beauty in stone. Beauty that led downward, into the underground chambers of sacrifice.

Alongside her, Robin lurched in golem-stride, blank eyes rolling inward, her quiet wails blending morose and grave with the eerie songs. Her insipid, slack stare did not register Leslie's presence, and Leslie feared she had done something terrible by bringing her into this place. But to leave her in the other . . .

Leslie ducked into the corner as a priest dressed in a long white alb and dalmatic garment embroidered with falcons and boars strolled by with a large retinue. Incense wafted along with the procession, and the rich, indescribably spiced scent burned her nostrils. Her vision shifted with the smoke. Before her, the people became translucent, with diamond glitter bones, sapphire veins, ruby organs, emerald minds, and thin topaz skins, shining with such brilliance that they were like glaring suns. Blinded, she reached for Robin's hand but grasped air.

Her heart beat with the frenzy of the drums and murmured with the hideous, inarticulate chantings. The sacrifices had begun.

Peeking blurrily through her lashes, Leslie spied Robin trudging along with the slaves and war prisoners and braved notice as she darted from her crevice. She tugged on Robin's arm, but Robin shrugged her away, as if her limbs had multiplied as other arms pushed her aside. The throng of feet clapping the stone hushed when the garbled prayers began, like spirit winds haunting hollow caves.

What, what, what? her mind screamed, confused and scared. Nowhere to run, no way to hide when they had Robin in their binds. No ideas, because the first body was laid upon the stone altar and the obsidian knife was poised above his chest, and her mind went blank with horror.

The priest bared the man's chest, and the victim's abdomen shrank with his fearful gasp, ribs of suffering and hunger shown, pasty skin vibrating with his rapidly throbbing heart. As the stony point entered his body the man writhed and convulsed on the sacrificial slab, making the streams of blood twist down along his sides. Pulling his skin away from his sternum, the priest cracked the flat bone and stripped the heart free. He ripped it from the man.

Steam wisped about the heart. Hot blood, hot life. The priest inhaled the man's soul and took his offerings to the idols, holding the pulsing heart to each of the effigies' mouths, breathing upon those same bloody lips to transfer the soul to the dark gods.

Again, wailful melodies hailed from sullen mouths.

"Lllesssssssslie," an effigy hissed, with smoke and spirits whorling and winding around the stone serpent-headed god.

Everyone in the chamber turned and faced her, eyes filled with black venom, mouths filled with blood. Knives filled their hands. Even those slated for sacrifice pushed toward her with hostility. Even Robin.

Light from their torches flickered with an unfelt draft and dwindled to a faint glow before extinguishing into darkness. Sliding along the walls, Leslie backed out of the room, and the carvings she had admired shifted beneath her hands, its lush ferns sprouting stone fronds and twining about her with a cement hold.

"Lllesssssslie." *Tsk-tsk.*

Fetid breath blew on her face. Abrasive-skinned palms rubbed the odors into her cheek. Burning, burning, their touch and that breath. She struggled against the wall, scraping her back, hips, and elbows against the sharp rocks, whimpering as she heard her blood drip, as she felt keen tongues lap and lick and split her bleeding flesh.

"Yesssssss." The slithery voice snickered in her ear, and every nerve in her body shrank and seemed to die, leaving her senseless.

For that she was glad when the torches were re-lit. She looked upon the face that owned that voice as it pressed near hers and its tentacled fingers twisted in her hair, in her mouth, and between her legs. Several of its crablike pincers waved in front of her, snipping off bits of her skin—freckles she had scrubbed with lemon juice to bleach her face with no luck; freckles she now wanted back. Its serpentine tail raised, and her head spun in the sight of its giant scorpion stinger. A red venom droplet clung to the tip. Beneath its arterial vellum, her father's face bubbled, and his mouth was wide with silent screams because the carmine worms that squirmed inside his mouth had eaten his pharynx and vocal cords.

Leslie screamed for both of them.

The aquatic-saurian god laughed, rumbling the walls, stirring the dust of the other ancients still sleeping in effigies, and brought the stinger within a millimeter of her left eye. In her visions, the face of her father was staring and weeping venom. Like sea salt in wounds, the stinger ground and stung her eye as it worked through the soft cornea, into the optic nerve, and beyond even her cerebrum, poisoning her very spirit.

"Ssssslleeeep the black ssssleeep."

And her eyelids drooped to heavy slits. Eyelashes looked like winking shadows and, at the rear of the sacrificial room, a flat boulder was heaved aside, utterly dark in its vacancy. The cavern of Death opened. The priest shoved Robin inside.

"No," Leslie's numb lips mouthed.

Carrion stink, the odor of maggots feasting, overwhelmed her as a cold wind blew out of the horrible abyss. It was the wind of the damned souls, of the living sacrifices who had fallen in heaps of rotting flesh; it was their final, collective gasp unto death trapped within the cavern.

"Sssssweeet sssstufffff." The dark god spread her legs with sticky tendrils and placed its sucker mouth against her labia. Leslie fought her submission to its gentle lampreylike sucking and licking, gagging on her revulsion, sickened by her hip-rocking eagerness.

"Sssssweeeet sssstufffff," it repeated with heated breath, hot touch upon her, tingling her skin, warming her inside.

"No," she said vehemently, shunning this orgasmic wasteland.

The god laughed again.

"Defy what you are," the priest chanted with hysterics as he sprinkled incense oil upon her, spice in the already putrid air. "Defy, defy, defy."

Venomous dementia tore at her—walls turning into gray mirrors; her face shimmering upon the mirrored surface in a rainbow mask; violet shifting into indigo, into green, into yellow, into orange, into blood. Her face flowed off her bones. Beneath her flesh, she was faceless, a black apparition of the nothingness she was.

"No," she muttered, shaking the gruesome head that couldn't be hers. *Madness in the sounds and sights of Hell.*

"Defy, defy, defy." Voices rose in high chimes.

Body jerking in response to the dark god's hard suckling, Leslie closed her eyes and stared at the walls of her mind, at the chamber of the Void within. There was no door to open, yet she walked through, trading one madness for another.

The Void

She had forgotten about Robin until she heard her friend cry in desperation, "Oh God, please don't leave me here. . . ."

Too late. She was drawn into the Void.

Chapter Twenty-seven

Wolfen howls pierced the quiet of the charcoal-choked sepulchre, and Coatl walked out into the night to seek the source of the alarms. Winds moaned against him. Ghosts moved through him, enveloping him with their gritty, cemetery perfumes. In Xibalba, something had gone wrong—he saw it in the humps of the misshapen dead, in their tumors and cysts, the teeth, bones, and hair of something else growing on them.

The sky shifted in dangerous degrees—wind-raced clouds, streaking radiant white on the black canvas, side-winded down to the barren land in clumps, dying heads with whipping tails; egg-white moons wrinkled in corruption; stars were bloated with mycetous cancers. Mountains disappeared from the horizon. The twin peaks of the Lord of

Mictlan's claws sank into the ground, and the curled talons stretched out and grasped the great emptiness.

Across Xibalba, blackness spread like a sporous disease.

A figure with exposed vertebrae joined Coatl and placed a hand upon his shoulder. Snails, with his fingernails as their shells, crawled onto Coatl's shoulder and oozed along his neck until they inched in the hollow of his trachea. Nails of the houses scratched into his windpipe.

"She means to take all of Xibalba into her," spoke the god of the dead.

"How can she do that?" Coatl's words escaped his throat instead of his mouth, not words really, but bubbling sighs and slick whistles.

"She is the Void."

Grim apparitions with blank faces and ear-shattering cries soared into the vanishing sky, still clinging to the clumps of dirt and grass of their graves. The vast ebon nothingness swallowed them and silenced them beyond silence.

"Nature abhors a vacuum," Coatl found himself saying. "Empty vessels won't remain empty forever." He watched the dark souls dragged from tombs flow into the empty sky. Awestruck, he repeated, "She is the Void."

"The Void rests within her and exists outside of her. Through her, a tunnel to a darker beyond." The death-god removed his hand. "Your route to bring her to us."

Teri A. Jacobs

Coatl backed away from the death-god, who slashed into the shining dead as they swirled in the cyclonic winds. Screaming faces whorled in fury and agony. Pieces of their spirits glowered in the god's grasp and teeth, and the god grumbled in ferocious thundering hunger. Their ghostly bodies squeezed together, bulbous wraiths sausage-linked, and the monstrous figure gnawed into their squalid bellies, bursting purplish, etheric innards.

"Else we devour you entirely," piped the demon inside Coatl.

"I will bring her to the Bat-God."

Apprehension prickled his spine. His skin itched from the awareness that something beyond the static ether was prodding his tranced body. Fingers on eyelids, fingers on throat. Eyes on his flesh and his soul.

Growling, Coatl balled his hands into fists and shot a probe into the beyond, where his body lay helpless. Enemy hands were indeed upon him, and Coatl spied the star-bright knife poised against his exposed throat.

"Release me," his demon hissed.

"Yes, release the tzitzimime." The dark god's greasy lips slid into a threatening grin. "Let the feasting begin."

Chapter Twenty-eight

Leslie floated in the icy black of the Void, drowning in the riptide screams. *Oh God, don't leave me here . . .*

The depths rippled with waves of screams, and an allegro symphony of pain pounded into her, its tempestuous ballet of misery spinning her deeper and deeper.

. . . Oh God, don't leave me here . . .

. . . deep at the bottom of the Great Empty . . . with these cold, cold tentacles of death wrapped around me . . . alone in the primeval nothing of the primordial god . . .

. . . Oh God, don't leave me here alone.

But in the absolute darkness, she was not alone.

Chapter Twenty-nine

He unleashed his demon. With his mind's sight, Coatl watched his inert body turn black, as if it had been scorched. Blisters bubbled on the blackened skins, and his demon erupted from his body. Coatl psychically flinched as he imagined the fiery ripping.

All shiny blackness, the demon rose before the cowering man and flashed ten silver talons, each as long as an army knife but sharper.

Stars aligned for doom, Coatl thought, grinning.

The shadow struck Sam . . .

The death-god interrupted and killed his vision.

"Bring the sacrifice. Her blood and spirit shall become our pulque."

We are but food and drink for the gods, the souls upon the winds cried and pulled upon him.

Shadows stepped from the shadow of the death-god. "And we will devour you entirely."

Voracious eyes of god and demons lit upon Coatl, daring him to fail their demands, and he bowed to the dreaded lord, feeling those sharp-set eyes cut into him, and once again promised to bring her to Xibalba.

Unless you kill Leslie Starr, you will fail, Jorge had warned.

He looked to the salivating grins of the shadows and figured that by delivering her to the dark gods and their minions he would kill her anyway. His hand delivering her to death would be the same as his hand thrusting the knife into her. Failure was not in *his* stars. He slipped from the howling winds and through the borders, the shadows following, their presence burning onyx flames and smoke.

The gray realm shifted in his sensorium. Embryonic eyes watched him cross the flowing carnage, the gurgling spew of flesh, and into a verdant ocean. Hurricane winds and cyclonic waters tore him into another realm, and Coatl was slammed with green tidal waves and beaten below.

Falling into a subterranean and subaquatic world, he landed on an alien shore. The sands coalesced into bits of bones. Skeletal arms reached upward, scrambling to pull themselves from the quagmire of grisly remains, grasping onto Coatl's ankles as he walked across the calcified sands.

The bones clicked in movement like a million hard shell crabs scuttling along the beach, and

Coatl ran through the piles of brittle decay. Winds moaned his escape when he entered a chitinous tunnel.

Dim and dank, the place smelled of brine and mold, and the insane chatter of the shells on the walls almost made him retreat.

But the clack of bony heels on the shelled path behind him pushed him forward. Coatl refused to glance back, partly because if he turned back, he wouldn't know what waited in front. Because he knew something waited. He heard it breathing laboriously, phlegm trembling in its throat. Even the shadows advanced like snails.

Sea smells intensified as he traveled deeper, and the ground became sodden beneath his feet. Coils of spines slipped along the ground and sloshed around his ankles. Horns split through the walls, their points heading straight for him.

Looking up, he stared into the mucoid eyes of a monster.

The thing had the head of an angler fish, semi-transparent fins fanned across the top of its slate-scale skull, red gills flapping at the crease of its wide jaw, its arced lure dangling an eyeball, which swung in front of Coatl's face.

In its livid iris, pearly larvae swam.

Coatl squeezed his eyes shut, searching for the portal to take him to Leslie; instead, he had a vision of the larvae squirming, crawling into his skin, feeding their way to the brain and making their nests within his cranium. Eyes open, he saw the fish-headed creature swing its massive tentacular arm back and bring it forward with brutish force toward him.

The thing knocked him down into the blackest of all worlds.

Through abysmal channels, Coatl crawled. His astral breath and heartbeat roared and thundered in the black chambers of this strange crossing, but he continued onward, despite the gripping fear of the death he sensed with every part of himself.

She waited at the end of the tunnel, if such an end to the profound darkness existed.

The raven-black droves of demons glided upon amorphous wings and soared beyond him. Brief glimpses of the meteoric menace in their eyes made him grateful he was not their fodder in the trough.

With stealthy approach, they came starved upon her in the darkness.

Chapter Thirty

A myriad of red blinking eyes surrounded Leslie, and grins streaked lightning-bright and dangerous in the black spans.

"Row, row, row your soul, darkly down the stream," they sang gutturally, their silver claws rocking across her.

"Scarily, scarily, scarily, scarily, life is but a dream," the demons finished in grottoed chorus and, with talons hooked into her soul, dragged her over an obscure threshold.

Into horror itself.

Her father floated in a fulsome repository of bloody and fleshly waste. At least parts of him floated by.

A brew of demons churned in the thick grue, feasting upon his remains, lipless mouths tearing off strips of soft, scabious flesh, teeth sinking into corpulent rot. Pieces of her father squished between their squabbling claws.

"Beware of me," he garbled, half-mouthed. Half his face pitched upon this dead sea; the other had forever plunged into oblivion. From his battered eye socket, maggots slipped out like tears and wriggled down his bony jaw. "I bring doom upon you."

"Why?" she cried, feeling small and scared as a child again, the spring sky raining butterflies, rainbows in the water, her father fishing her drowned body from the lake.

"Because nothing should live after it dies." His voice sank below, and her father was gone.

Fetid water spewed from her mouth once more. An unending stream vomited, and memories bobbed on the surface of her mind, blue face down. *Her father cried as his hands rocked her tiny, water-filled body*, she remembered. *A Mexican Indian handed her father a potion, bubbling tar-black liquid, and her father poured the vile pulque into her mouth. Demons smoke-swirled within her, their barbed tongues in her throat, cutting death from her insides.* She remembered the pacts her father made with this man, the priest of Mictlantecutli and the man L.W. claimed tricked her father into bringing the darkness he meant to destroy.

The taste of a filthy, dead-fish lake was in her mouth, flooding more memories into her.

Beneath leek-green water, she sank, but her bubbles rose to the sunlit surface like glittery balloons, pop, pop,

pop with the last of her breath exploding. The murky water stilled to a dead calm. She floated along with the grainy debris of algae and fish scales, totally immersed in this world, its slime deep in her throat and lungs and on her flesh, changing her into something like the sinuous grasses that wrapped green blades around her ankles.

Beautiful, she thought as the water rocked her, gently cradling her to its soft bottom. Streams of sunlight tried to reach her as though with golden arms. Mayflies landed on the sparkling surface, and she wished she was closer because she loved their shining azure bodies and their lacy wings. They were fairies, dancing in the wind, singing their hushed songs. But the only sounds Leslie heard were the distant rumble of boats and the waves lapping at the rocky shore. Sleep, sleep in the cool mud, *the waters sighed.*

Eyelids slinking down, feeling like snails over her eyes, she breathed the air inside and left the world outside.

She breathed the sun, breathed the stars, breathed the light that washed over her.

Glorious light, glorious breath, but darkness swam around her, nests of moccasins disturbed by a gargled voice, and stole the breath with viperish kisses. Laughter, laughter in the deep. Someone was raising her body with laughter.

The spring sky rained butterflies, rainbows in the water, as her father fished her drowned body from the lake.

A man laughed in the shadows, bringing shadows with his laughter.

And the lake wept from her cold body.

How had she forgotten it all?

Oily demons reached up from the putrid, icy floes, slapping pus-slick arms around her, pulling her under, reminding her why she would want to forget, and the water, like sewage, poured into her mouth. Down they pulled her, deeper. Down into the decay-silt bottom. Down where parasitical gods fed off the dead and dying.

The *smell* of this place overpowered the stench of fear and the heady-sick odors of rotting viscera and flesh. It was the smell of the dead rising from sweet, mucosal waters, so damn desperate to be born into darkness.

Leslie swooned until skeletal hands steadied her. But the hands had an even stronger smell of death and a deadlier grip.

Those hands were upon her.

His nails needling into her skin, the Dark Man pulled her against him, and she felt the shackles of ribs beneath his cloak and feared he would keep pulling her close until she was trapped inside him.

"Shame I have to hand you over to the Xibalban gods."

Hard shaft of bone pressed against her pubic mound.

The deities drew around them, and she stood the carrion for vulture-faced demigods. Their eyes were like mouths, with fangs lining their eye sockets and bloody spittle hanging shiny from those sharp incisors and, when they blinked, their fangs snapped together. Narrowing the distance, the demigods blinked more often, as the tasty sight of her increased their hellish appetites.

The vulture-faced immortals sported colossal erections too. Another attribute of their hungering.

Leslie wrenched her arm from the Dark Man's hold, ready to flee.

"Nowhere to run, nowhere to hide," he stated with a bone-faced grin. "Dreaded darkness everywhere . . ."

. . . her father being unmade, his flesh uncurling from his bones, his bones crumbling into dust, his dust scattering into darkness.

"Everywhere," he repeated.

. . . his physical body lying in darkness and birthing a thing darker, and Sam caught in its midst . . .

"No," she agonized.

"Nowhere to go but with me. Else they devour you entirely."

Sycophant demons rushed upon the demigods, opening jaws wide, moaning morbid bliss as the gods' scarlet cocks thrust into their mouths and cracked apart the demons' mandibles.

Others rushed upon Leslie.

With scythe fingers and sickle teeth, they ripped into her spirit-flesh, reaping hunks of crimson muscle and creamy tendons. She howled in harrowing pain.

"Say you'll finally give me that dance."

. . . her father spinning away forever . . . her cousin joining the spiraling dead . . . bring it to an end.

She answered yes, but no human sound came out of her mouth. Instead, millions upon millions of garbled star-buzzing voices shouted.

In her mind, she saw clouds of deep red light burst upon the darkness in nuclear mushrooms of glowing blood, in a cannon-blast shrapnel of amputated radiance, in exploded pieces of pulsing hearts. She felt the blast-waves and blows within her. Darkness became light, and light became darkness.

Languidly falling through the dark chaos, Leslie was taken into Xibalba.

But something other than her soul had followed the Dark Man.

Chapter Thirty-one

He held her slack spirit-body against him and pushed through the passage into the place of phantoms.

Winds of raging spirits and sands besieged upon them, like hands of granite and teeth of graphite trying to grapple and tear her from his arms. He pulled her back. The phantoms twisted around him, forcing their way into his arms, determined to pry her away. Grit and nails stung his eyes. Airy fists struck and bruised him. Wresting her from the grappling dim ether, Coatl broke her free and dragged her down the ruined pass.

The towers of rock had fallen, ground into powder by the winds, and covered the path with massive dunes. Behind the dunes, the serpent lay uncoiled, its scales splayed open from hood to tail, its many ribs standing monolithic, austere statues of blue bone.

Unarguable signs, the dead abode was dying, itself.

Coatl glanced down at Leslie. Her eyes were glazed and staring at the black-streaked sky, and her lips formed soundless words. Sweat shimmered on her skin, the mercurial sheen disguising her as if she were some magnificent being carried down from the stars upon celestial storm winds. Within her, he felt that dark space threaten to spill from her glistening pores.

"What do you have inside you?"

"Nothing . . ."

Unblinking eyes shifted from the sky to his skull face, and he had a glimpse of that mystery in her swirling pupils, black holes looming to obliterate anything in its path. He felt drawn into her, into that oblivion core, and briefly lost every sense of himself.

Something happened in that brief encounter. Across the southern and western horizons, clouds of necrotic ash churned in the whorling winds and turned the sky the pitch of bottomless wells. The darkening clouds spun above Xibalba, casting a shadow of such magnitude that it seemed to suck the land into the deepest depths of existence, almost to the point of making it nonexistent.

As tornado winds roared and sundered the Underworld, the shadow of the nether-beast rushed toward them.

The palaces in the background fell to rubble as the voiding winds approached, and by the time the winds passed over, the rubble sifted away into nothing. In front of the monstrous destruction, Xibalban princes and legions of demons fled.

On the backward-bent legs of a rooster, the demon Izpuzteque sprinted through the blood river, yawping an alarm. Xochitonal, roused by the disturbance in her death-flowing river, pushed from the shore and headed for Izpuzteque. The demon sprang upon the alligator first, its raptor-razor claws ripping into the leathery armor and splitting the river guardian apart. Dead souls mewled through the gray-meat crack.

Dead souls yawning the black of Leslie's mind.

Coatl snapped from the fear that stalled him and turned his back on the ooze-dripping dead and their ravages on the demon. Digging his nails into her cold hand, he pulled Leslie across the blood river and through the deserts, away from the wasting winds, away from the spirits.

Another fiend appeared. Nexetepehua flew upon them, fiery wings spread fifty feet, its horrible mouth spewing clouds of ash, stinging into his eyes and burning into his windpipe and lungs, burying him in darkness.

But it wasn't Nexetepehua burying him in darkness.

Masses of ebony spirits had risen from the ground and enveloped him, their density crushing him. In the quake of the fiend's squalls, the crunch of his bones echoed empty.

They buried Nexetepehua within their remains, the wall of wraiths muffling his tremendous cries into acute silence, and Coatl feared for himself as he shrank within their cryptic embrace.

Stifling fear of stifling death, he willed his skeletal fingers into nine-inch bony nails and pointed them at Leslie's throat, ready to anger the gods in order to save his mortal life.

"Twinkle, twinkle, kill the Starr." Lunatic giggles bucked from his collapsing throat. How much he sounded like his demon, absent at this moment but present in another moment, taking care of another Starr.

He pressed inward, his nails sinking through the skin and into the spaces of her throat. Her screams whistled and vibrated against his fingers.

Hideous noise in return, the dead withdrew and whirred around him in hostile winds, creating some kind of black vacuum, its motor running high, its intake valve waiting to open.

He kept his fingers in her throat as he led her through the wraith-winds.

Coatl braced himself against their assault, but nothing touched him except the cold. Cold like he'd never experienced, coming from the dark of the dead, and he shivered in dread from the subzero breath of whatever was hidden in the circle of death.

Even Leslie trembled against him. The inner muscles of her throat spasmed against his fingers as she swallowed.

"What is in there?"

"Nothing . . ."

Whatever it was, it was turning the Underworld into cold darkness.

The fore winds of the massive twister whipped at their backs, and Coatl hurried across the remaining desert, listening to the screams behind him as the princes and tzitzimime were rampaged in the storm.

On the edge of Xibalba, the last mountain stood, but stones rolled in an avalanche down its steep side. The entrance to the Bat-God's cave was already half blocked.

Rocks assailed him as he shoved Leslie into the dwindling hole. Death wounds peppered his astral flesh.

"Oh, God, don't leave me here," she yelled.

But he had no choice. The final boulder sealed the cave's only entrance and exit.

She'd have to make it to Camazotz on her own, or perish along the way.

Either way, he wasn't going to wait around to find out.

"Unless I kill her, I will fail." And he escaped into the warped channel to find her body and put the stone knife into her heart.

Chapter Thirty-two

The avalanche roared down the mountain and shook the ground, felling her, and her hands smacked onto the gummy floor of the cave's tunnel. In the semidark, she had trouble figuring out the substance on her hands as she raised them for closer inspection. Dark and sticky like tar, smelling organic, though, like the waste products of blood and decay.

It covered everything, the floor, the walls, the ceilings, and she caught the crud shifting sluggish on the rocky surfaces.

Down the tunnel she heard indescribable sounds, sounds that worked into her brain and stirred a frenzy of immense fear. She preferred silence at the moment, the kind of silence that told of the horrid secrets laying in wait, because these noises made no secret of the atrocities they were capable of.

But the way the breeze curled around her, wrapping her within its tropical perfume and sweet breath, beckoned her forward.

She turned to the entrance, where not even a wisp of air could squeeze through piled rocks, and decided she had no choice but to find the source of the paradise breeze. She stood and walked farther into the cave. Fear trickling down her spine, she wondered if she would find a lava lake at the end of the tunnel, its demon-winds intoxicating and rendering her incapable of proper reasoning and caution. She sensed danger here, all around her, in fact. The flowery scent on the air almost overpowered that sense.

Pits opened along the path several times, and she avoided them by sheer luck, not caring to look at what was inside them. The wafting stench gave enough inkling.

Buffeted by a draft, Leslie flattened herself against the wall, waiting for whatever forced the air from the humid depths to follow.

The sound of flags flapping . . . or vampire capes . . . or wet-skin cloaks . . .

Air rushed above her head, disturbing the side part. Instinct abreast in her, she ducked. Her hair was hooked by something flying over her, and she cried out as the hair separated from its follicle plugs and pulled away. Leslie touched the spot, and her fingers came back wet.

Giant bats.

They crammed into every space along the ceiling once they settled from their flight, and she shuddered at the appearance of their faces. Or rather at the disappearance of their faces as the dark of the cave hooded their horned heads.

Keeping her body low and her eyes fixated high, Leslie worked her way down the tunnel, and, in return, the bats watched and waited for her to make a standing mistake. The farther she crawled, she noticed the breeze no longer had the odor of flowers. It was heavy with copper and salt minerals.

Light bled along the walls as it flowed from the cavernous chamber ahead.

The bats shrilled.

Take her . . .

Dust dwindled down in scaly streams as the mountain quaked. Shaking as well, Leslie moved into the chamber.

Take her . . .

She came within inches of the cave's bloodcurdling dweller.

Take her . . .

Bone-hook tips gored into her sides and its bloody mouth pierced her throat, and Leslie's screams gurgled in her mouth as the Bat-God took his long-awaited prize.

"Give us the Void," the dreaded god hissed into her ear. His breath was of clotted blood and decay and smelted ore.

Devour, devour, devour, chattered the bats that crowded the cavern.

More dust rained down from the ceiling, and the mountain groaned thunderous apart. Through the split, Leslie spied the spinning black winds of souls.

Something was happening within her. She felt her insides spin as well. Something powerful was drilling out of her.

"Yes," she told the Bat-God. "I'll give you the Void."

And the world went dark and blank, and she found herself deep in the Void, which was both beyond and within.

She heard screams, those of the Underworld and those of the physical world, and her heart curdled and wrenched. Loudest of all, Sam was crying for her help. . . .

. . . Leslie blinked and squeezed her eyes shut again as a whitewash light glared back at her. It left bloody afterimages in her mind, and when she reopened her eyes, she still saw red and gagged on the tubes in her throat, which hindered her screams.

A man stood beside her, his skin bright red and wet, as though he had bathed in blood.

Her vision cleared, and his sanguine face dripped off, revealing his true flesh, dried and yellowed-brown like a harvested tobacco leaf.

The man who tricked her father into raising her from the dead was beside her.

Jaundice-eyed, he stared at her, silent until a series of hacking coughs doubled him over, and she smelled his sickness in the recycled hospital air.

Still, she feared the frail Mexican. The blood she saw on him might not have been as imagined as she thought.

He had the eyes of a viper. Venom-filled, perhaps, instead of diseased, with shadows in his midnight pupils.

After the coughs subsided, he wiped the phlegm off his hand, smearing scarlet stains onto his white T-shirt, and placed that hand above her head. Heat passed between his hand and her face, and sweat broke out on Leslie's brow as though the summer sun burned down upon her instead of tawny flesh and bone.

Then the lines of his palm shifted and crackled apart the skin. Blackness sifted through the pores and opened sores, wisping down like noxious smoke, snaking through her nostrils, choking her breath away.

"Beware the shadows," he sneered, lowering his hand within an inch of her face. She breathed in his ebon spirit, breathed in fumes. "I sense their coming. Beyond the window, it is not night that descends but the denizens of the Underworld. Look . . ."

Leslie obediently turned her head—spinning white walls—and glanced at her room's panoramic view. Winter night, silent night, of fluttering snow, of sleigh-bell winds, of darkness with silver-frost teeth.

"Twinkle, twinkle little Starr, how we plunder where you are," the darkling winds sang. "Up above the grave so high, like a dead one in my eye."

"Die again, my little Starr." His hand covered her mouth and nose, pinching off her entire breath, and Leslie writhed on the hospital bed.

Chapter Thirty-three

Human wails and demons licking at his flesh.

He opened his eyes.

It wasn't demons licking at his flesh but blood splattering onto his body and dribbling down like tongues. *Blood sacrificed onto him, anointer of his dark baptism.*

From the corner of his eye, Coatl caught his demon toying with Sam, its talons making venous wounds. Sam struggled to slip away from the demon, but his bloodied hands slipped instead on the wood flooring. The only thing escaping was his scream.

"Make sure the dead star doesn't shine," Coatl warned the shadow, thinking of the h-man's divination.

Says the night will be painted indigo as twilight, with no moon but bright stars. Says it is the dead stars burning.

Beyond the room and window, the night had indeed brightened with the snowfall. White reflective in the sky, like the scattered remains of angels.

He smiled.

The shadowy fiend slashed its talons into Sam's abdomen, and Sam's shrieks turned into crimson splashes. Hurling Sam through the window, the demon cheered, its voice perfectly blending with the shattering glass, and then leapt after.

It grew quiet, save for the tender swoosh of snow beneath a body being dragged.

Coatl groaned as he lifted himself from the ground, as he felt every tight sinew reject the notion of movement, but he needed to insure other stars didn't burn even after he'd left them blotted in darkness. He walked with pins and needles under his step toward the dresser.

With near-arthritic fingers, he picked up the stone knife and brought it to his mouth. The blade's edge kissed into his lips.

Delicious on his tongue, his blood, his knife, the thoughts of it kissing Leslie good-bye forever and ever . . .

Chapter Thirty-four

. . . cold beyond her, all around her, within her.

Sinking in hyperborean depths, Leslie drifted away from the living world and all its senses. Encapsulated in cold. Numb. Utterly and damnably numb and sinking and shrinking smaller and smaller. Losing all sense of self slowly. The bubbles of her memories and thoughts exploding soundless in the icy floes. Her awareness bubbling away from her, she surrendered what she was and all that she would have been to the cold beyond her, all around her, within her . . .

Hot within her . . .

Electricity jolted through her body, bright-slamming into her head.

As if strung by live copper wires and snapped by a manic puppeteer, Leslie bolted upright, aspirator and intravenous tubes pulling out. She gasped, the air wailing into her throat like inverse screams, as shadows crowded the hospital bed. Unmoving, the shadows were a hovering darkness beside her.

She fell back onto the mattress, stiff shock reeling in her system, alarms ringing, and the flash and jolt hit her again. A long shrill of alarm dwindled into hiccuping beeps. Her sight focused in the brightness, the nearest shadow a doctor in green scrubs holding two aluminum-lined paddles.

Other faces filled the dim background, some solid, some insubstantial, as the Starr family ghosts crowded beside the corporeal. Her father had sidled next to her mother and stared at her with gruesome eyes, flesh hanging and streaming down like red-glistening tears. Reacting to the chill surrounding her, her mother shivered and brushed the goose bumps along her arms. She looked to the ceiling, trying to find the leak that dripped onto her.

"Daddy," Leslie whispered, weakly raising herself and trying to slip from the bed. The sheets tangled around her feet, and the doctor pressed his hand on her, pushing her back down.

A hand raised in greeting, her father turned toward her, but his face never showed. Only a hollow of horror stared, as though the Void had eaten his face.

Indeed, all the dead in the room looked erased, blackboard blank. Chalk-wisp bodies with slate oval faces.

A static of feeding stars crackled from absent mouths, and Leslie feared the Void had found the bodies it needed in which to walk the earth. Dead bodies for dead spaces.

Rod walked through the throng of harrowers, strands of their essence sticking to him like cobweb silk, waited for the doctor to finish taking vitals, and wrapped his arms around her when the doctor cleared the way.

"We thought we lost you," he said.

Maybe you did, she thought, feeling more than withdrawn, feeling empty. She barely registered the pressure of his embrace, her body seeming a cloak of threads, fibers, material immaterial of senses. She was aware of only one thing: the thrumming of the Void within her.

Leslie gently pushed his arms down. "Do you know what's happened?"

Heartache creased his already battered brow. "I walked in on some man trying to kill you. Has everyone gone crazy in this town? Do they dump psychotropic chemicals in the water to induce mass hallucinations and hysteria? I feel fucked up myself after what's happened. I don't understand . . ."

"Where's Robin? The girls?"

"The girls are in the waiting room. They wouldn't allow children in the rooms. Mallory's not dealing well with . . ." His gaze drifted to the other side of the room.

Leslie cocked her head. On the other side of the room, the dead Starrs had gathered around a bed and were in the process of ushering something white into Robin's prone body. Arms were chains; hands were grappling hooks. The thing hung a foot above the body, writhing on the hooks, shrieking bat-shrills.

It turned toward Leslie, terrifying her with its cadaverous eyes of sunken whites void of pupils, and with its cavernous mouth, multiple rows of icy fangs dripping in its gape.

"The guardian of spirits," murmured a Victorian ghost, drifting in lavender and petticoats, caressing Leslie's ear with her frosty tongue. "A caged and feral guardian that needs to feed constantly, and we are its keeper. Lucky, aren't we?"

"But what are you doing with it?" Leslie asked, and those in the room who breathed air glanced at her, perplexed by a question that formed from thin air, from nowhere.

The ghost of her Aunt Josephine placed a chilled finger on Leslie's lips. "We will feed it."

Then she took Leslie by the hand and led her off the bed, through the confused crowd, and over to Robin.

"The Starrs don't merely drift through space, my dear. We have our higher duties, and it's time you learn. Your father has shielded you too long from your heritage."

She placed Leslie's hand on the guardian of spirits. That hyperborean touch, freezer burning into her palm, the feel of flesh that has lain in the deep of the ocean or of space, where no light has ever given it warmth or life. Thing of death beneath her hand, she nearly fainted with fright. It was like the worm of the Void come crawling into her presence finally after years of knowing she wasn't alone in "there."

Tears formed in her eyes. She'd left Robin alone in the Cavern of Death, her soul wasting into the dark, her body waiting to be found by this wailing horror.

"In time, it finds a bit of everyone," Josephine said, her voice like cool air whispering from the air-conditioner vents.

Leslie struggled with her breath, choking on sobs, her lungs collapsing as if shrinking from the terror of the thing that collected pieces of every living—*dying*—soul and tore off the last remnants of life. Her hands shook on the cold, cold beast. Josephine guided her shaking hands, pressing them down on the white death, and Leslie cried out, her skin sharp-stung by its semiflesh, as if she submerged her hands into an ice bath.

She went numb as they pushed the guardian into Robin.

She wondered if everyone who looked upon the scene thought it was a coincidence that the moment her hands contacted Robin's slightly rising chest, the heart monitor flat-lined. Or if they suspected the truth, listening to the machine's yowl.

Leslie fell to the floor, weeping in strangled heartache and guilt. On the ceiling, darkness swirled in dense clouds with red-glowing eyes.

Chaos flowed through the room, like a corpse slow-floating in the ocean tides—the telephone rang, or rather tolled, long drawn-out gongs of brass muffled by the insistent machine shrilling Robin's death, by the operatic screams of those witnessing Robin's flesh disappear from her bones, by the shrieks of the thing that ravaged her. All of it, roaring waves of violence and fear.

The black terrors scuttling along the ceiling dropped down, steel-tipped kites descending, wings flared, fangs bared. Leslie cried out to warn the doctor as darkness settled upon him, but no one heard her over the din.

With a lightning flash of talons, the demon struck the doctor. His skin blackened with burns, and the demons rushed him, piercing blisters and seared flesh with their arrow-tipped tongues, splitting his mouth and jaws apart as they tried to fit inside. The doctor's blood and pus splattered the floor. In a matter of seconds, they reduced him to gutty puddles.

The dead surrounded the living, defending them with crashing blows to the shadows that darted around them and attacked with calculating measures. Around and around and around they spun, intermittently breaking into the center to slash at their prey, the nurse at the moment, her face stricken, her arms striped with bleeding cuts. It reminded Leslie, as she stood ignored in the hunt and stunned, of marlins herding schools of fish into a cyclone and swimming through the circling fish until every last one had been gobbled up.

Little by little, the numbness that afflicted her subsided, and she shrank from the carnage, feeling helpless even though the Void within her rattled her bones.

"Release it," Josephine said, chilling her soul, but she felt if she let go of what built within her, the whole world would be swallowed into its immense black maw and broken down into nothing within its infinite entrails. *Karma monster.*

Still she needed to act. Her mother and Rod couldn't hide behind the dead for long—her father already seemed to fade, a flashlight running low on batteries, and Leslie knew she had the charge.

Something propelled her to pick up the receiver, maybe the way the phone buzzed her name.

Breath of demons winded through the room and knocked the receiver from her hand, knocked the cradle onto the floor, plastic noise shattering. Then an eerie quiescence descended upon the room. Such quiet, the static emitted from the phone was heard loud as the crackle of a raging bonfire.

"Rock-a-bye-bye baaaabbbbyyyy . . ." the legions sang as black smoke filtered through the tiny holes of the mouth- and earpieces.

The shadows came.

Chapter Thirty-five

Lips on the stone knife, Coatl closed his eyes and hunted Leslie's body with his mind. He found her in a drab white room amid bedazzling black chaos, and his heart quickened at the psychic sight.

Leslie's soul had returned to the body.

How? Dead stars still burning?

But he knew she stood alive, in the center of seething shadows, not in the center of the Bat-God's cavern, with the dreaded lord's hooks and fangs secured to her soul and syphoning her dry.

And she was frigid with fear and fury, and even removed from her physical presence, he sensed the voiding mana about to obliterate all the barriers holding it back.

"Shit," he whispered, hanging his head and opening his eyes.

Teri A. Jacobs

"Ssshhhhhhh." Smoke hissed from his human-skin medicine pouch.

Coatl frowned, and more smoke puffed out with bilic giggles.

Along the teal walls, the smoke curled and curled until it formed a clouded circle, and within the circle three spaces cleared, making the hollows for two eyes and a grinning mouth. A smoky tendril reached downward and loosened the ties on the pouch. His chest tightened as the tendril lifted his trophy from the medicine bag.

Charlotte's tongue.

The gossamer coil levitated the desiccated piece and brought it inside the smoke-mask's mouth.

Impossible, he thought, yet anxiety filled him as if with ashes.

"Oh, anything's possible in love and war, yes?" The tongue worked well; the words only slurred a bit without substantial lips. "You started this war, but I'm with the other side, dear."

Light always defeats the dark. Remember that, some other ghost had said.

The smoke-mask thickened, and it looked as if blackened skin seeped from the air and covered the face—looking more like Charlotte with each breath and blink.

"How can this happen?" His hand convected warmth to the knife, and his palm sweated. Yet chills escalated along his spine.

"You brought a part of me back . . ." Smoke consolidated into a grisly mass, a manic face of nightcrawlers and ice crystals. "And her powers bring the rest of me. . . ."

Chapter Thirty-six

Black fiends gurgled from the faucet and toilet in geysers of putrescence and hissed noxious through the vents. They swarmed into the room from every crevice. Razors and teeth and rage exploded within the tiny space, splattering blood and clots of flesh across the sterile walls. So much blood, the walls looked black.

Arms thrashed in the blackness, as though they swatted away killer bees, or twisted to free themselves from the tangles of the black widow's web. Stung and snared nonetheless. A nurse's body bulged with the infestation of a shadow, the swollen lump of abdomen moving with its implanted fetus, and her face ballooned with bruises and popped eye-plugs from their sockets. Oily muck like sewage spilled through the split seams of her cheeks. The demon's laughter bubbled in her bloody filth.

Leslie ground her teeth as she watched in horror, still unable to move. Her aunt had vanished with the rest of the dead when the shadows came, mouthing for her to bring it all to an end, to bring on the Void.

"Save us from the doom I brought," her father moaned, his voice dwindling away more slowly than his apparition.

Across the room, her mother's face turned to a scarlet net, a mesh of tattered skin and blood.

Leslie's knees buckled, and she slumped screaming to the floor, not only reeling in the gut-wrenching, heart-eviscerating, mind-macerating sight, but *sensing* her mother's agony. It flamed on Leslie's face and in her belly, wick of invisible umbilical cord lit with burning coal stuff. *Not again, not again,* her mind wailed in shock. She couldn't bear to watch the shadows take a parent again, couldn't wait idly until they wiped her mother into nothing.

Release it.

Her entire body shook. The building shook. Hands clenched into fists and her jaw locked in anger, she stood a tight vessel for the power within her. Pressure built and wound and expanded until she thought the cork of her skull would blow off.

Release it.

Pain screwed from the top of her head down along her jaw and brow and into her vertebrae. Her vision distorted, and she saw nothing but dark shadows and the light of those they meant to devour.

Release it.

Inside her, the Void thrummed faster and faster. Tremors seized Leslie, and she felt as if every cell in her body was put into a blender and liquified. Liquified, then evaporated, and the Void was released with her howls.

Then the darkest dark erupted into the room.

The Void filled the room with utter blackness and emptied it as well. Its substance, neither solid, liquid, gas, nor plasma, but something of a non-matter nature, burned and froze into the shadows. The demons melted away. The demons evaporated.

The shadows were devoured entirely.

But still more came through the window and the walls and the pipes, and the Void's ebon energy descended into the dead, recruiting reinforcement troops.

Leslie hooked her hands around Rod and her failing mother and pulled them outside the room, glancing back one final time before she fled the quaking building.

The dead were rising. No features on their faces, they wore the mask and mouth of the Void, and the dead charged the enemies in their charcoal-cloud uniforms.

Towing her mom, leading Rod, she ran down the buckling corridor. Tiles of the floor cracked apart and flew upward, crashing, shattering along the ceiling and walls. Mayhem was intent on tearing the hospital down as more shadows broke through to her realm center. They reached the outside doors by the time the sounds of the roof falling on the second floor boomed.

Outside, in the suffocating dust and shrieking dusk, she remembered the two little girls inside.

Leslie felt her heart lodge in her throat as she raced back into the unstable frame. She didn't care about herself, ignoring the wince of glass shards in her skin as windows imploded, focusing only on finding Jenelle and Mallory.

"Help us!" they yelled, hidden beneath the waiting bench.

Leslie hurdled a fallen beam and crunched across the rubble of plaster to reach the girls. Crouching, she held out her hands and coaxed the girls to scramble from the bench before the bottom floor turned to ruin. The ceiling groaned in agreement, and white dust sifted down upon her. Leslie blew the chalk from her mouth, begging the girls, "We have to go now!"

"What about my mommy?" Mallory cried.

Every answer caught in her throat. *Robin screaming as the priest closed the cavern-tomb. Such an anguished face. Her eyes pleading, pleading, pleading not to be left alone in the dark. A haunt before she had even died.* Died. Dead; her mother was dead.

Grief wrung Leslie's insides and wrested swollen tears from her eyes. Mallory saw the tears streak down Leslie's dusty face, making clear paths, and her little lower lip trembled.

"Please . . ." Leslie whined, shaking her empty hand at them, unable to grab either child beneath the bench.

Neither child moved to reach for Leslie's hand. If she wasn't mistaken, it seemed Mallory had even shrunk farther away from her. Didn't she realize the building would collapse on them? The depth of Mallory's shock and sadness seemed to testify that perhaps she did and had decided it was better to go down with the building than to stand up and walk through life without the only person who'd made a life for her.

Sunlight and shadows. Her father slain by the latter. Her sunshine never to shine again. Leslie understood, sometimes wondering herself why she hadn't jumped into the brambles and wrestled with the shadowers, happily succumbing to death, skipping the happy empty life.

Losing that key person proved to be more pain than she could endure, having never gotten over it, never forgetting, never allowing herself to truly love again for fear of losing all over again. She sighed. She'd left Owenton not to escape Jake and the other horrors, but to shield herself from pain, not real pain but the *possibility* of pain.

She was afraid to love and lose. Demons were nothing compared to that.

"Mallory, don't be afraid. We'll find our way out together."

Don't do what I did. Don't hide from life; don't lose time by running away from it when it already has you in its traps. You'll lose something then, same as the wolf who'll chew his own leg off to free himself from the metal jaws, she silently begged, her phantom heart, like the wolf's phantom leg, aching for relief.

Blue-spark zing, wire cables snapped from the ceiling and swung down on Leslie. She ducked as the electrical heat buzzed over her. The hairs on her arms raised like Moon's hackles—God, she hoped Andy had kept Moon safe, or that Moon had kept Andy safe. To avoid the tingling sting of the air charged by the wires, she flattened herself to the ground and crawled on the brittle detritus.

"Girls, you have to come with me *now!*" Frantic, Leslie propped her shoulder against the frame as she dug beneath it to snag a child. Curse the man who decided to bolt these things to the floor.

"Mallory . . ." whispered a harrowing voice, a perfect mimic of cold, brutal winds blowing through reeds.

"Mallory, Mallory, Mallory . . ." came the voice drowning in a bog.

A stagnant stench wafted in the room, of a polluted lake brimming with dead catfish. With it, the cold of a dead winter lake came, not so much a bitter breeze, but a frost.

"Mallory, go with Leslie," ordered the icy voice, cracking with a mother's heartache.

With her breath held, Leslie turned. She found Robin's ghost shimmering blue as frozen corpses in the scintillating light. Snowflake tears fell from her winter-white eyes and fluttered down her cheek, and the blood-red slash of her mouth sputtered an anguished chant of denial, "Mallory, Mallory, Mallory . . ."

Arms without substance beckoned the children from beneath the bench. The girls went to her without hesitation, and Leslie didn't wait for their reunion; instead, she grabbed their tiny hands and dragged them out of the lounge. Mallory screamed for her mommy and fought every step, which further separated them.

"Hush little baby, don't you cry . . ."

The ceiling crashed down behind them and tore away the lullaby, but Leslie thought she might be able to finish it for Robin—"Mama doesn't want you to die."

Chased by the booming clamp of ceilings to floors, the three raced toward the exit. The girls no longer needed coaxing. Every second counted if they were to survive, and they were lucky—amazingly, most of the hallway withstood the shakedown, only crushed in the distance behind them.

But then explosions rocked the floor and toppled the runners. Charcoal smoke and flames billowed in the corridor ahead, blocking their way. Intense heat licked at their skin. Dirty air sucked away their breath.

Within the smoke, beasts with coal-clump faces leered at them.

Jenelle and Mallory, too much smoke in their lungs to even scream, cowered against Leslie, and she had no idea what to do, whether to make a break for it and hope to push past the fire-and-brimstone demons, or let loose the Void. *Fight fire with fire.*

"The Void won't save you and the girls from burning. It will only save you from dying at the hands of the hellish beasts," Robin murmured, her voice crackling and hissing like ice and wind, and she wrapped them in her cold embrace.

Frigid air burned white-hot oxygen into their lungs. Her dead hands cooled their singes.

It seemed Robin pulled them into the space of spirits, of white darkness and gossamer faces, and they moved through as if swimming in Arctic waters, their flesh beyond feeling, their minds sluggish, their eyes glossy with delirium. Leslie lost all sense and drifted along in tow, unable to discern what was real.

For a split second, the lump of a demon had hulked in front of her, its breath steaming on her and melting the protective ice sheath. Something blacker than coal swooped down on it. She saw nothing more but heard a sharp crack, of rock or bone splintering apart.

Nothing more but white. Clouds. Fog. Mists. Snow. Spirits.

In a blizzard of confusion, Leslie panicked, constricting throat, dizzy-rushing blood, bewildering visions, almost as if she had slipped from Robin's arms into something unsafe. She felt locked in coils.

Icy coils and icy fangs.

Leslie screamed and thrashed in the mega-cold grip.

Blinding white pain sent her into darkness, the dark of its insides, and she had the vision many described as they neared death, a tunnel of light opening in the darkness, but it wasn't warm and it wasn't peace. What she saw was light flooding into the mouth and throat of a leviathan, and her point of view came from its belly.

This is death, huh? Leslie thought.

In the light, silhouettes waited for her and called her name. She heard Rod's voice urging her to join him and, with her heart twisted with sadness and guilt because he never would've come to Owenton if not for her, she gladly went to him, resolved not to miss another opportunity to love him. *Dance like no one is watching and love like it will never hurt.* Love couldn't end in Eternity, could it? Then it couldn't hurt, and it was finally safe to let go of her fears.

She walked through muck, her feet sinking, her legs shaking from the effort of moving, and fell into his arms.

"I thought I had lost you again," Rod said, holding her face between his large hands, and she thought it strange that his hands felt like bread fresh from the oven.

Little by little, the woozy haze dissipated, and with streetlights spotting them, the sight of his face struck her with brutal clarity. Gauged cheek displayed pink blubber and bone, and his mouth stretched into a carmine grimace all the way to his left ear. He stared at her with a blood-bruised eye.

"You have to get to a doctor." It was all she could think to say.

He nodded but said, "I don't think there are any left, though."

Leslie turned her head, reeling with a dizzy spell, seeing the collapse of the hospital swaying in her view as if it still rocked in the Void's quake. Fires burned like sacrificial pyres. Black smoke billowed and disappeared in the night sky, but the stench of roasted human flesh was more than evident enough of its presence.

On a sour note, the media had a rational explanation for the hospital's destruction—mysterious fire instead of mysterious shadow ire.

"What happened in there?" Rod asked, as if he had read her mind.

Leslie held his hands, pulled them away from her face, and wrapped them around her waist. She hugged him fiercely, burying her head against his chest, breathing in his manly scent, wanting to hold him forever.

"It's not done happening." *Forever could happen sooner if she didn't finish the fight.* She added aloud, with a tremor in her voice. "Don't ask questions; trust me on this. Take the girls and my mother back to Cincinnati. Go now, before it's too late." Again, Leslie had that eerie premonition that Cincinnati was about as likely a future destination for her as Atlantis.

"Leslie . . ."

"No arguing. If you don't go, Jenelle and Mallory may end up like Trisha's children." Cruel as the demons, she pushed away from the embrace, regretting that, even at this moment, she couldn't bring herself to tell him that she loved him and wanted nothing more than to keep him safe from harm. No matter how much she feared letting him go and never seeing him again once he did leave.

Leslie rubbed her arms as the wind reminded her that winter hadn't vanished and watched Rod's ruined face crumple with emotion. Too much had occurred in the last couple of days for him to gather the strength to deny her. He walked away dejected and confused toward the girls.

With the wind whispering *violate you* through the charred tangle, Leslie sat by her mother's side and gently took her hand. She realized she'd never held her mother's hand before—that was something she'd done with her father—and cried for all those tender moments she'd missed. Indeed, she'd missed the moment again.

Her mother had died.

"No, no!" Leslie wailed, gripping her mother's cold hand tighter, hoping the pressure would bring her back.

She bowed her head and wept against her mother's hand. Everything inside her hurt, even her tears as they rolled from smoke-burning eyes. *Wretched;* the word, sounding like an ax hacking into hearts, perfectly described how she felt.

Mallory approached Leslie with her thumb stuck in her mouth. The child understood and, without a word, clasped her arms around Leslie's neck. They clung to each other, both suffering the loss of their mothers. Mallory's heart rabbit-thumped against Leslie's chest, and Leslie held on to her with maternal love/rage.

With her eyes closed, she could imagine herself as Robin, trapped behind the rock and locked in with the forever howling dead, sensing the danger around her little girl, impossibly pounding her way through the worlds. An unstoppable force, a mother. Leslie squeezed Mallory and brushed the soot from her silken hair, understanding that she was her surrogate mother now. She had to protect her by any means.

The wind bit into their wet cheeks, and they wiped their tears before they froze onto their faces. Intensifying, the wind whistled through the skeletal trees and rattled the bones of the few houses along the street. The sky darkened with more than the night, with more than the harbinger storm.

It snarled with the teeming voices of the shadows.

Leslie jumped to her feet, took Mallory's hand, and nearly dragged her across the sidewalk to the parking lot, where Rod tried to work his key in a frozen lock. Perched on his hip, Jenelle stared behind them as they approached. Her almond eyes blanched with fear and her mouth worked with soundless screams.

The wind screamed loudly.

Behind her, Leslie heard the fibrous flap of numerous wings, *thap-thap-thap*, like leather thongs stuck through fast-spinning rotors.

"Rod, hurry!"

He turned at the alarm in her voice and dropped the key when he looked at the source of her fear.

But Leslie didn't dare glance back. A sheath of ice covered the remaining stretch between them and the car, and Leslie scooped Mallory into her arms and slid across the patch as though she had trained for ice sprinting in an Olympic event, going for the gold, one step ahead of the silver.

Leslie couldn't stop her momentum and braced herself for impact with the car, twisting in order for her hip to strike, protecting Mallory from the crash.

Snapped from his shock, Rod set Jenelle down and stepped in their path. His broad body cushioned the collision.

Still, the sudden thud knocked out their breath and dazzled them with star-sparkling pain.

Precious seconds passed as they regained their composure. The shadows gained on slippery ground.

"The key . . ." Leslie gasped, crawling on the ice to find it.

"I got it," Jenelle announced.

"Go, go," Leslie barked, snatching the key from Jenelle, unlocking the door, and shoving the girl inside. She motioned for Rod and Mallory with grand sweeps of her arm. Her teeth were gritted with terror.

The demons came like a wall of odiferous smoke, billowing black across the parking lot, reeking of death.

"Don't look back," Leslie said, slamming the door shut after Rod.

As the engine chugged and revved, the vacuum motor within her churned into action. Every nerve vibrated with its force. The shadows seemed to pick up on her vibrations as well, stalling in the air, contemplating and plotting with palpable leeriness in the blood-glowing eyes.

Sleet zinged through the air and against her skin. She didn't run for cover, didn't raise her hands to shield her eyes, and didn't budge from her stance against the shadows. Bombarded by the icy bullets, she gathered her strength to endure. No matter how much flesh she lost, she wouldn't lose her soul to those darkest gods and their minions.

She had enduring strength, thanks to their life-long pursuit of her—her father and mother, Jake, her friends, their ceaseless taunting and torture of her dreams and life. She had prevailed, and she had what they were afraid of now.

The Void oozed out of her rictal grin.

Sludge of darkness, the Void settled on the ground, swirling like a tempestuous black sea. It flowed turgid beneath the clouds of demons, and waves rose high, slapping down fragments of them, washing them down into its fathomless bottom.

She saw nothing but darkness gnashing darkness until the shadows escaped into their other realm. Silver lightning ripped into the sky and beyond.

The Void pulled her along. She followed on her dark leash, feeling a growl rumble within her throat, wondering if she hadn't transformed into a were beast when she became this dark chaos. But did she wear the dark blank mask of the dead?

"You need no mask. You hide your face in the shadows well enough," Bruce had said with a voice not entirely his own. Had he seen her other face behind the human mask?

A face of shadow-skin and starry eyes? A face of the Void?

The Void's face. Then she was the Void. She was the decimating, nulling force. Jorge and her father probably didn't count on bringing anything but her life back after she had drowned in the lake, but those few moments in the black empty that is death enabled it to hitch itself to her, because hadn't it claimed her already?

As Leslie walked down the street, she shook with cold and nervous laughter. Every time she blacked out, every episode that baffled the experts, was her way of keeping one foot in the grave, in the place where she truly belonged. *Because nothing should live after it dies.*

Ironic that she should happen upon the dead and hear their unstilled voices begging for her to release their dark chains. But she needed the dead to help fend for the living, and so she called them up from the forever-night limbo.

In the neighboring cemetery, the ghosts sprang from the ground at Leslie's command and waltzed into the street, an icy parade with a freezing wind march. Her father led the ghostly bands toward the lake, the lake she'd drowned in as a child, the place of the horror's beginning, the place where it should end.

Chapter Thirty-seven

The Charlotte ghoul dropped from the air and landed on tendon-balled feet. From her grinning corpse head, her tongue wiggled along her gory lips, and black stringy saliva trailed down and hung from her gaping mouth.

One drop hit the floor. Oblivion pooling, and the inch of floor disappeared completely. Not quite a hole, not quite anything. Nothing was there, in fact. Nothing at all but an empty space leading nowhere.

With a bawdy sway of rotting hips, the Charlotte ghoul sauntered his way, and Coatl backed into the wall to avoid her fingers, which stretched toward his throat. He plunged the knife into her.

Her chest opened and pumped out darkness, as if it were blood, except this flowing ichor melted, thawed, and dissolved the knife before it returned to its pulsing wound. The flesh of his fingers also dwindled at its touch. His bones smoldered away to his wrist.

Coatl screamed worse than Jake ever had.

Responding to its host's cries, his demon hefted itself over the windowsill and the shards of glass. Winds of wounds seeping pus followed the demon inside, and Coatl heard the snarls of the other shadows coming along on the tumultuous winds.

"My battalion, my dead dear," he said, shrinking down the wall and slinking away from her as she turned to face off with the legion of a different darkness. "What weapons have you got against the shadows of gods?"

"Nothing . . ."

Seconds ticked away, the beat of his heart waiting for the next moment.

Laughter roared from the two foes.

With grandiose body-whipping, the demon and the ghoul clashed in the middle of the room, their dangerous ether combusting, and fire and smoke wafted. Slaughter-tainted flames burned along the ceiling. Bile-tainted smoke fogged on the floor, and he soon lost sight of his legs in the smoke.

He watched the torture with rapt eyes.

"Devour her," he called.

"I don't think so."

Hands gripped his knees and knocked him into the fog. Hands bearing large slivers of glass thrust into his stomach, and he tasted blood as it was pushed up from his gut into his mouth.

"This if for Charlotte . . ." Another sharp thrust. "And for Leslie . . ." Again glass knives cut into his flesh.

"Fuck you," he spat.

His blood shot onto Sam's face and dripped into his lunatic grimace.

Cold agony shifted through his wounds, and Coatl cried out for the gods to honor their bargain and grant him immortality.

"The gods will forsake you." The Charlotte ghoul lifted him and smothered him in an embrace. "Only another part of the religious cycle of saviors."

She laughed.

"Salvation, an empty promise." The Charlotte ghoul crushed him harder in her macabre hug. "No escaping the darkness of death . . . dreaded darkness everywhere . . ."

Her kisses sucked away his breath and his flesh, and her razor-wire arms cut him away from the world. Powerless to struggle, he was rendered to suffer the awful tendrils of darkness that snaked from her eyes and mouth, which wrapped around. In the vise-grip of the terror from Leslie's mind, Coatl sank into expiring sands of time.

He felt his body sink in freezing water.

Darkness above, darkness below, he crossed over into a place beyond phantoms and death.

Chapter Thirty-eight

Hoarfrost cracked beneath her feet as she walked down the gravel road. The wind blew silently. The waves lapped at the shore, blue-green silk wisping against ice, the softest of sounds. No other noise accompanied her to the lake, not even the chilly whispers of the dead who followed her.

Too long in the winter elements, her skin had gone numb. Fifteen minutes ago she had felt her fingers and toes burn, her cheeks sting, and her chest hurt, as if icicles were stabbing into her lungs. Now she felt nothing.

She was as cold as the winter, in her body and in her heart.

A good soldier, she thought sarcastically.

Screams cracked the dark placid air. Awful spine-curdling screams, both human and inhuman, echoed around the lake and churned the gentle-bobbing surface tumultuous.

Avoid acoustic shadows, my dear. By the time you hear the battle, you're already walking among the dead.

"No," she whispered, but the dead nodded their black-hooded heads.

Her mother's house stood on the slope without a light in any window, and her unfeeling heart distressed her. A flood of emotions swelled within her, going from bad to worse, as she ran up the backyard and rounded the house to the front. Fishing the spare key from beneath a Wildcats-painted rock, she unlocked the front door and went inside.

"Andy? Moon?" Leslie called. She took a step in through the doorway but kept her hand on the knob, prepared to bolt back outside with the league of specters if anything unsavory should seep down from the dusky corners.

Only the creak of the floorboards answered her.

She hated being alone at the lake. The utter quiet unnerved her, its silent noise oppressive, as if something lurked behind the door, holding its chortling breath until it hurled itself from its hiding place with deafening roars. In her head, her anxiety clicked like solitary heels on concrete steps, going faster and faster, running from the invisible yet very present dangerous other whose footfall followed close at heel and matched the pace and sound.

The wind stole the door from her hand, and it banged closed. Leslie hurried across the room, away from the door and whatever might have approached on the unseen side. She walked to the basement door, took a deep breath, and opened it a crack.

"Andy? Moon? Are you down there?" She strained to raise her voice above a whisper, but her throat refused to open up its narrowed tubes. Trying the light switch, she sighed in resignation. No electricity, of course. The high winds probably had knocked the wires into the trees, as they did with every storm. Only once had she enjoyed the absence of artificial light—a summer's evening of severe thunderstorms and tornado warnings, with the sky eerie in chartreuse resplendency.

Moving through the dark house, she periodically called for Andy and Moon, hoping to find them beneath a bed or tucked into a closet. Nothing but darkness and wind thrumming against the windows. At least until she entered her old bedroom and found an alabaster face floating in the dark.

The shock stifled her screams.

Then she chided herself for not removing the mirror, which caused more than a few night-fright incidents. But it had been an inspiring thing, and she had decided to do a self-portrait with this concept, of a white face like the moon hung on a black sky. The larger-than-life-size picture, titled "Starr in the Night," still hung above her ivory- and opal-crackled mantel, flanked by wrought-iron candle holders and smaller prints of a sullen Moon cat.

She had set the automatic timer and sat before a black screen, wearing widow attire and a somber expression—thoughts of her father dying in broad daylight by the hands of shadows not belonging to the day having supplied the grave-eviscerated mood. The portrait had turned out better than she had expected, and she had surprised herself by refusing to sell the piece, despite a lucrative offer. It reflected her haunted self. Something she couldn't share with anyone but the smoke fairies drifting disturbingly graceful and distorted from the amber-glowing candles.

All her visions for her dark art stemmed from this place.

When she was a child, yet old enough for her mother to leave her alone to watch the boys, she would run through the house, turning off the lights, nearly screaming by the time she made it back to her room in the dark. The click of the lock snapped her heart into a new beat, into gruesome raven-terror rapping. She would place her ear against the door and listen for something wicked to move on the other side. She had always felt something in the dark. The shadows.

With her jaw aching from being clenched and her eyes watering from fatigue, she wouldn't turn out the light as she had crept into bed to fall asleep. She had been afraid of never waking up, of being thrust into the utter dark alone, unable to see, hear, feel, or think of anything but the blackness stalking her. Afraid of the shadows.

Some things never changed.

Leslie crossed the hall to her brothers' room and stopped in her tracks as a baby's cry or a cat's wail shattered the stormy silence.

"Moon?"

Beyond the sliding glass doors, the *yrowl* sounded again and strangled Leslie with its chilling pitch. Bad thoughts crossed her mind in vivid images, of demons skinning her cat, stretch of his midnight fur and pink lining, cushion of his belly with its fat clumps and twitching muscles.

She rushed to the deck doors and pulled the blinds' cord. The blinds zipped open, revealing Moon, his face pressed against the window, making steam against the glass, staring with his moon-lit eyes. He was alone, shivering in the cold, his fur matted with balls of sleet.

She tugged the door open and it argued, with metallic scrapes and icy crunches. Moon didn't wait for the door to give him adequate breadth and squeezed through the narrow slot, bounding as far away from the winter's mantle as possible without leaving Leslie's sight.

As Moon shook himself dry, the ice pelted the walls and the brass vent with crystal chinks.

Leslie breathed in relief and snatched Moon into her arms, snuggling her lips against his icy-wet scruff.

"My kitty," she breathed into his lake-smelling

fur. "My brave, stupid kitty, wandering in the dark all alone and without a scratch on his hide. Thank God . . ."

And for that moment, Leslie believed in God and mercy.

Until the winds shrieked with the kettle brew of shadows steaming into the sky.

Moon clawed his way from her arms, shunted himself back outside and leapt from the deck's railing to the ground. Hackles rising, her cat padded beneath the shadowy eidolons and stretched his lithe body upward. He slashed at the thickening air.

The shadow's laughter rumbled all around.

Scrambling after him and down the stairs, her feet slipping more than stepping, Leslie rushed into the middle of the yard with Moon.

"Devour, devour, devour," the demons sneered, flowing black and evil onto the ground. "Here pussy-pussy . . ."

Talons stroked the arrow points of their erect shafts.

The Void hummed a dark symphony within her, and the shadows backed away, crouching to the ground, waiting in seething coils for the coming destruction.

As her shaking hands brushed against Moon's scruff, he bolted from her.

"Moon!"

He kept bounding away and disappeared in the thickets of the wood.

"The goddess of the moon brings mysterious

shapes in dim half-light of night and its oppressive silence." Her father's voice drifted slow and easy upon the wind as the dead strolled from the lake's shore toward her and the menacing vapors of hell.

"The starry sky of night will be consumed by the fires of the rising sun. . . ."

"You must hurry and bring it to an end . . ."

"Yessss . . ." all the dead hissed, their faces of black maws opening on the shadows.

In the dark and light of conflict, Leslie stood, waiting for the Void to show its deep and ravenous emptiness. She felt nothing.

Nothing as the shadows lunged upon the dead, whirlwind blades of talons slicing apart their grave corrosion.

Nothing as the lake boiled up the dark gods of the Underworld, their terrible grins stretching across their terrible faces.

She tensed at the sound of steps crunching on the frozen path.

The Dark Man is coming. . . .

Turning, she expected her nemesis but not the darkened figure limping toward her. It was a much greater shock. Blood covered his hands, and severe lacerations had mangled his face.

"Three times a frightening charm," Sam muttered through scarlet-tattered lips.

"Whose blood, Sam?"

He collapsed a foot from her and curled into a fetal position. "Partly mine. Partly Buddy's."

Buddy with his intense eyes, eyes she should've figured for the Dark Man's.

His dreaded gods were rising, *from the deep, dark waters*, and everything she ever feared—darkness, death, and despair—escalated within her, bringing the stirring of the Void she'd finally yearned for.

"I'm dying, you know?" He pulled his knees tighter to his chest and held them with his crossed arms.

Pain needled into her eyes, and her sight grew dim. She saw only darkness and light. The shining dead in a glory of frost ripped apart the shadows, splattering their darkness onto the white-bright ground. The lords of Hell rose darker than anything in her diminishing vision, except perhaps Sam.

Sam, dying, shrinking from her in body and in spirit.

"No."

A declarative word. Her declaration of war.

Nails into coffins, an intense pounding inside her skull almost forced her to her knees. Blood trickled from her nose; she tasted it rolling onto her lips.

"Devour you entirely," the shades of dreadful gods drooled. Their glimmering talons clasped her. Clasped Sam. Deeper into him, grating his flesh, gushing more blood from him. His deafening cries begging . . .

"No!" Her voice stormed from her throat.

Not again. Not ever again, her mind growled, expelling images of her father dying in brambles and shadows, of her mother's face adorned in red lace and shadows unstitching her, of Robin sacrificed to death and its guardian, of Sam dying with blood on his hands and shadows wanting to devour him.

The Void's power hammered right through her skull. Black-satin shrouds fell on the demons and their malicious creators.

Smothering.

Winds tore into her. Dark winds raging lavender and cemetery perfumes wailed, "Snare them in the Void and take them forever down into cold darkness."

Take her . . .

A hint of dawn smoldered on the horizon . . . *the starry sky of night will be consumed by the fires of the rising sun . . .* and Leslie knew she had only one option. She wished she could've wrapped up her fragmented life, pieced together her loose-ended relationships, but time played a cruel hand.

She had no more time.

Staggering toward the lake, weighted by tons of demons, their claws unbounded in fury on her flesh and her soul, she held onto them in return. Her spirit-mantle wrapped around them.

Smothering.

With one step, she entered the lake. *Down in deep dark waters.*

Leslie spun into the depths, into cyclonic blackness and cold, mucoidal bubbles trailing upward from her as her breath was crushed from her body.

She trapped the shadows and the gods of death

in the Void, in the deepest dark where no sound, sight, sense, or sentiment existed, inside herself. *Her father's champion.* Leslie Starr shone no more, drifting in the black space only as the nothing she'd become.

The Void.

Epilogue

Andy Starr cast off the lid of the hamper and climbed out, thanking God for his lean and mean, limber build. Rubbing a cramp from his calf, he thanked L.W. as well for the dog-headed charm that guarded him from the dangers he'd heard sleet upon the roof and the ground.

Sleet of icy talons. He knew. Every so often he would catch a glimpse of the outside, of the shadows feasting on fallen corpses, in his mind. A gift he never enjoyed, no matter how much L.W. tried to convince him otherwise.

But it alerted him to the unnatural quiet beyond his safe hamper.

A mournful cry called him outside.

Once beyond the door, he nearly tripped over Leslie's cat, but Moon didn't seem to notice as the cat curled around his ankles, purring loudly. Not a happy purr but one of pain. He sensed that.

Andy inhaled the chill and danger lingering on the air and pressed forward despite the clenching of his gut, a sure sign to run. All the bad feelings hit a high by the time he reached the lake's shore.

The morning sun burned atop the lake, giving it an unhealthy glow, as if the lake had turned to blood.

For some reason, Andy sensed his sister down there, down deeper than the bottom. He frowned, not understanding why this didn't bother him.

Maybe because he sensed something else too.

A Dark Man lurking beneath the water and laughing.

MARY ANN MITCHELL

CATHEDRAL OF VAMPIRES

They live among us, unnoticed. They survive on our blood. They are vampires. Among the most infamous and powerful of these creatures is the notorious Marquis de Sade, his perverse and unholy desires still unquenched after two centuries. But his off-spring, vampires of this own making, have hungers and desires of their own, and one of the strongest is the need for revenge. From California to Paris, from underworld clubs to ruined cemeteries, and eternally young woman and her half-vampire companion will stop at nothing to find Sade and put an end to the master vampire's reign. But as they will discover, there is more than one type of vampire . . . and killing any of them is never easy.

Sips of Blood

MARY ANN MITCHELL

The Marquis de Sade. The very name conjures images of decadence, torture, and dark desires. But even the worst rumors of his evil deeds are mere shades of the truth, for the world doesn't know what the Marquis became—they don't suspect he is one of the undead. And that he lives among us still. His tastes remain the same, only more pronounced. And his desire for blood has become a hunger. Let Mary Ann Mitchell take you into the Marquis's dark world of bondage and sadism, a world where pain and pleasure become one, where domination can lead to damnation. And where enslavement can be forever.

___4555-9 $5.50 US/$6.50 CAN

MOON
ON THE
WATER
MORT CASTLE

It's a strange world—one filled with the unexpected, the chilling. It's our world, but with an ominous twist. This is the world revealed by Mort Castle in the brilliant stories collected here—our everyday lives seen in a new and shattering light. These stories show us the horror that may be waiting for us around the next corner or lurking in our own homes. Through these disquieting tales you will discover a world you thought you knew . . . and a darker one you'll never forget.

JOHN SHIRLEY
Black Butterflies

Some nightmares are strangely sweet, unnaturally appealing. Some dark places gleam like onyx, like the sixteen stories in John Shirley's *Black Butterflies*, stories never before collected, including the award-nominated "What Would You Do for Love?" These stories are like the jet-black butterflies Shirley saw in a dream. They flocked around him, and if he tried to ignore them they would cut him to shreds with their razor-sharp wings. Shirley had to write these stories or the black butterflies would cut him up from the inside and flutter out from the wound . . . into the world.

__4844-2 $5.99 US/$6.99 CAN